NESTING IN TEXAS

MARY LAVOIE

Copyright © 2023 by Mary Lavoie

First paperback edition May 2023

Edited by Jennifer Sommersby Young

Book cover design by Bailey McGinn

ISBN 978-1-7388455-0-7 (paperback)

ISBN 978-1-7388455-1-4 (ebook)

www.marylavoie.com

NESTING IN TEXAS

by Mary Lavoie

My mother chose humor in a world filled with darkness.
She taught me that strength isn't undermined by sensitivity,
and being hopeful is an act of rebellion.
Mom, this is for you.
(Even if you could have done without the sexy bits.)
I miss you always.

CHAPTER ONE

*E*lmira Bondell flew down the highway in her blue Toyota Tercel, imagining flames in her wake, trying not to think about the bedbugs that might be burrowing past her clothes into her skin. Driving fifteen hours hadn't put enough distance between her and the Detroit apartment she'd almost rented. She kicked herself as she remembered sitting in her car outside the sad-looking building, dialing the number on the sign. Anyone being honest with themselves never would've pulled into that lot. Dilapidation wasn't Elmira's style.

The place was a dive, but Elmira needed to work on herself too, so the idea of rebuilding together appealed. After speaking on the phone, the landlord appeared in the doorway, waving, impatient or unwilling to brave the mid-January cold. They walked up the steps to the third floor while he promised the stained hallway flooring would be replaced with laminate by year's end. His shiny new sneakers and the food stains on his shirt led Elmira to believe he made a lot of unfulfilled promises. Even still, she could handle a fixer-upper, get her hands dirty with a renovation, and deal with a seedy landlord. At the least, she could hire someone to change her locks.

As the landlord turned the keys in the three deadbolts, Ellie tried not to imagine why so many of them were needed. She clung to her frenzied optimism.

That the unit was larger than expected was where the list of positives ended. The linoleum in the entry was peeled back to expose layers of grungy browns before exposing a match to the building's stained hallway. Beige carpeting covered the rest of the living space with a patchwork of stains and held a smell reminiscent of a petting zoo. The former tenant's belongings were left behind, broken, and overturned. Judging by the paraphernalia strewn about, the place had been ransacked, maybe even raided by the police.

Carpets weren't a problem, they could be pulled up. The mouse droppings in the kitchen corner, however, churned her stomach and presented larger issues. The unit was gruesome, but the most off-putting fact was that the landlord would not step inside. That's when she saw it. It might have been the last of her frayed nerves, but she could've sworn there was a beetle being chased by the biggest cockroach she'd ever seen in her life.

She ran.

Again.

Elmira turned up the radio, trying to forget about bugs in the nauseating, unhygienic pigsty. Blaring static had her pressing the tune button to find local stations. The first had a country song about a soul-sucking ex, the next a western twang about an adulteress, and another press took her into *she took my dog and broke my heart* territory. It couldn't be avoided; she may not have been cheating on her fiancé, Daniel, but any closer to the altar and she'd be a runaway bride.

Elmira clenched the steering wheel and settled on an innocuous pop song, but her thoughts couldn't be blocked out any longer. An hour after leaving Canada, she'd missed the cake tasting. Looking at the time, she noted that she had officially missed the meeting with the florist, scheduled for an hour ago. Her ignored cell phone flashed missed-call notifications from her wedding planner, proof of her shirked duties. If Daniel was waiting for her, he would be wearing his stiff suit, emailing from his phone, put out. Had he made the effort at all? Did he notice she was gone?

No, twisting the issue wouldn't do any good. Daniel had been career-minded when they met, and that didn't change after he proposed. They both had time-consuming jobs they'd worked hard for, and that's how the relationship worked. They understood that about one another: careers came first, so it made no sense for that to be the reason for running from him. *If* that was what she was doing. She didn't want to untangle the whats and why's, all she wanted was to forget her responsibilities for a while longer.

The winter-bare trees standing sentinel along the I-30 kept the cities a mystery. In Texarkana, she jumped from Arkansas to Texas without preamble. If it weren't for the flatlands and the enormity of the cloud-blown sky, she could've been anywhere. Driving so fast down the I-30 had made it easy to forget how far she had come. One more border crossing sat between her and Mexico, but that seemed a little too gauche, a little too far to run without the law chasing her.

She would stop for something to eat, then she would turn the car around and head back north and face reality. Apologies would be handed out to Daniel and any clients whose time was wasted by Elmira's juvenile behavior. She would continue with her life as a rational human being because there was no need for the jitters. Elmira would take this as a wake-up call to self-care, something that could, and would, be handled.

As a hardworking woman who was just now achieving her goals, how could it all be thrown away over a teensy little melt-down? No, she wouldn't waste her business management degree—she'd worked too hard for it. While most of her classmates were partying, she'd been committed to her studies and her student placements. While her peers were falling in and out of love, she was happy to be single and focused on her degree. Well, after that *one* failed dalliance, anyway.

Now, long since graduating, she had a prestigious job with a salary that was nothing to scoff at and had been offered a huge promotion that no one in their right mind would turn down. As the owner of a modern condo in Westboro, a once up-and-coming and now affluent neighborhood in Ottawa, retail therapy was always within reach. And there was Daniel, a lawyer with high aspirations and endless focus on his own goals. Calling herself lucky felt dishonest; she'd worked herself to the bone for everything in her life and had no right to be unhappy with any of it.

So why the preemptive runaway-bride act? It must have been cold feet. Once the gas tank and her belly were filled, it would be back to the grind and back on track.

Celine Dion's *Because You Love Me* ringtone came through the hands-free.

Elmira braced for impact. "Hello, Mother."

Eliza Bondell was firm and demanding but had her act sewn together with such seamlessness, it made it forgivable. With an active mind and a curvaceous body she kept in shape despite her hush-hush age, she won over crowds with her smile and sharp wit. Growing up in her mother's shadow had been hell. Elmira learned from a young age never to complain. True, she might have never grown into a successful businesswoman without Eliza pushing her to do more and be better, but therapy made Elmira aware that she was equal parts thankful and resentful. Some parents gave hugs and cupcakes, her mother gave her enrichment programs and kale.

Her father ... he'd given her dual citizenship.

"Hello, Mother? You go missing for two days, in that death-trap you call a car, and all I get is a 'Hello, Mother'?" Elmira tried to cut in with an apology, but her mother stomped on the attempt. "You will be happy to note that I was there for your missed consultations with the wedding planner, and I've had your assistant cover for you at work."

"You went to my appointments? Was Daniel there?" Elmira had wanted to ask if he was upset but sensed a dramatic flair in her mother's tone. No matter the truth, Daniel would be painted as devastated. It was always safer to keep to the facts with Eliza Bondell.

"Elmira, do you think he could afford to lose time with clients? Honestly, when he got the notice that you weren't there, he called me and—"

"He called *you*?"

"Of course, he did. He knew that he could count on me. So, the cake is going to be red velvet, and the florist agreed that we should go with the mix of red roses and white lilies—"

"I'm allergic to lilies, Mother."

"No, you're not, dear. Besides, you can drop a pill for that. You are to meet with the wedding planner tomorrow to nail down the venue. Are you going to make it, or shall I?"

"Mother, I am not marrying Daniel." Thus began another out-of-body experience.

Her mother paused. "Of course, you are, Elmira. This is what we have been working toward. This is your path. Wherever you are, just turn around and come back. Daniel doesn't even have to know you've left town."

Many things came to mind to say after hanging up, such as, '*You* have been working toward this, Mother, and I want off the train,' or 'I feel so lost, I need some time to think.' She *should* have said, 'Stop changing my ringtone and get your own life.'

Instead, she managed a confident "goodbye, Mother" before turning off her phone and throwing it onto the passenger's seat.

Elmira drove on with a death grip on her steering wheel, muttering incoherent blasphemies as the claustrophobia-inducing trees along the I-30 opened to barren plains. The flora was depressing, browns and dry yellows, but a hint of hopeful green grasses tried pressing through. She soon stumbled into a small town, and rather than speeding through, she decided to stop at the restaurant-gas station.

The squat, rectangular building was not unlike many greasy spoons along the interstate, set apart with a fresh mural along its brick wall. Elmira admired the artist's clean lines and patriotic bent with energetic red, white, and blue as she pumped her gas. Once she pulled into a parking space beside the diner, she closed her eyes, and held the bridge of her nose in an attempt to dispel the overwhelming tension a five-minute conversation with her mother incited.

Once her shoulders fell from her ears, she grabbed her purse and fumbled out of the car. Having never driven for so long before, she hadn't expected to be so stiff. She rolled her neck from side to side before she trudged into the diner, expecting it to be drab and to carry the heavy odor of deep-fried decades, but it was clean and bright. A career waitress wearing a retro blue uniform, white tennis shoes, and a name tag that read *Kelly* led her to a table. Elmira flushed red as the locals gave sideways glances. Maybe they weren't used to strangers. Insecurity made her do a quick presentability check.

"Can I get you something to drink, honey? The coffee's fresh," Kelly asked with a sympathetic tilt of her head, insinuating that Elmira looked as rough as she felt.

"No coffee, but do you have any orange juice? And maybe a newspaper?"

"This *is* the South, darlin'! And don't you have the sweetest accent? I'll be back in a jiff." The woman sashayed behind the counter and came back with a local gazette. Elmira sped through the menu, though she found it difficult to choose with her stomach gurgling. Asking for the special without knowing what to expect, she smiled at her own spontaneity before remembering that driving across the continent was a touch more adventurous than ordering a mystery meal.

Feeling eyes on her, she hid the best she could behind the newspaper. There were agonizing fluff pieces about craft shows and bake sales, and it was heavy on high school sports reporting, making it clear how tiny Littleton was. Her food arrived and Kelly let her be after calling her *sugar* a few more times. Elmira might be an out-of-towner, but she was pretty sure the waitress was pouring on endearments a little thick.

Half focused on her meal and glossing past articles about raffles and local clubs, it took some time to find an article of interest:

Littleton Resort and Spa to Revitalize Tourism

The article featured a picture of the mayor and a former boxer named Guy Manning in a pre-fight stance, the resolution too poor to make out facial expressions. Elmira rolled her eyes. Named Guy Manning *and* a boxer? Now there's a man with something to prove.

The journalist lamented Littleton's history of heart disease, diabetes, and issues tied to food insecurity, driving home the point that the town and its people had been suffering a mere decade before. Then it went on to break down what had helped them win a recent award for health and wellness: diet, exercise, trails and green spaces, community outreach, and health services. Not to mention the arrival of a new grocery store chain to the area. Apparently, all thanks to a not-for-profit the towering former boxer began.

While the health of the townspeople had improved, the economy needed a boost. Manning was championing the idea of a wellness spa and resort, but the mayor believed it would ruin the small-town appeal. Elmira was no expert but thought a spa couldn't hurt, as long as it didn't try to be too ostentatious. The best resorts always knew and worked with the area they were in — rustic in small towns, modern in big cities. The mayor was playing a game of politics and might want to do a little more research, in her humble opinion. Was Guy Manning angling for the next election? What a drama. Elmira ate it up with her toast.

The next page was a full-spread ad for a real estate agent, a southern belle so beautiful that the page required readers to stop and appreciate. Despite the simple black-and-white print, Elmira could've sworn that the woman's white teeth sparkled. Underneath were pictures of a few of her listings, including a condo for lease. It was a newer build, and although it lacked small-town charm, it was unlikely to be a roach farm. After having read about some of the town's history, Elmira felt a pull and dialed the Realtor's number.

"Goldie Morrison," came a voice like wind chimes—sweet and energetic.

"Hello, this is Elmira Bondell." She channeled her inner businesswoman for confidence. "I'm looking at your listing in the *Littleton Times*. Is the condo in the picture still available?"

The woman was silent, possibly processing Elmira's words or her accent.

"Yes, it is. The unit has had some traffic. If you are interested, I'd suggest you come on by as soon as you can." Elmira could feel the woman's smile—it was infectious. "If you're looking at the *Littleton Times*, I'm guessing you're in town?"

"That's right," Elmira answered.

"I'm available anytime today, but I happen to be at the property right now if you wanted to come on by?"

Elmira agreed, paid Kelly, and asked for directions before leaving with the paper under her arm. When going to a meeting with someone as attractive as Goldie Morrison, looking halfway presentable was a necessity. Feeling another stab of insecurity, Elmira fluffed and primped her hair in the car's vanity mirror. The real achievement was getting her overgrown bangs off her sweaty forehead.

After pinching her cheeks for color, she leaned back in her seat, accepting that it would be impossible to feel confident next to the blond bombshell, so she shrugged off the silly bout of jealousy. Why is it grown women feel the need to compete, anyway?

Soon, she was slowing and counting unit numbers to a modern-style condo that rose out of nowhere. It had sharp angles, large windows, and a model waiting to show it off. The Realtor was immediately recognizable, her coiffed hair toeing the line between cute and a caricature of every Texan woman from television. She looked as reputable as she was beautiful in her pantsuit.

Goldie waved like a beauty queen, flagging Elmira down, inviting her to what could be her new home, her new life.

Elmira could not breathe.

Accelerating as she drove past, hunched over as if it were possible to hide herself, Elmira held tight to the steering wheel until her sweaty palms began to slip. It wasn't the commitment to a new home or the intimidation she felt looking at the attractive woman she'd ditched. The condo reminded her of her place in Ottawa—a modern and trendy abyss.

Her eyes cut to the rearview, paranoid that the real estate agent might have chased her across town. Once certain that she wasn't being followed, she pulled into a construction site parking lot, kicking up dust, and slammed the brakes to avoid hitting a tree. She stared out the window, as yet unable to break the grip of her white knuckles, wits ever so slow to return.

As a rule, she didn't drive often, so this was her first long haul. A car accident in her youth had torn her ACL and ended her dreams of becoming a professional dancer. After extensive physical and psychological therapy, she tried not to think about the accident. Reliving the trauma wasn't helpful.

"Get it together, Elmira." An echo of the words her mother had repeated at least once daily as long as she could remember, chiding Elmira into submissive success. Valedictorian, top-university, a high-salary career, and engagement to a man going places, Elmira had a fantastic life filled with beautiful things. Catching her wild-eyed expression in the rearview, she leaped from the car in an attempt to escape her unfamiliar gaze.

Looking off in the direction she'd come, it dawned on her that she must've driven right to the edge of town. Texas was a lot different from what Elmira had imagined. The hair was about right, but the landscape was different. There were a lot more trees than she'd expected, untamed plains rather than vast desert. The pockets of overgrowth provided a welcome sense of privacy, and she rested her hand against the tree she'd almost hit, stroking it with a silent apology.

"Now, don't you worry, little miss," came a deep rumbling voice from behind her. "The tree would've won."

Having thought the work site was empty, Elmira turned in alarm. The man stood six feet tall and was covered in sawdust, sweat, and tattoos. His body was lean with defined muscles, a body built for action, not pumped up for appearances. It was a strong and capable tool, and he was comfortable in it.

Elmira reddened, realizing she'd been staring for too long, and brought her gaze back up to his face, taking in his rugged good looks, light, sun-kissed hair, stormy blue-gray eyes, and supple lips in a tight half grin surrounded by stubble.

Danger and sex rolled into one, the kind of man who never looked at her twice.

"I'm sorry," she said, offering her hand. "Elmira Bondell."

"You in the market?" he asked, motioning behind him.

"I'm not sure." Elmira bit her lip to keep her sob story from falling out. "Shops or residential?"

"Both, actually." The man wiped his forehead with the back of his hand.

"You're hot," Elmira said, instantly regretting her words as the man gave her a raised eyebrow. "I mean, you're sweaty ... uh, would you like some water?" She face-palmed in embarrassment as she turned back to her car to retrieve a bottle from the package she'd picked up at a 7-Eleven halfway between Littleton and home. "Forgive me, it's been a long few days."

"Nothin' to forgive. Noted the license plate. You're a long way from home." The man was still smiling as he accepted the water and studied the unopened cap before twisting it off and throwing it back, emptying the bottle. He wiped his mouth as he turned toward the building when Elmira didn't volunteer anything. "The lower units there, with the picture windows, are going to be small, boutique-style shops. The doors to the right of them lead to apartments above."

Elmira focused on the building for the first time. There was something about it ... vintage Americana with the curved arches of the stonework and flat roofing. It was out of a Western, but not cliché, managing to be both dignified and homey.

"It's nice to see a traditional-style build."

"Ha! I take it you saw those other new builds in town?"

She curled her lip, expressing her distaste.

"I agree. Ice boxes for ice princesses."

"These are ready for life to begin." She knew he was watching her as she moved closer to the building. She felt her crazy rising and had the strangest desire to shock him. "I'll take the one on the end." She pointed to the right side of the building.

The man chuckled. "Sorry, miss, but they won't be ready for about another month. I could take you to the office and talk you through all the steps ..."

"It looks like the exterior is almost done," Elmira said, not breaking her appraisal of the apartment complex.

"It still needs—"

"There are lights on in there, so the power is ready."

"Power, but temporary fixtures. They're not ready for a woman's touch yet."

"I'm in the mood for a fixer-upper." Elmira tried to be sassy. The thought of being there as the unit was born thrilled her. This would be the kind of building people would say, 'If the walls could talk,' and she wanted in on it.

"Then pick up your phone and get on Tinder, miss ..."

"Elmira."

"Miss Ellie," the man patronized, stepping closer, forcing her attention back to him. "I don't know how they do things back in Canuck Land, but here in Texas, buildings have to be on the market before you can move into them."

Bone tired, Elmira didn't have enough fight in her. "Please, I've come a long way, and this is the first place that has felt right."

The Adonis stared her down. Seeing that she wasn't going to flee, he groaned his acquiescence. "When do you need it by?"

"Tonight," Elmira said. His eyes nearly popped out of his head. "Please." She didn't have to try at puppy-dog eyes.

"Well, shoot, Miss Ellie! You do know there are laws around buying properties? The paperwork alone won't roll through that quick. And there's a small thing about escrow. Not to mention citizenship, which might not stop you but will slow the process down."

"My name is *Elmira* and I have dual-citizenship. I'm sure if you talk to your boss, he'd let it roll. I'm willing to pay extra for your troubles, a lump sum up-front. They could charge me as a renter until the escrow lifts. Charge first, last, insurance, whatever is needed?" She was not proud of begging and couldn't explain why she was doing it without even seeing inside. It was a gut feeling—and joy at getting a rise out of the construction worker. "Besides, I have a fantastic lawyer who can make it work. We could do a liability waiver and all of that." She waved her hand, not knowing the logistics, but confident it could be done.

"All right, Miss Ellie. Stop by this address with all your info, and Arleen will help you out." He handed her a business card. "Do you at least want a walk-through?"

"That would be lovely." She pocketed the card without

looking at it as he led her to the building and pulled open the door. It didn't yet have a doorknob or lock.

"Assuming the deal clears, we'll have locks put in by this afternoon," he said, reading her mind.

Elmira followed him up a narrow staircase to the main level of the living space. Her face lit up. The unit was open concept with high ceilings and tall windows. Otherwise, only the bare essentials had been put in.

There was plumbing right under a short but wide west-facing window where the kitchen sink would be. Elmira went to it, imagining colorful but neat curtains framing the horizon accented by a green thicket around the development. The sunsets alone would be worth the begging. Along the highway, she had wondered what such growths hid. Here, it felt comforting and protective. Otherwise, there was nothing but sky.

Elmira heard the contractor shift his weight, and she shook her head to dispel her reverie. It was, after all, a time for business, not daydreams. The kitchen island had been roughed in, an electric fireplace had been installed across the room, and another door led to a powder room. She peeked in, finding there was already a toilet and a sink. *Perfect.* Another door hid a tiny closet. Down the hallway were bare frames waiting for drywall.

"How many bedrooms is this supposed to be?" she asked.

"Two were in the plan, but it's still flexible. I could take out this wall and make the master bigger."

Elmira thought about it. "What if you leave it as is and make this an open area instead? Could be an office."

"Could do that, I suppose ..." The man considered the idea. "Would bring the resale down, though."

She waved away his concern. "If it bothers me I can add it on later, right? It would save you some work and get the place done faster, yes?"

"You busting my balls already? A door frame doesn't take

13

much, could do French doors if you want it fancy," the man countered, raising an eyebrow in good humor.

"Hey, I'm just trying to make this easier." She held up her open palms in mock defense. The place was perfect. A blank canvas—she and her potential new home could be built up at the same time. Elmira found the ensuite, which she immediately considered *her* bathroom. It had a toilet and exposed pipes for the sink and bath. "I've always wanted a claw-foot tub. Think that could happen?"

In second grade, her entire class had been invited to Chelsea Ardmore's birthday party. Elmira hadn't fit in with the other girls, and she'd been excluded from most of the games. When the parents announced it was time for hide-and-seek, she'd wandered off, snooping around the house. They had a piano and messy shelves. There were pictures everywhere of the happy family. One was an old picture of her classmate and her siblings in a bath overflowing with bubbles. They seemed so joyful. She'd imagined she was the baby of the house and found herself hiding in the claw-foot tub, waiting for someone to find her. Her mother had been the one to come for her, and that was that. Elmira should've hated that tub. Instead, it became a symbol of the familial love that she so craved.

"I don't see why not, but you pay out of pocket for upgrades. If you make your way over to the office, they can get things started." The man regarded her with chagrin like he knew a secret. It made her want to check her back for a kick-me sign.

"If you want a bed for the night," he said, pausing for effect.

Elmira narrowed her eyes at him as her cheeks grew warm.

"There's an antiques shop about four doors down from the office and a resale shop a block down from that," he said while winking at her.

She wrinkled her nose at the thought of a used mattress after the Detroit incident.

"You can order a mattress in town too. Not sure what they

have in the shop, though. Might have to go a day or two if you're fussy. Nearest motel is about an hour out if you don't want to rough it while you wait. If that's all, I'm sure we'll be runnin' into each other soon, Miss Ellie."

She didn't correct him this time. Ellie. It could be her alter ego —quirky and fun. She squealed with delight like a schoolgirl and threw her arms around the tall stranger in thanks before speeding back to her car.

She pulled the sexy contractor's card out of her pocket as she approached the town's main strip. The card heading read:

Guy Manning, CEO
Regal Construction Inc.

CHAPTER TWO

*G*uy Manning hadn't been surprised to find a woman in his parking lot that morning. Women found their way to him one way or another, but he had found this one refreshingly desperate. He'd been checking on some work that had been done in one of the units when he heard her car peel in, and he'd thought there'd been an accident. Instead, he found the small woman in rumpled clothing, face paler than a ghost, about to hug a tree.

Normally, he would've considered calling the cops—you never know how crazy a stranger might be—and as a boxer, he'd seen it all. He'd expected her to be a delusional fan out for a joyride, but it appeared that she had no idea who he was. Or she was trying to play him for a fool. He'd had his share of beautiful women throwing themselves at him with dollar signs on their minds. Fame made paranoia a defense mechanism, it had taught him not to trust women too soon.

It didn't help that the readings on his crazy meter wouldn't go down. She wanted to buy one of his apartments on the spot? If it'd been a man, Guy would've told him to take a hike, but something about a damsel in distress—he couldn't help his southern hospitality. Her credit or background check would probably come back bad, and then he could send her packing. That's why he was rushing back to the office. He couldn't leave Arleen alone if this woman turned out to be dangerous. He would never forgive himself if someone got hurt because of him. Out of the boxing ring, anyway.

Guy made a quick stop at home to change. A T-shirt and cleaner pair of jeans were his usual choices before heading into the office—one perk of being the boss—but he decided that Miss Ellie needed a clear picture of who was in charge. He donned a tailored suit and tie but drew the line at shaving. He wanted to make a point, not pretty up for the girl.

It was a block-and-a-half walk to the office before he strolled in, wearing a cocky smile like he owned the place. He did own the place. Guy Manning came from money. It was no secret his father's side of the family was full of blue-blooded doctors, or that his mother had built an empire. Dr. Edward Manning, a well-known orthopedic surgeon, had an established career before meeting his young wife, but they were secure enough decades later that he'd taken a break to support their adopted son Liam while Ivy's career flourished.

Knowing he started life with a big boost had driven Guy to become a self-made man. Though his parents were affluent and influential, he never asked for money or help with connections. He knew that didn't mean that his name wasn't a draw, or that banks were more inclined to take a chance on him ... but he did the work. His brief boxing career had been a success, and Guy was proving he could succeed with his fists *and* his business sense.

People would always talk trash. Some said he'd left the ring out of fear of losing. The truth was that although he loved his sport—pounding flesh, assessing, and taking down his opponents—he didn't love the lifestyle. In the beginning, the women and the parties had been addictive, but it got old. There was something unfulfilling about blackouts and nameless women scratching notches into their bedposts. His focus became all about the business of boxing.

In walked Amanda. Barbie doll Amanda with the heart of ice. He hadn't quit boxing because of a woman, but *that* woman ... she manipulated, exploited, and sucked all joy from the fame, cash, and the fights. She played him hard to advance her own career, and to be frank, for the fun of it.

Hearing Arleen going through the paperwork with Miss Ellie, he decided to add an emergency contact form. The lady wasn't from around these parts and might need some intervention. She didn't seem like another Amanda, but routes sometimes crossed into stalker land. If she *was* going to tailspin, he would like to know which way to point her.

"Hey there, Arleen. I see you've met Miss Ellie. You got my email about the specifics of this contract?" He stepped into the room, intentionally taking up space.

"Yes, sir, a temporary rental agreement that will lead to ownership, most unusual. We've been working on some paperwork. I need your signature on a few things." Arleen's eyes widened at the sight of him in a suit, then turned to her customer. "He's going to have to sign the same waiver as you since you didn't want an inspector—"

"Not a chance. Miss Ellie, we do things by the book around here. I will see if Marlin is available ASAP."

"That's not necessary, Mr. Manning," Elmira said.

He warmed at the formality of his name. Judging by her croak, the suit had chastened her.

"It's as much for our sake as yours," he said. This woman didn't have the good sense to protect her investment. She had to know that her check would bounce. Maybe she was hoping to find something wrong with the place, then she could sue him for all he's worth. He wasn't having it.

"So," began Arleen, raising a discreet eyebrow at Guy, "all the paperwork is in order. We will send it to your attorney to have a look-see. And as per Texas state law, the property will be held in escrow for about thirty to forty-five days, assuming all is on the up-and-up."

"Yes, I've already called ahead. He will make it a priority so it can be pushed through today." Ms Ellie sounded confident but Guy suspected she had no clue what her lawyer would have to do to move this mountain.

"All right, last thing is the rental payment. Would you like to pay first, last, and fees by check?" Arleen asked.

"Do you do direct deposit? I'm sorry. Left my checkbook behind. I read in the newspaper that there isn't a hotel here yet, and I don't fancy sleeping on a park bench while waiting for the bank to catch up to all of this."

Guy leaned against the door frame and chewed on his cheek. The woman was trying to ignore him behind her.

Arleen sent a sharp glance his way, and he nodded. "That *should* work." Arleen gave her the necessary information, Miss Ellie pulled out her cell phone, and a few minutes later, she let out a girlish squeal.

"When can I pick up my keys?"

Guy pulled out his own phone and opened his business account app, accepting the payment. The wide sum paid by Elmira Bondell was sitting pretty in there. He glanced at her, not wanting to give away his surprise. "I'll have the locks put in by noon. You can come back here after that to pick them up. Assuming Marlin gives the OK, and the background check clears."

"Background check?" Miss Ellie whirled around.

"Yes, ma'am, we need to keep everyone safe."

"You don't think I'm—"

"Don't know until you know." Guy fixed Miss Ellie with an assessing gaze, hoping to read her reaction.

"I understand. I hope it doesn't interfere with the move-in."

"You got something to hide?" Guy asked.

"Of course not!"

He noted that she flushed pretty for a grown woman.

"Then no need to worry. The first should be back in time for dinner." He had texted Arleen to make sure she submitted it before anything had even been signed.

"First?"

"Single-day background checks are less thorough but will bring up any red flags."

"Well, I'm certain I won't have any *red flags*." Her frown turned on a dime, and she stood smiling like a damned fool before looking him in the eye. He couldn't tell if they were gray or green from the distance between them, but he was unnerved. She wasn't flirting or checking him out the way she had at the site. He wasn't a vain man, but he knew his looks were appreciated. It was as though Miss Ellie didn't notice him that way anymore.

He didn't like it, nor did he like not liking it.

His looks were one weapon in his arsenal, first to disarm and second to scare off. A lot of women appreciate a muscled man from a distance, but the tattoos, minor scarring, and his hint of a crooked nose kept enough of them happy to look from afar.

"We'll see," was all he could muster.

"Marlin is available at one o'clock," Arleen told Guy after hanging up her phone.

"Do you not trust your craftsmanship, Mr. Manning?" Miss Ellie had the gall to ask him, catching on that he didn't trust her as far as he could throw her.

"Wouldn't want a pretty young thing like yourself to get hurt on my watch. Now, you best be off shopping. Beds. That way," he said, pointing out the window to the left, leaving Ellie blushing behind him as he disappeared into his office, victorious.

THE BACKGROUND and credit checks both came up clean. Guy soon found himself googling her, and all he could find were some newspaper articles about a businesswoman in Canada. There were no pictures. Both articles were from Ottawa, Ontario, Canada but the list of accolades was long enough for someone in their fifties, not thirty-two-year-old Elmira Bondell.

Next, he scanned the major social media sites and came back empty there too. She was an enigma, and he found it unsettling. But she had been right about one thing—craftsmanship did matter to him. Even though he might have been relieved at Ellie not being able to move in, he couldn't allow it to be because of his work.

Guy spent much of the day organizing and helping his crew. They finished the drywall and some other minor finishing ahead of the inspector. If he'd gotten Ellie to choose carpet or tile, he might have gotten a lot more done before she moved in, but she had been so insistent on moving in the same day that he figured she needed a dose of reality. It wouldn't be the first time a trust-fund baby tried to work her way into Guy Manning's world, and he took a measure of joy from toying with them when he could. He no longer had any interest in princesses. He appreciated a strong woman who didn't turn to money to solve all her problems. Miss Ellie would be running scared in a few days without a shower or a mirror. He flinched at the thought.

The woman had money, or else she wouldn't have been able to get this far in the process. Her clothes were well-made pieces, despite their bland and rumpled appearance. Yet, even though he didn't want to admit it, she didn't strike him as vain. No dress-to-impress attitude, her hair was overgrown, and she wore little to no makeup. He considered her a looker, but it was evident she didn't prioritize her curb appeal. Heck, the way she drove into his life, she didn't seem to take much care of herself at all. And he didn't have time to house-train a puppy.

Heavy footfalls coming from below alerted Guy that Marlin, the inspector, had arrived. He wiped his hands on a spare cloth and made his way down to meet him in the main space.

Marlin Black was tied for the title of Littleton's oldest citizen, and he dressed the part, wearing his Gatsby cap and suspenders. It was amazing to watch him come up those stairs. He was slow, deliberate, and made a show of banging his cane on every step. Three years before, he couldn't make it up the stoop of his wife's store, but Guy had worked out a rehabilitation plan to help Marlin rebuild his strength after his heart attack. Guy didn't take credit for Marlin's success—he'd worked hard and deserved every ounce of the pride he took in it. Guy made the map, but Marlin had to climb those mountains. Since then, they'd shared a mutual respect.

"Don't you know you're supposed to finish the work before folks move in?" The old man shook his head as he surveyed his surroundings.

"Good to see you, too, Marlin."

"And don't the lady know she should be here? Could swindle her, and she'd be none the wiser." His bushy gray eyebrows twitched with indignation.

"Who's to say what she knows?" Guy responded, keeping his thoughts about the woman veiled by his tone. "Lucky for her, we do things right."

The old man grumbled. The dark, leathery weathering of his skin held his grimace well, exposing nothing of the man's soft core. He broke out his tablet, an image at odds with the old-timer persona he otherwise projected. Guy knew he was taking notes, following the letter of the law and the man's own code of what was right and just. They went step-by-step through the apartment in near silence, except when Marlin quizzed Guy about specifics. It didn't take long before they'd finished the tour.

"So, how'd I do, boss?" Guy asked. It wasn't his first build, but he was still new to the business. He wanted to make quality homes, homes that would stand the test of time.

Marlin scanned his notes before meeting Guy's gaze and cracking his first smile. "Not bad, kid. I'll have another walk-through once you're all done here. I'll be back in an hour. Two if the truck's not loaded by the time I get back to the shop."

"Miss Ellie came your way for the bed, then?" Guy asked with a surprised chuckle. He'd been hoping she'd throw a little wealth their way. Business was tough in a town that didn't get many visitors. It surprised him because he'd expected her to be the type to order from swanky designer stores in Morocco and let everyone know it.

"Ha! She had a field day. That girl's going to keep you busy."

"I'm sure she will," Guy groaned in return.

"Now, now. The lady's a fruit loop, but she seems harmless enough." High praise coming from Marlin. He turned to the steps, grimaced, and gritted his teeth the whole way, tough as nails.

As the bell on the door of Moira's Antiques chimed, a calm washed over Elmira. The shop was huge and filled to the brim, shelves were heavy with overstock, and furniture was stacked on top of one another. The smell of wood polish and copper added to the mystique of the place, making her feel like she was starting a treasure hunt. It had taken the owners half an hour to notice her, and only after she'd come across them while following a trail of faucets and hanging lamps. They were seated in a corner taking inventory and chatting over tea.

Moira started the shop soon after she and her husband had married. At nineteen years old, she'd already developed a 'terrible habit' of holding on to things. They'd held a yard sale to help pay for the cost of their new home and had been surprised at how well they'd done for themselves.

Their mutual love was evident. As they sat across from each other, they would argue playfully as they told Elmira, a complete stranger, their stories. They reached across to hold the other's hand as they shared the harder bits, having been one of the first interracial couples in town to make their relationship public. Elmira was jealous of the deep reverence they had for each other, despite the weight of bigotry and contempt they experienced even now.

After their chat, Moira left her husband with the books and led Elmira through the shop, telling stories of how things came into her life. There was a Victorian brass bed bought from an old hospital a few counties over and curtain rods from the nursery of quintuplet girls. Other fixtures and some small pieces of furniture, while far from ostentatious, had names attached to them that meant nothing to an out-of-towner but enriched the experience, nonetheless.

It was the kitchen sink that did her in. The thing was a behemoth, but it had history. A country-style, enameled cast-iron sink that had come from a ranch outside Littleton where four generations of the Williams family had lived. Elmira pictured all the dinners that had been finished by doing the washing, all the mud-caked hands scrubbed clean, and all the babies that might have had their first baths in it. It was no longer just a sink. It was an artifact of familial love, and the thought of leaving it behind caused Elmira's heartache too much. So, she bought it and the rest of her things and arranged for delivery later that day.

She left Moira's on a retail high and moved on to the Salvation Army down the road. Once done picking up minor household items, such as towels and linens, it was on to the local appliance and home store, where Elmira ordered basic appliances and a mattress with assurances that they would receive everything early in the week. They could process orders but didn't receive them on weekends.

She then found a laundromat and decided to wash her new linens as well as all the clothes she had in her car, mostly gym wear. Elmira's great escape had happened on dry-cleaning pickup day, giving her some clothes to wear while she washed everything else. Loading the washer with American coins was a new experience, the clink of them satisfying. Instead of waiting around, she decided to take in the local sights.

Littleton was a vibrant town that could've come right off a film lot. Store signs were hand-painted, buildings were old but well-kept, and people nodded and said, "How do you do."

Even the trees conformed to good behavior. Though their leaves were sparse for the season, their branches arched skyward poetically. Soon Elmira came to what could only be the town square where a statue of a man with a musket stood among the trees near a gazebo, where some townspeople were eating lunch at picnic tables. Knowledge of American war history was not one of her strengths, as such, the man's identity or what side of what war he fought for was a mystery. There was no sign posted to remedy her ignorance, which suggested he must be a town legend, or a work of art rather than a historical piece.

It reminded her of the National War Memorial back in Ottawa. She passed it almost every day and yet knew precious little about it. She felt small and insignificant next to both statues. What had she done to make the world a better place? It wasn't a new feeling, but at least they emboldened her to learn. Could she do something about it, though? She didn't know the way forward, but maybe learning some history would at very least teach her what not to do.

As she ruminated, she collected her laundry and drove back to her new property, parking with more intention this time. Guy Manning leaned against the wall by her door, looking like a classic rebel, only without the cigarette dangling from his lip.

One had to gawk. He was wearing the same worn jeans she'd seen him in earlier, distressed with a fresh coating of dust, and a simple white undershirt that hugged his muscular frame. Tattoos unapologetically marred the flesh of his forearms and biceps, and Ellie found herself wishing she could have time alone to analyze the artwork without the man who wore them. He was pure sex and angst, and she was certain the angst was because of her presence. You'd think a guy would be happy having sold the apartment, but she affronted him somehow.

Half expecting him to spit or light up or something to show his distaste, she made her approach. She never had been popular with men like him. Still, his reaction to her seemed over the top. She consoled herself with the fact that her attraction was superficial and greeted him with a smile.

"Hello again," she managed, looking up at him, which wasn't unusual for her considering her five-foot-nothing frame. The setting sun formed a halo behind him, and she shook her head to loosen the thought.

"Your load from Moira's came in," he said, and Elmira's smile faded.

"Was something broken?" she asked, picturing the sink cracked in two as she surveyed the lot. There, along the side of the building, sat a pile of her purchases, right in the dirt. She opened her mouth to say something but then let it close to pursed lips. Of course, she should have been there to receive them.

"You expecting poor Marvin to carry up all your crap?" Guy asked. "Because he would have, you know, he would have tried to move it all on his own. He'd have gotten hurt too. Lucky I was here to do your work for you."

"His name is Marlin. I suspect you know that and are trying to make a point?"

This response deepened the shade of rage red on Guy's face. "I don't know how many servants you got back home waiting on you hand and foot, but here, you do your own damn work." He began walking to his beat-up blue pickup, having nothing left to say to her.

"I'm sorry," she called out. Leaving additional tasks for Guy hadn't been intentional, and certainly not for Marlin, who had been so kind to her. Guy had left her things outside to make a point, and assuming nothing had been broken, it was a well-received punch. She hadn't meant to act prissy and could blame it on her state of mind, having not slept, and the whole running-away-from-life thing, but all were poor excuses to mistreat other people. His rage was degrees out of proportion, but she guessed he was feeling more protective of Marlin than he was mad at her, though it was too close to call. Were fighters known for their anger control? She thought not. This punishment would be taken in stride.

As Guy drove off, she turned to her pile of things and planned it out: carry the smaller items up first. The curtain rods are an easy load, and the bag of knobs and things could go in a spare laundry basket. But when she went to the door, she found it locked—and Guy had driven off without leaving the keys.

She sat down and started biting her nails. On the one hand, she was in the wrong and would need to give a proper apology. On the other hand, he was cheesed off and more than a little scary. He'd been a boxer, so who knows what kind of hostility he carried within. Having never been a fan of confrontations, even without the threat of violence, Elmira decided it would be best to give him some time to cool down. Sleeping in her car wouldn't be so bad now that she had blankets. She could call the office in the morning.

A resounding howl came from the thicket not far off in the distance. It could be a dog ... or ... Elmira pulled out her phone and Guy's business card. There was no one in the office, the message told her, and they had closed at noon and wouldn't be open until Monday.

Feeling her eyes well up at the humiliation of having to call him personally, her heart pounded. It rang once, then went to the machine. Another howl, then an answering chorus rang out. She dialed again.

"WHAT?" his deep voice cut through the line.

"I'm sorry," Elmira managed through her breathlessness. "You never gave me the keys." More silence on his end. "I tried the office, but it's closed, and I don't mind meeting you or Arleen"—*please be Arleen*—"somewhere to get them. I'd hate to inconvenience you any further. It's just that, well ..."

"Well, what?" he asked through gritted teeth.

"I think I heard a coyote ... Are there coyotes in Texas? Maybe it was a wolf, I don't know." The levy was breaking—alone in an unknown place, with a new home that shouldn't have been bought, running away from issues she hadn't known about until miles away from the comfort of her own little bubble, *and* she may be imminently attacked by coyotes. Everyone had a limit.

"Yeah," he spoke in a low, slow drawl. "We got coyotes here. But it's them badgers and bobcats ya gots ta watch out for. New builds takin' up their land and such."

Elmira's heart pounded with fear until she recognized the expectation in his silence. Exasperated, a groan escaped her chest. "You're laughing at me, aren't you?"

"Might be," he answered.

Counting to ten to rein in her biting remarks, she reminded herself to be apologetic. "I'm sorry I wasn't here for the delivery. I wasn't trying to be ..."

"A jerk."

"I was going to say thoughtless."

Silence.

"I'll be there in five." He chortled as he hung up. She wasn't sure that his coming back was such a good thing anymore. She'd rather face a bobcat.

Instead of sitting in her car worrying about Guy Manning thinking her a huge tool, she decided to risk the possible coyote and start making sense of the mess left outside her apartment. She grabbed the extra hamper she'd bought in town and filled it with the smaller items. She then set to lining up the larger items closer to her door.

Storming into town and throwing down enough cash to start a homestead didn't read as the most rational choice to make. She was getting used to the sideways glances but didn't want to be thought arrogant or ostentatious. It was the first time she'd been excited by a project in a long time. Not even her wedding plans excited her as much as seeing if the kitchen sink would go well with the handwoven curtains from the Salvation Army. If she was nesting, it was on the wrong end of the continent, but she couldn't help the smile as she considered her pile of treasures.

Elmira heard the truck pull in but wasn't ready to face Manning yet. Something about the man was disarming. The way Guy's body moved like a lion, almost lazy with confidence as he stalked toward her, couldn't be ignored. The incredulous way he appraised her with every glance suggested he was running a risk assessment; it kept her on edge. Her body responded with a dry mouth and tightening deep down, yet there was much more to note about the man before fainting at the sight of him.

She'd felt burned so many times by prom king and queen types that she refused to overvalue outward appearance unless it could benefit a business deal. But it was intriguing that he'd made the switch from boxer to businessman. Elmira knew better than most how important having a plan B was, especially to athletes. No stranger to businessmen, it was her job to understand them, and he seemed well-rounded. Although, being part of his own labor force made her wonder if he had control issues. Shifting her gaze, she couldn't deny that the man had vision. The craftsmanship of the building in front of her spoke for itself.

"You scare off the coyotes?" he asked from behind her. The sneer she'd envisioned as she turned to meet him turned out to be a well-meaning grin. She considered banter but decided to get to the heart of the matter.

"I am sorry for neglecting to be here for the order today. I plead insanity."

"You'd win that in court." He dangled a key in front of him as he walked toward her. He seemed more wary than enraged. She would take what she could get. "I might have seen red a little too fast. Marlin is like family to me, and to be honest, I'm not sure what to make of you yet." It was more of an apology than she had expected from him.

"I get that. Thank you for coming back." A prickling of tears tickled her eyes. She swallowed and carefully arranged her features to mask her feelings. He already thought her crazy, he didn't need to see her fall apart. Ragged from traveling, she wanted nothing more than to lock herself behind a door and curl up in the sleeping bag. Feelings had to be held in a little longer.

"Let me help you," Guy said.

"No, no, thank you, though. I appreciate it, but …"

He wasn't going to listen. He headed straight to the heavy pile and seeing it was no use, Elmira unlocked the door for him.

"Figures you'd find the heaviest damn sink in the county." He lifted it with a grunt and manhandled it through the doorway. She fought the urge to tell him to be careful with her prized possession. They carried her new things up the stairs, hardly speaking to each other. He even helped her with the bags and boxes from her car.

"So, I take it you enjoyed Moira's?" he asked once the last of the load was up.

"It's amazing. I swear I could spend a month in there."

He peeked into a basket and lifted out doorknobs with old-style keyholes. He raised an eyebrow at her, and she laughed.

"I know, not all of it will be relevant here. Everything had a story, you know?" She told him how the knobs had come out of an old schoolhouse and how the curtain rods were handmade by a blacksmith in Austin just a few years ago. "Who knew that was still a thing?"

"And that monstrosity?" he asked, pointing to the sink he'd placed by the window it would soon live under. She wanted to tell him about her vision of four generations of the Williamses babies having their first baths in it. About how she wished it could spill secrets—how had so many of them ended up staying in the home? What bound them to it? Were they still there and renovating to suit a new generation?

Instead, she said, "Isn't it glorious?"

"How about I bring up the catalogs and swatch books from the truck? Look through 'em and put in your design requests as soon as you can. I'd suggest you focus on flooring and cabinetry first, then maybe wall tile for the bathrooms. You can go fancy on the shower tile if you want. With the claw-toothed-tub it won't get in the way of installation timing. Not sure how long delivery will take on that, though. If you choose a more basic model insert, it can be in and usable within a day or two tops. Anything else shouldn't greatly affect your day-to-day living."

"Thank you," was all she could say before he was out the door and back a few minutes later with a crate of goodies for her to peruse. He laughed when he saw her excitement.

"Into interior design, I take it?" he asked.

"I've never thought about it much until today. Can I tell you what I'm picturing?"

He leaned back in response.

"OK, I'll save it. I don't want to go too off trend, though. I want to make it my own, but I don't want to make it unsellable."

"Already thinking about leaving us?"

"I don't know what I'm doing here," she admitted with a shrug. "I love this building, though. Have you been in the business for long?"

"A bit," he said. "What are you thinking, Miss Ellie? Between that sink and the claw-foot tub you asked about, I'm guessing a country theme?"

"It's that obvious, eh?"

"So, you *are* Canadian."

"Yeah ..." She laughed. "So, I'm thinking a country/Victorian marriage? The warmth of the country items coupled with industrial pieces? I think the stuff you're dealing with would be the country items—reclaimed wood floors, country kitchen ... but the rest I want to be rather stark. Subway tile, maybe black-and-white honeycomb flooring. Does that sound remotely doable?"

"Should be. Check through the book in there. It'll give ya a better idea of what's included and what's going to cost more. If you have anything selected, I can place orders first thing Monday.

If it's in stock, I can start laying things down for you in the afternoon. I'll drop by tomorrow and see where you are with everything."

Elmira pulled out a paint swatch book and flipped through it with glee. "Thank you, Mr. Manning. For helping me with my things and for my new home." They shook hands, and she felt her skin flush at his touch. The humor in his eyes locked her in place.

Mercurial. What a confusing man.

"Call me Guy. See you tomorrow, kid," he said with such authority that she felt like a twelve-year-old girl instead of an adult businesswoman. He took the stairs like a dancer, and she heard him lock up behind him. Did he keep a key? She should've felt disconcerted, or maybe indignant, but instead found it oddly reassuring. He would need access for the ongoing renovations, anyway.

The next hour was spent moving her things to the appropriate rooms. Guy had left a small toolbox behind, and before long she was attaching doorknobs where she could. She considered putting up the towel rods but thought it might be best if they painted first. The pile of samples called to her, and soon she was knee-deep in rainbow swatches, envisioning her home. Should she go with a continuous color theme? She sat on the floor and closed her eyes, trying to picture her new world.

Her *real* home was done in earth tones. Who was she kidding? It was beige. Her new home would be colorful.

She found paper and a pen and began taking notes for her meeting with Guy the following day. She knew he thought her a pain, and the kitchen she envisioned wouldn't help matters. Dreaming felt good, though, and she hoped it wouldn't be too hard to bring to life.

The space took over her imagination. If she weren't careful with her choices, the space would have too many hard finishes, what with the distressed hardwood and cold, clean tile. She wanted whimsy and soft femininity; her palette was clear skies and colorful sunsets. She wrote down the names and numbers from swatches of purples, blues, and yellows. That done, she considered twiddling her thumbs, but the sun was still up, so she grabbed her keys and drove back to town, hoping to find the hardware store still open.

For a few good hours, Elmira didn't think about what she was doing there. She focused instead on improving her space and found some flowerpots to hang in the windows and a fern to improve air quality. She ate dinner at a local restaurant that had candles on the tables. It was when she crawled into her new sleeping bag in her new room on the unfinished floor of her new apartment that the truth rolled in again.

She was on the run, and no amount of nesting would fix her problems, especially when she wasn't prepared to ask herself what those problems were. Was forgetting for a while longer, pretending to be someone else, such a bad thing? Maybe that's how she would stumble upon her truth.

CHAPTER THREE

*G*uy pulled into the lot around noon carrying a couple of sandwiches and bottles of water. When he'd apologized for leaving the church lunch early, Pastor Thomas made sure he didn't go without something to bring to the newest member of Littleton. The Pastor was so excited about adding to his flock that Guy hadn't the heart to let him know that he doubted she would be sticking around, or that she seemed more of a new age spiritualist than churchgoing religious. Guy believed everyone was entitled to their own beliefs, but it would make it harder for Miss Ellie to become a part of the community.

He'd kept a key for practical reasons—installations could be done at odd hours, and she wouldn't be required to stay home. Also, she seemed the type to lose things, but he was a gentleman and didn't intend to use it unless necessary. As he raised his hand to knock, a loud bang came from above. His key was out, and he flew up the stairs to find Miss Ellie trapped under a ladder, paint roller still in hand.

"Are you hurt?" he asked as he assessed if it was safe to move the ladder.

"YOU SCARED THE BEJEEZUS OUT OF ME!"

"I scared you? I thought you'd knocked yourself out!"

"There's a doorbell for a reason!"

"It's not installed yet!" He decided to leave her where she was.

She muttered profanities as she wiggled out from beneath the ladder and checked herself for damage. As she was red-faced from embarrassment and otherwise looking like hell, Guy decided he would be charitable and give her a minute to regain her composure. He dropped the bag of sandwiches beside Miss Ellie's notebook on the floor and took stock of the room. It had been painted. And she wasn't on the first coat either. He couldn't decide if he found this enterprising or another sign of psychosis.

"Sorry for yelling at you. You took me by surprise is all."

"You good?" he asked, tossing her a towel from a nearby hamper.

"Yeah, I'm fine. It's time for a break, I guess." She did her best to wash herself clean of paint in the powder room.

"Pastor Thomas asked me to bring you some lunch and an invitation to his service next week." His gaze swept the walls. "You been up all night painting?" On his hurried way upstairs, he hadn't noticed if the entryway had been painted, and he checked himself for smudges.

"Yeah, don't worry, I started down there, so it should be dry. Let me just say how thankful I am that the plumbing is up and running. A sponge bath after painting is way better than the alternative." She yawned as she settled on the floor. "Thanks." She unwrapped the sandwich, then savored a bite before swallowing before continuing. "I wrote down a list of finishings for you, but there are a few things I was hoping we could tweak."

Guy was surprised that she didn't dawdle with small talk, but he didn't mind the segue. It wasn't as though he were there to talk about the weather. Talking through her ideas for the place, Guy became excited about it too. It wouldn't be too labor intensive, and she had charming ideas that fit with his vision for these buildings. He wouldn't admit it to her, but he didn't even mind the bright blue she had chosen for the main space.

Although her style was more flamboyant than he'd considered, Miss Ellie was keeping with the spirit of vintage aesthetics just as he'd imagined at the project's inception. He took some notes and appreciated her asking his opinion on her choices and for ideas that would be more appropriate for local tastes. Picking out paint and getting it on the walls showed him that she was relentless and driven.

After a couple of hours of going through her selections and haggling over what was included in the cost of the building, Guy checked the time on his watch and whistled. "I'm sorry, Miss Ellie, but I've got family dinner to get to."

"Thank you so much. It was fun bouncing ideas off you." It struck him that he'd enjoyed it too.

Guy gathered his things as she tidied the bit of mess left over from their sandwiches and her stomach rumbled. She laughed. "Is there a restaurant in the area you'd recommend?"

"I could name a few, but it won't do you any good. Everything that's open on Sundays in the county is closed by now."

Ellie's face fell. She hadn't considered the possibility.

"You must be a city girl." He chuckled.

"Yeah ... I mean, Ottawa isn't huge compared to others, but there's always something open. Serves me right for not thinking ahead." She made like she'd fluffed it off, but Guy could tell she was disappointed. And seeing as how he knew her lunch had been meager, he took pity on the new girl in town.

"Well now, how about you join us for dinner?" It was a reluctant gesture, but her bafflement made for an amusing payoff. This lady wore it all on her sleeve.

"I wouldn't want to impose ..."

"My folks always make more food than we can eat, and it's Sunday in the South, after all. It wouldn't be Christian to turn you away." Miss Ellie was hesitant to accept, so Guy added, "They would love to meet you. The town is buzzing about new blood here."

"I'm not newsworthy! Really!" Ellie's eyebrows shot up so high that Guy chuckled again.

"Don't worry. Everything is newsworthy in a small town." Guy decided he wasn't taking no for an answer, and soon he had her following him to the other side of town toward his childhood home. Checking in his rearview mirror to make sure Ellie hadn't chickened out, Guy shook his head. What was he getting into with this woman? *Charity*, he told himself, as she tried to fix her hair while driving.

A few minutes had passed when he looked up again and saw that he'd lost her. He took a quick U-turn and found her in her car on the road's shoulder. The engine poured smoke, and she was bouncing her head against the steering wheel. He knocked on her window, feeling like a patrolman.

"Might want to get out before it explodes," he called to her with a grin. She opened her window without turning to face him.

"Don't tempt fate!" she shot back with much less humor.

"Come on now, pop the hood. I'll see what I can do."

She got out of the car and came to pout at the engine.

"You all right?" he asked. She was so tense that her head tilted, and he thought he saw her eye twitch.

"It's been a heck of a week," she admitted as Guy poked around at the engine, careful not to burn himself. "Do you know what you're looking at in here?"

"I'm no mechanic, but I get by. I'm guessing it's overheated. I've got some coolant I can pour in for you." He had no idea what he was talking about, but he didn't think it would cause any damage, so he got coolant from the back of his truck and her car magically started.

"Thanks. I owe you one. Do you think it's safe to drive?"

"Yeah but be careful. I'll keep an eye as we go. My folks aren't too far now."

~

ELMIRA FOLLOWED Guy up to a two-story family home with large bay windows and a garden with hedges waiting to decorate the veranda come spring. The front door was large, made of knotted wood, with a section of colorful stained glass at the top. No paint bubbles on the siding, no scuff marks anywhere. Freshly painted window frames and a veranda that hugged right around the building punctuated the feeling that this home was well loved.

"Are you sure your parents won't mind me showing up unannounced? They might think I'm a vagrant."

"That would make it easier to accept you. Southern hospitality at its finest!"

"I don't want them to get the wrong idea about us. I mean, me. I mean, you know ..."

"Are you seriously worried about meeting my parents?"

"Well ..." Without a doubt, it was true. Growing up, Elmira had always dreamed of the perfect mom: cookies at Christmas, a kiss on the forehead at bedtime, pride tempered by warmth and love. Seeking out these things from other parents taught her that a mother's unconditional love applied to their own children, so she'd pushed that longing down.

There was nothing soft about Eliza, a fact that gave Elmira the upper hand. If Guy's mother was vile, she would know how to stay composed. Her approach would be clinical, and she would not get attached. If she was perfect, well, she could deal with the emotional fallout later. Above all, she would remember that she was an adult and didn't need validation from anyone. Even mothers.

She took a box breath as they stood in front of the door: in three, hold three, out three, hold three.

"You do that a lot, don't you? The deep heaving thing." Guy looked at her, causing a rush of defensiveness.

"What? Breathe? Yeah, I try to remember to do that."

"Hey, Ma!" Guy called out as he pushed open the front door

of the cottage-style home. Ellie's recent foray into real estate had her wondering what a place like this would cost. She had no clue what to compare it to. The wraparound veranda invited guests to stay awhile. Even with plants devoid of leaf or flower, Elmira could imagine soothing blooms come spring. What struck her was how familiar it felt, like every family home she had ever seen on television and wished she could belong to. One didn't just live in such a place: the house was a family member. Longing hit her as she gazed down the porch to where a swing hung. She imagined losing her teenage self in a book there, or running up to a knitting grandmother, crying over a scraped knee and receiving kisses and tickles until the catastrophe subsided.

"Come on in, Ellie. Oh, hey, Cujo!"

A gorgeous golden retriever galloped into the foyer, and pressed his way between Guy's legs, demanding love, flopping to his back upon receiving it.

Elmira stood in the doorway and admired the scene. The bright foyer offered a view of the craftsman staircase. The woodwork was well kept, original to the home. With its twisting angles, it was made for prom reveals. To the left of the entry was a den where a piano lounged. Down the hall were French doors to what must have been a home office. She took it all in while the dog demanded love.

Elmira's mother had never allowed pets, and she and Daniel had never discussed it. He didn't seem like an animal person, and she had gone without for so long that she felt disconcerted when in the company of a pet. She respected their status in a family, but she didn't know what to do with one. The otherwise debonair dog managed to wiggle himself two feet forward, still on his back. He heard her laughter and stood abruptly, turning to size her up.

"Cujo, this is Miss Ellie."

The dog turned from Guy to her and back again, feigning his composure, then cocked his head sideways as if to ask, *What's her deal?*

"I don't know, but as far as I can tell, she's not dangerous to anyone but herself," Guy responded sagely.

That was all it took for Cujo to jump on Ellie and knock her to the ground, licking and prancing as he went. Elmira was equal parts elated and terrified but gave way to nervous laughter as she guarded her face.

"Now, Cuj, you best stop that," said a demure southern drawl.

The dog stepped back, distancing himself from this stranger he'd licked from top to bottom.

Ellie saw Guy's mother for the first time. Her hair was a strategic mix of blondes and grays that allowed her to age in her own time. She had to be in her fifties but even with telltale laugh lines and crow's-feet, her skin glowed. She was a woman of means, taller than Ellie but with more feminine curves, and Pilates-toned muscles. Her eyes were the same shade of blue-gray as her son's, not to mention intelligent and shrewd. All the while, she was warm and exuded love for her son, from whom she accepted a hello hug. "Guy, you didn't tell me you were bringing someone home. I might have put our best foot forward."

Ellie stole the opportunity to look around. The vast entryway was pristine. Even from the floor, she couldn't find any evidence of shirked house duties.

"Sorry, Ma, it was a last-minute thing. This here is Miss Ellie. She's the one who bought the condo. Doesn't have an oven hooked up yet."

"Oh yes, the Canadian girl. You have taken the town by storm, haven't you? Might I offer you some coffee or iced tea? Maybe a cocktail?" she asked with perfect courtesy, ignoring the fact that Elmira was still on her floor, covered in dog slime.

"It's Elmira." She fortified herself with her name as she glared at Guy. "Pleasure to meet you, ma'am."

"You can call me Ivy." At the sound of heels behind her, Ivy continued, "And this is Goldie Morrison, Littleton's premiere real estate agent. I believe you've heard of her."

"Ha! Yes! Hello! What are the chances?" Elmira squeaked out in panic as she struggled to her feet. "I have quite a low tolerance to caffeine." There was a defined pause as everyone took in the awkwardness. "But a glass of water would be lovely."

"Well, all right, then. Guy, your father is out at the grill." And Ivy glided toward the back of the house.

"Low tolerance to caffeine?" asked Guy as he led Elmira down the hall.

"Yes."

"Is that so?" Goldie, the blond bombshell, asked in clear enjoyment of Elmira's discomfort.

"Yes."

"Hmmm" was the collective response.

"No, for real, I can't touch the stuff."

"If you say so." Guy and Goldie shared a knowing look as they continued to the rear of the house.

"I tried taking a couple of caffeine pills in university once, to get a few more hours of work done one night ..." Guy looked at Elmira like she had a dunce cap on. "It didn't end well." She finished quickly, leaving out the clowns and the waking up two days later.

"How was your grade?" he asked with a twitch of a grin forming at the corner of his mouth.

"Aces," she said, averting her eyes from those lips, leaving out the fact that she had needed an extension on that particular assignment. He saw her as a crackpot, which was fine, but she didn't need to fuel the idea when he was looking so attractive. She chastised herself for falling victim to his pretty face. Thirst traps like him didn't get under her skin. She wasn't immune to their appeal, but she craved connection more than basic attraction. All quite aside from the fact that she was engaged and shouldn't be noticing broad shoulders and angular jaws or considering the softness of lopsided grins.

They entered the backyard, and Elmira was awestruck. The

garden was pristine. There was even an old wood tree house and a tire swing hanging from an ancient oak.

"Ed, we have company! This is Miss Ellie. Poor girl doesn't have a stove to cook on!" Ivy cooed, breaking Elmira from her thoughts as she detected a familiar tone—judgment basted with kindness.

"Well, you have come to the right place. It's a pleasure to meet you." Ed Manning was older than his wife but carried himself with a handsome dignity. Guy had the same broad shoulders as his father, an athletic build, but where Guy held tension Ed was relaxed. He was graying, his eyes a lighter shade of blue than his son's, but he had a gentle manner about him.

"Let me help you with the drinks, Ivy." Goldie bowed out with grace that Ellie both admired and was thankful for. She needed a break from their knowing looks.

"Pleasure's mine, sir," said Elmira. "Your home is so beautiful."

"Why, thank you. Hope you like steak!" Guy's father flipped a huge slab of meat and Elmira smiled in response, unsure of what to say. She didn't want to be rude, but this back-and-forth banter of pleasantries was alien to her. She knew how to make deals, how to run a business, and how to deal with her mother, but outside of those structures, she floundered. Especially when she wanted to make a good impression.

"So, what is it that brings you to our little town?" Ivy asked as she and Goldie returned to dole out drinks. Ivy then settled into a wicker chair, sipped her iced tea, and got right to the heart of things Ellie didn't intend to reveal about herself. Her gaze flicked to Goldie where she sat near Guy.

They looked perfect together.

Elmira's face reddened. Of course, they were a couple. Home builder and Realtor—it was *too* perfect. She felt an unnameable feeling creeping in but pushed it down, unexamined. She had seen a show once that talked scientifically about how people choose mates in the same league of attractiveness, so it only made sense for

Guy and Goldie. Even the names worked magic. Ellie looked back to Ivy who was also admiring the match.

"Well, I was headed to Mexico, but after I read an article about Littleton, I decided to see if it would be a good fit."

"Isn't that adventurous! What is it you do for a living? Must be flexible if you are able to be so impulsive," said Ivy.

Goldie snorted at Ivy's hint of belittlement.

Ellie knew she deserved Goldie's ire for leaving her on the side of the road. "I'm basically a manager, but I've been considering a change."

"What about technically?" asked Guy, enjoying the awkwardness of the situation.

"Pardon me?"

"We talk slow sometimes, Miss Ellie, but we don't need things dumbed down for us," Guy answered, grinning as he took a sip from his drink.

"Oh, I didn't mean ..."

"Don't let him fool you. We know you didn't mean to be rude, don't we, Ed?" Ivy fanned the flames.

Ed responded with a grunt, paying extra close attention to the steaks.

"Well," started Elmira, flushed and eager to get off this track, "I am between titles at present."

"What a shame. Tough to lose a job," Ed said, throwing her a kind smile.

"No, what I mean is that I got offered a promotion."

"Is that so?" asked Guy with a smirk, sensing a punch line.

How dare he patronize me? I am an independent, smart businesswoman!

"Yes, it is, but I'm not sure if I want to accept." She knew she should share much more to even get close to polite, but when she was met with silence, she didn't continue.

"So, this is going to be a vacation home, then? I thought you snowbirds preferred Florida." Ed laughed, and Ellie was thankful for the respite from the hot seat, though not knowing how to respond, she asked the only appropriate question she could think of:

"Could I use your washroom?" The question somehow earned looks of bafflement.

∼

ELLIE TOOK her time doing her business and washing up. She splashed water over her face and paused to dissect her image in the mirror. Her hair was overgrown and out of place, and her skin was flushed from embarrassment. It wasn't the first time on this trip that her reflection alarmed her, nor was it the first time she'd felt so disconnected.

In high school she'd been invited to what was touted as the biggest party of the year. Of course, her mother would have forbidden it. And, of course, that was the appeal. She hadn't intended to go to the party, not until her mother decided they should review the video she'd taken at her ballet rehearsal with the express purpose of ripping it apart. Elmira hadn't eaten much in days since her mother had put her on a juice fast to keep her form for the recital. She'd barely kept up with her schoolwork, and her energy was depleted. Her mother, on the other hand, was fueled by a bad day and a bottle of wine.

Ellie was used to her mother's condescension and critiques, but that night she was downright hateful. When her mother broke out the scale and the measuring tape, Ellie felt something snap. Instead of changing into her leotard for her mother to measure every inch of her body, she threw on a pair of jeans and a crop top and climbed out her window.

An hour and a half later, after the Jell-O shots, the room began to spin. That was when Elmira found the washroom, puked, and washed her face, alone as ever.

She'd seen the shadows around her eyes, saw the gray pallor, and knew that it wasn't only the alcohol. Her mother was poisoning her like a parent who slips rat poison into their child's food to get the attention of doctors and sympathy from friends. The difference was that her mother was monopolizing her talent, feeding off her daughter's glory, and poisoning her sense of self-worth. Elmira's joy was dying. Even through her stupor, she knew it was time to make a choice: she could try to reclaim the joy, or let her mother keep driving her life.

She wanted to feel alive again when dancing and had managed to convince her mother that she needed more than celery juice to fuel her through the competitions. After she broke her knee, none of that hard-won freedom mattered anymore. Letting Eliza steer her wherever she liked was the easiest thing to do.

Elmira rehabilitated her knee over time, but it didn't matter. It was never quite strong enough to complete leaps and extensions with the precision necessary to fulfill either of their dreams. Having always been a good student, and without dance to draw her away from her studies, it was easy enough to pivot. Easy for her to let her mother develop a new dream for them when all her hopes had crashed.

Standing in the Mannings' home, Elmira appreciated just how far she had fallen. She'd never driven so long after the accident, and she would've never risked driving overnight through a country virtually unknown to her.

She shook off the thought. The accident wasn't something to dwell on. What was done was done.

What she saw now in the Mannings' mirror was different from what she'd seen as a drunken teen. She couldn't quite put her finger on it, but it made her feel raw. Could she still be anyone, do anything? Was she a blank enough canvas?

She heard everyone outside transitioning indoors for the meal.

Ellie grounded herself before entering the dining room. While she was in awe of Ivy's home, she knew now that Ivy was a shrewd woman who missed nothing. Not to mention her clear and obvious plan for her family, a plan that included Goldie. One that she would not tolerate someone stepping in on.

Ellie decided to do her best to play the part of the impulsive out-of-towner. Heck, she already had a nickname! No one knew her here, it was her chance at reinvention.

"Now, if I had known you were coming, Ellie, I would have taken the spice down a notch. You might want to avoid the rice. It has some kick." Ivy shared a private grin with Guy.

Ellie smiled wider, a defense mechanism mastered as a child. "Thank you for the warning, Ivy, but I love spicy food!" she replied while taking a heaping spoonful and passing the dish down.

"None for me, Miss Ellie. I can't handle the stuff myself," Guy said.

Elmira glowered at him, unsure why he was so jovial, but not trusting it. She'd almost forgotten she was supposed to be playing the part of a carefree adventurer when a young man stumbled in, throwing his football pads and duffel bag to the floor. He was the inverted image of Guy, with dark hair and eyes, a lanky teenager but muscular enough. The age difference between brothers had to be at least fifteen years. But Ellie didn't have time to muse. His energy was a show she had to watch.

"Sorry, Ma, practice ran late," he said as he tallied the contents of the table, stealing a roll while pulling out his chair. "You trying to kill Miss Ellie here?"

"Yes, death by rice," Ivy deadpanned. "How on earth do you know Miss Ellie?" she asked, overjoyed to have another son home for dinner.

He laughed as he heaped food on his plate, winking in Ellie's direction. "She made an impression. You know how the town talks. She's big news! And here I find you trying to set her on fire."

Ellie thought this was another case of Texans underestimating their northern neighbors. She would show them. She ordered Thai food all the time—she could handle a little southern zing.

"Now, Liam, you go wash up. And take your gear with you. I can smell your bag from here."

"Yes, ma'am!" He was up in a flash and running down the hall.

"Where does that boy get his energy?" asked his mother as everyone, except the Canadian, watched him bounce away, missing Ellie eat a respectful forkful of rice with determined nonchalance.

Her mouth went from normal to molten with a single chew.

The room erupted with warnings and chairs dragging back from the table as they noticed the expression on her face. It was unlike anything she'd ever felt. She liked spicy food, but this was not flavor—it was pure heat. She considered whether there might be acid in her mouth. Had she been poisoned? She was on her feet, flapping as though hand-fanning could cool her inflamed mouth.

Guy stood beside her, cussing something she couldn't hear through her panic and handing her his water glass. Ivy and Goldie covered their mouths in shock. His father grabbed the bottle of orange sports drink sticking out from Liam's duffel, taking off the lid and handing it to a still-panting Canadian wimp. She guzzled it as fast as she could.

It. Did. Nothing.

Ivy disappeared into the kitchen and returned with a gallon of milk, fiddling with the cap and looking for a glass. Ellie charged her, grabbed the bottle, and poured milk down her throat, making a mess of her clothes, forgetting her lactose intolerance and unable to care when the melting of her esophagus abated enough for her to recall.

She accused each person of murder with a glance.

"Are you OK?" someone asked.

"I'm fine," she croaked as she took the napkin Goldie offered from across the table.

"Whoa! What I miss?" asked Liam as he ran back into the room.

"Well, Miss Ellie tried her first bite of your mother's ghost pepper rice," Ed explained, as though good manners could undo the disaster in front of him. "You two are still the only ones who can stomach it."

Ellie wanted to yell at all of them, but her years of training in the art of mother pleasing provided the good and proper response: "I'm sorry, Liam, I drank your Gatorade. I will buy you another sometime." She began calculating how long she had before the dairy would take hold. "Thank you for having me. For now, I think I will get home. Good night." She turned to leave, careful not to slip on the spilled milk around her.

"Gatorade?" Liam said before his eyes widened. "Aw, naw, that wasn't Gatorade. That was Coach's Go-Juice ..."

Ellie stopped in her tracks as an overwhelming wave of defeat rolled through her. She visibly shrank, knowing the answer but praying to be wrong. "And what exactly is Go-Juice?"

"Dunno, mostly caffeine, I think." Liam shrugged.

"Oh, Ellie, this isn't your night," Goldie said with obvious care.

Ellie couldn't take pity on top of everything else. She wanted to scream, but all she had left was her face, and she intended to save it.

"Would you like a ride home?" Guy asked with his perfect body and his perfect family standing around him. The sound of his voice uncorked the bottle of rage she'd hidden inside.

"No, thank you." She seethed. "I wouldn't want to spoil your dinner any more than I already have. Bye, now." She waved over her shoulder as she made a hasty exit.

"SHE SURE KNOWS how to leave an impression, doesn't she?" asked Ed, smiling as he sat back down to eat. Goldie and Liam followed his lead.

"You *should* make sure she gets home safe," his mother told

Guy as she mopped up the milk. "It'll be dark soon, and I would hate to see her get into an accident."

"I'm sure you would, Ma," he goaded as he kissed her forehead by way of apology. "I'd better catch up."

"That girl is all sorts of trouble. She didn't even wait to say grace before eating."

He paused, surprised at his mother's opinion of Ellie. Sure, she was a train wreck, but trouble?

"I'm being friendly. She is a client, after all," he responded before chasing after Ellie, uncomfortable with the need to defend her.

He caught her as she was fumbling with her keys. She glared at him with pure rage.

"Now, what are you mad at *me* for?"

"You could have warned me, you know!"

"I did warn you. So did Mom AND Liam. Not my fault you're a damn fool." As soon as the words were out, he regretted them. "I'm sorry, darlin'. Let me take you home and get you settled in."

"Forget it. I'll be fine. Thanks for the dinner invitation." She drove off, barking her tires in her haste.

Guy watched her disappear into the distance, surprised at the direction his thoughts went. Miss Ellie was sexy when she was mad. He shook some darned kinky thoughts out of his head and went back in to salvage the family dinner.

CHAPTER FOUR

The house was quieter than Ivy liked it to be. It was the sound of the nest emptying. Even her Liam flew the coop as soon as he finished gorging himself on dinner. She and Ed silently ushered dishes and serving platters back from the table to the kitchen to be cleaned and put away. Ivy, as always, was the first to break the silence.

"I don't like that girl one bit. She seems to aim for demure, but something is off with her. You don't think she's dangerous, do you?"

Ed grunted something.

"Sorry, darling, I didn't catch that."

"I said that Guy can manage her."

"I don't know. His heart is so big, and a girl like that comes with baggage. Our boy is a gentleman who carries luggage and likes solving problems. I hope he sees the crazy on her face."

"Mind if I go clean the grill before it's full dark?" Ed asked.

"No," Ivy spat. "I don't mind." Ed left Ivy alone to tend the dishes. It was almost a blessing, she chose to think. If he had been in there, he would've stuffed things in the refrigerator any which way. Methodically, Ivy packaged leftovers for lunches and washed dishes as she imagined a long line of women had done for the Manning men before she was even a thought. If something had to be done, it might as well be done right, and Ivy was nothing if not organized. Her husband of thirty-two years scored the grill clean as she listened to him and scrubbed the dishes.

It wasn't that she thought Ellie could do any physical damage: she was tiny compared to Guy. He *had* been a boxer for too many terrifying years. But even he had to sleep sometimes. No, there was something about her. She was trying too hard, but what had bothered Ivy was the way Ellie had made her feel. Old. Matronly. Like a damned finished novel. Ma'am, indeed.

Ellie had ogled the Manning home like it was some kind of museum of happily ever after, and yet she met her passive-aggression blow for blow. Ivy hadn't intended to act so petty with the girl, a visitor to her home and her town. There was something irksome about her evasive maneuvers. Authentic people didn't need to run and hide in the bathroom, for goodness' sake.

Ivy remembered the first girl Guy ever brought home for family dinner—Susan Gale, when they were about thirteen. Susan was smitten, and Guy was a gentleman. Later, Ivy learned that Susan had been bullied at school, and Guy had dated her to help her feel better about herself. That was the kind of boy he was.

Then there was Rita Barton at sixteen who was diagnosed with bipolar disorder. Guy had talked her off the gymnasium roof when she'd decided she was going to end it all. Marie Klintock had been beaten by her father, Alexa Bloom had an eating disorder, and Andrea Holding had been taking pharmaceuticals in an attempt to maintain her grade point average. Oh, and Anna Beth Murrey ... she was a nice girl. Ivy wished she knew what had happened to end that relationship. She imagined Anna Beth was too low-key for her son. Too together. Too boring after all the drama he'd soaked up.

Things changed when he started his boxing career. He stopped bringing home strays, or any women at all, except for Goldie, but they maintained that their relationship was professional. Still, a mother could hope.

All Ivy wanted for her children was for them to be happy with someone they could call their soulmate. Guy approached relationships from the wrong angle, and it was happening again with this Ellie girl whom Ivy didn't even have the family name to google. Why he and Goldie weren't an item made no sense to her. They were both good-looking and driven. Easily they'd become Littleton's power couple, the same as she and Edward were.

Ed came back into the house, put the barbecue tools on the counter, and grabbed a beer from the fridge without a word.

"Going to watch the game, darling?"

"Yup." He continued on to the living room. Ivy watched as he followed the exact path he'd used hundreds, if not thousands, of times over the years. Feeling tired and restless, she turned back to the washing. Maybe her son had gotten his inclinations from her. Charity was the family business.

She removed her pink rubber gloves and hung them to dry, then pumped some lotion onto her hands, promising to keep an eye on her son this time.

ELLIE SHOULD'VE STAYED LYING fetal in her sleeping bag. While her guts were settling, her nerves were not, and the floor wasn't cozy enough to keep her. For the first time, instead of feeling excited about her new place, she felt lonely and stupid. That morning she had lain in a cocoon of blankets and sweatpants, hoping a depressive haze would swallow her. Her heart still pumped too fast, forcing her to get up and move.

Windows were washed, dust and debris swept, and door handles were shined. The yet-unpainted walls whispered accusations, so she used up the last of her paint. When she surveyed the room again, the place was as spotless as an unfinished space could be. The walls seemed gray instead of blue as the early-morning sun filtered through her windows.

The buzz of her cell phone brought a welcome distraction. Her voicemail was full of *motherly* advice. It sounded like Eliza was harassing Ellie's administrative assistant, so Ellie sent out a few apology emails to her employees, let Human Resources and her boss know that she would be away, but ignored the absurd amount of unread emails.

Nothing from Daniel. The feeling of isolation was unyielding and she only had herself to blame. Her mind taunted her for the softer things she was made of until she couldn't take it anymore. It was time to face the world.

It was unbelievable, even to her, that her car had broken down again a couple of blocks away from the Mannings' house. The tow-truck guy said he'd be at least an hour, but she didn't have that long. Her choice had been either to turn back and make Guy's family aware of what dairy did to her system or run as fast as possible. The twilight howling had kept her motivated, but her shoes didn't survive that run and neither did her feet. The thought of wearing her running shoes made her cringe with all the blistering sores. So slipper boots were the only choice.

It was a cool morning for this part of Texas. She was thankful Ottawa had a cold warning in effect when she'd left. Otherwise, she might not have had her warm and cozies with her. She threw on a soft, blue wool toque with a furry pom-pom taking the stairs two at a time, despite the tenderness of her feet. As she walked toward the only café in town, she felt the chill in the air. It was nippy, her nose stung, but there was no sign of frost and none of the wet cold she was used to between seasons. This cold was dry, a little insidious, but not powerful enough to sneak past a sweater.

Day was breaking. Somehow, she had survived the night. Her body hummed. She felt as raw as her feet. Worse than angry, what she really felt was fragile. A warning sting surfaced behind her eyes that had nothing to do with the cool breeze running down the main street. Monday morning pedestrian traffic was bustling, and children dragged their heels to school with heavy backpacks. A few runners, wearing spandex and water belts speaking to their expertise, nodded as they passed her. A certifiable mess, though she may be, it was not on her bucket list to land in an American loony bin. She nodded back but hugged herself to self-soothe more than to preserve warmth.

The lineup for warm drinks was long, but fast moving. The warmth of the shop was relaxing, along with the smell of cinnamon, and fresh baked goodies. It was a simple setup, a display beside the cash register, a pickup area farther down the line, and plenty of seating. Wood paneling had been painted white, so the effect was clean but scuffed with wear and tear.

While ordering, Ellie's elbow knocked over a box of straws. "Sorry! I suck today!" she tried to joke, but the barista's deadpan was too strong for her weak wit. Ellie took the table in the corner. She sipped at her decaf soy latte with caution, trusting no one. It tasted nondairy, but eyes had been rolled when she'd asked for soy, so he could've switched it to make a point. She had tried to be as polite as possible, but you never know who might be willing to mess with your food. Her stomach accepted the drink's warmth, which was more than she'd expected after having been thrice poisoned.

She nodded and smiled at everyone who bid her a good day. Noting the apprehensive double takes sent her way, she took off her warm cap in hopes of drawing less attention to herself. She found herself missing Ottawa for the first time. She could've sat in a million different cafés and had no one acknowledge her for hours, as long as she paid her way. People might have given her a wider berth in light of her inability to stop tapping her hands and feet, but they would've kept their stares to their periphery. That's what she wanted: anonymity.

How sad is that? she asked herself. *I miss being avoided.*

Realizing that she'd reached bottom, she decided to give the fetal position another try. Before she could stand to leave, she locked eyes with Goldie who was headed toward her.

"Merde," she grunted.

Goldie, with her Nashville hair and boudoir eyes, looked like she bathed in sunshine and kittens and not at all like a woman who would run across town to get to a toilet as Ellie had done the night before. As Goldie moved, her hips gave a signature wiggle that Elmira knew she could mimic but never master. Ellie was a fitting nickname—childish and awkward, like a knobby-kneed filly. All she could hear as Goldie approached was a va-va-voom in tandem with her strides.

"My goodness! Miss Ellie, you are vibrating. What's going on? Are you OK?"

Ellie almost cracked. The one person in town that she wanted so badly to hate was the only one who cared enough to ask, and out of genuine concern.

"You know what this is. You were there. Or were you too busy sucking up to the future in-laws that you missed it?"

Goldie's eyes went wide.

Ellie knew she was being petty but couldn't help it.

"Ha!" Goldie's eyes filled with unexpected mirth. "We all thought you were exaggerating about that whole low-tolerance thing. It gives you fire in your belly! We gotta get you to a doctor."

"Hey, Gold! Are you still meeting me at ten? I'm not going to have time to pick up those swatches from Decan's for your buyer. Holy Hannah, what's wrong with you?" Guy Manning asked as he strode toward them, unwashed in his low-key sweats and overworn T-shirt, glistening with perspiration, glowing with health.

If the caffeine had worn off, Ellie would've looked away, bashful, completely embarrassed, and ashamed of her dry mouth and the warm pulse emanating from below. But it had not worn off, so instead, she remembered to be angry.

"WHAT'S WRONG WITH YOU?" She launched out of her chair, slamming her drink down hard enough that most of it splattered on the table. "What's wrong with *you*? Mr. Perfect, eh? You invite me into your family's home, all southern hospitality, when you were in fact bringing fresh meat to the lion's den! If I wanted my life judged and dissected by someone's mother, I would call my own!"

"What am I missing?" Guy looked sidelong at Goldie for help.

"Apparently, she wasn't lying about the caffeine. I'm going to call Doc."

"No need, Goldie. What seems to be the problem, miss?" came the voice of a weary lawman with a dark complexion and a conspicuously large sidearm.

Ellie could not believe it. "SERIOUSLY? Who called the cops? I mean, really, people?"

"Ma'am ..."

She knew she was overstepping when he went from miss to ma'am, but she couldn't stop herself from interrupting.

"I'm sorry, sir. There has been a misunderstanding. Last night I was drugged, against my will, and I am trying to sit here by myself while I come down in a safe environment."

His eye twitched, and she might have only imagined his trigger finger doing the same.

"Why don't we take you down to the department and talk this over."

"Oh no, no, no, no, no ... You don't understand, Officer ..."

"Sergeant."

"I cannot be locked up right now. I will go completely insane. I cleaned my condo last night. I could clean the cell, but I don't think you'd give me a toothbrush. And I have a thing about jail cells. They are too small, and you can't get out of them ..."

"Sergeant Wilco," began Guy with familiarity and respect, "what Miss Ellie is trying to say is that she's harmless. She came by the house last night and accidentally had some of Coach Klein's Go-Juice, but she has a low tolerance for caffeine, so she's a little hopped up."

"A little?" the lawman asked.

"Well, it *was* a whole bottle."

"HA!" busted out the sergeant, breaking his steely manner all at once "Miss, you are lucky to be alive. What were you thinking, drinking all that Go-Juice?"

"It burns, it burns?" Ellie answered. "There were ghost peppers involved." The truth of her encounter with the milk, she would take with her to the grave.

"Now this is a story I want to hear from the start, but you can't stay here acting like this."

"To be fair, her place isn't big enough to run laps in," Guy answered for her, cracking a smile. Luck was on his side, and he knew it. Ellie couldn't kill him with the police right in front of her. Her alter ego was supposed to be foolish, not a fool. She made fists and puffed up, trying not to cry.

"So helpful, thanks!" she snarked as she gathered her things and pressed forward to leave. The sergeant blocked her way.

"Seems you might be a hazard to yourself."

"You're kidding, right?"

"No, miss. Until you come down from this frenzy, I'm going to have to keep eyes on you at the station. Unless you want to go to the hospital."

"It might be the better option," piped Goldie. "No offense, Ellie, but you might burst a blood vessel or something." Goldie's worry for her caused hot embarrassment to crawl over Ellie's skin. Ellie bit her tongue as her eyes began to well up.

SOMETHING HAPPENED to Guy when he saw that tiny tornado's eyes threatening to tear. It was the last thing he expected of himself, but he panicked, and all he wanted to do was scoop her into his arms and hide her face against his shoulder. How had she gotten to him? How had he gone from mistrust to wanting to protect her?

No. He would not be melted by a Canadian fruit loop.

"Sergeant, I've got a better idea." All eyes were on him—the sergeant's, Goldie's, and every other damn person in town who'd appeared to watch the scene.

Guy didn't know when it had happened—in high school maybe, or when he got nudged for his first professional fight? Maybe before then, when the parents of his friends came asking him to help their kids with schoolwork or to talk to them about their problems. What kid needs that? But he helped out. It was never his intention, and he fought it long and hard, but at some point, the people of Littleton came to depend on him for their well-being. He'd be damned if he didn't use some of that power to help Miss Ellie. The power dynamic between them would change if she kept up those puppy eyes of hers, maybe it already had, and that was terrifying.

"Community lab. Fifteen minutes. Is the football field free, Coach?" he asked, picking a short, burly man out of the crowd.

"If it wasn't, it is now!"

The room was abuzz. People were on their phones as they scurried out the door and in the direction of the high school. Ellie's body hummed, but there was now more energy outside of her than within.

"This is so exciting! I've got to go change!" Goldie was off as quick as the rest of them.

"What ...?" Miss Ellie's confusion made Guy feel a spark of something joyful.

"Can you run in those things?" Guy asked, looking at her boots. "We will pick up a pair of cross trainers next door." Ellie stared at him blankly. "Hustle, shortie!"

His authoritative voice had her following him out the door and down the street. People were blitzing out of shops like bees leaving their hives. Ellie moved in an agitated state of autopilot as Guy escorted her into an abandoned athletic store. "You must be, what, size five?" he asked, picking up a pair of pink children's running shoes.

"You do realize I am a full-grown woman, right?"

His eyes trailed down her neck to the curve of her breasts, still farther to the delicate slide of her hips to her legs and back up again, unable to tamp down his carnal longing.

"Besides, I don't think I can wear tight shoes right now." The sudden meekness of her confession disarmed him.

"Why not?" he asked with a gentleness neither of them had expected.

"They got pretty beat up on my run home last night," she said, looking at a pair of shoes to avoid eye contact.

"Run home? I saw you drive off."

"The car broke down a couple of kilometers after that, so I ran the rest of the way." Her mother had called her daft for buying a used car but she hadn't seen a point in buying new just because she had the money. Public transit and Ubers made up the majority of her travels, and when she did need to drive it was never far. Her world was usually very small.

"Why didn't you call me?" he demanded as he led her to a bench and pulled off her fuzzy boots. "You're telling me you ran across town in the middle of the night, in the dark, along the side of a highway, knowing full well about the coyotes?"

"I thought you were kidding about the coyotes! Besides, the Go-Juice, as you call it, kicked in." She wasn't telling him something, but he let it slide. Guy hung his head in exasperation. She kept bouncing and twitching, unable to keep still.

He let out a long whistle as he looked at her feet. Some of her sores had bled through her socks. "What were you thinking! What were you running in, razor blades?"

"Flats, actually."

But he wasn't listening. He was up and grabbing the first aid kit from behind the counter and sitting again at her feet.

"Do you even work here?"

He glared at her in response as he gently removed her socks, grimacing as he pulled them away from her sores. She seethed when it hurt but didn't tell him to stop. He applied antiseptic bandaging to the blisters, blowing on them to ease the sting. "This is a terrible idea. I should take you home."

～

ELLIE HAD no clue what the terrible idea was, but she felt as though Guy was talking about her. She hated to admit it, but she liked the way he'd looked her up and down. Right then, she needed to be cared for. That didn't mean she didn't resent him for it, and for making her body respond to him.

"You know, I have no idea what your grand plot is, but the entire town seems to be in on it. You wouldn't want to let them down."

"After I quit boxing and came back home, I found out that the town was ranked in the top ten least healthy towns in the state," he confided, moving his doctoring to her other foot. "A few family friends were sick. Diabetes, obesity, all that. So, a few times a week, I would get people together to work out. They started calling the sessions 'community labs,' like it was meant to be official. Well, it caught on until most of the town started coming. I made up some basic pamphlets on healthy eating." He laughed then. "I was a bit of an asshole about it, though."

"You?" she teased, smiling at him as he knelt in front of her.

He smiled back before shaking his head. "It was basic stuff, but I was rude about it. I was still in a fighter's mentality, you know? *Don't eat crap! Eat real food!* And people started listening, changing the way they were living. Now we are ranked one of the healthiest places to live in the state."

"That's amazing. You did that?"

"No," he said, losing his easy smile. "They did. They worked hard. They changed things. I'm glad to say the message has softened since then. I realized that the article was bunk—weight isn't a true indication of health. Health doesn't have a number. It had a lot more to do with what foods were and weren't being imported to the town. That, coupled with a lack of stress-relieving activities, had more to do with people's health than anyone's laziness."

"Looks like you might be a pretty good leader."

"I just gave them a kick in the ass."

"And that's what they needed. It's obvious this town loves you."

It was Guy's turn to be embarrassed, and it was obvious he didn't like it.

"Yeah, well ... I quit doing the labs. Other people have stepped up. I was going to run one for you to burn off all this crap in your system, but you shouldn't be on your feet. I'll take you home."

"Please." She rolled her eyes dramatically. "People are waiting on us. And Sergeant Wilco is going to be keeping a close eye for my arrival."

"No, people are waiting on me. No one who saw those sores would want you working out on them. Go home. I will cover for you with the sergeant."

"These are nothing. Hand me a size seven in those shoes there and go write the shopkeeper an IOU for me." Guy raised an eyebrow at her. "Getting a bigger size will leave room so the bandages won't rub as much," she said through gritted teeth.

"I'm not going to be the reason you wreck your feet."

"I've had worse."

"Bull."

"Try being a ballerina with a show mom who forces you to practice on split toenails. You think I got all these calluses from gentle use? This is cushy. I can do this."

"You?" He crossed his arms, again calling bullshit. "A ballerina? In what alternative universe?"

"The one up in Canada," she said, mocking his tone.

He frowned. "Your mom did that to you?"

She paused, feeling sick to her stomach. The last thing she wanted to do was share her sordid childhood with Mr. Perfect. "I was driven enough to do it to myself. Are you going to give me the shoes or what?"

He smiled his knowing, one-sided grin as he handed her a box and went back to the register. It hurt that he assumed she'd lie to him about being a dancer when it had once been her identity. She opened the shoebox.

"These are kids' shoes!"

"My mistake," he threw over his shoulder.

AT THE FIELD, about 150 people were already stretching. Coach was guiding them through the motions, but everyone put a little extra energy into it when they saw their golden boy running to the front.

"All right, everyone, this lab is for Miss Ellie," he called out. "She had a little too much Go-Juice, and she needs to work until she drops! Let's show her how it's done in Texas!"

For the next hour, Guy guided the town through high-impact drills, moving through the crowd to correct postures. Ellie had expected him to ride her, make fun of her, to tell her to push harder, but he only stopped beside her once.

"Good job, Miss Canada! Nice form! Keep it up!"

The only person not under his spell was a woman who sat on the hill overlooking the field. She wore an oversized black-and-purple hoodie and ate from a family-size bag of chips, pausing only to drink from a jumbo Slurpee. She watched everyone like they were part of a stage play. Maybe they were, and Guy was their puppeteer.

Guy didn't hassle Ellie, making her just like everyone else on the field, taken care of in the least intimate sense. She watched him when she could, sweat beading down her brow, her feet on fire. She saw him for the kindhearted man he was. He talked to everyone, helped everyone, teens to the elderly, regardless of how fit they were. She admired him for that, his charisma, but also for the simplicity of his approach. He helped because people needed it and asked for nothing in return. And she was his latest project.

Ellie lay in a heap on the grass, pouring water shared by a stranger down her throat. She saw that with Guy in charge, Littleton became a community, and a great one at that—a town whose residents supported one another, even the strange new girl.

She felt sad for Guy. It must be lonely being a demigod.

CHAPTER FIVE

*A*s the crowd dispersed, Guy answered questions and said goodbye to everyone. Most asked him when the next lab would be. Gentle referrals were given to the current schedule being run by the Community Lab Group. It had been developed so that he wouldn't have to manage things, because the truth of the matter was, he'd gotten bored. He loved boxing, but he got bored with being knocked around, bored with the threat of concussions. There were injuries cited at the press conference held to explain things to his fans, but the heart of the matter was a little trickier.

Boxing was an accidental career path. When he reached the cusp of sixteen, he rebelled against being the choirboy the town's parents believed him to be. Young and angry at the world for deciding who he was, he began picking fights at school. Admiration was the last thing he wanted.

At first, the teachers didn't believe that he'd started the fights until he was caught in the act. The teacher, Mrs. Barstone, brought him to the principal herself. He was sure he'd at least get a suspension. That is what they'd been giving out to all the other degenerates. A crackdown on teen violence.

"So, you have been starting these fights, young man?" asked Principal Lautner like a cop setting up for a confession.

Guy kept quiet, craving punishment but not yet able to see that himself.

"I think all these fights have something in common," Mrs. Barstone said. "All of Guy's victims are bullies themselves."

"I noticed," Principal Lautner said, scratching his scruffy cheek. "I do not condone vigilantism but reports of bullying *have* gone down since the usual suspects have all been roughed up." The principal finished with a conspiratorial smile.

It might have been true, but Guy had only targeted them because he knew they would fight back.

He was instead given a slap on the wrist and a pat on the back. Mrs. Barstone, who was a fan of boxing, suggested to Guy's father that his son start training because he had good instincts and energy to burn. It wasn't fair, but the only other way Guy thought to rebel would be drug use, which wasn't his style. Guy was angry and too resentful of the other kids his age who got to mess up. He kept getting that pat on the back and higher expectations to reach.

He channeled all his anger into boxing and built a career out of it until he got bored and quit. Even when walking away from multimillion-dollar deals and endorsement offers, everyone said he was 'smart to quit in his prime'. Anyone else would have gotten flack for being a quitter. That became his rebellion in the end— people let him fluff things off, so that's what he did. He never gave his all because they would expect more. They called that *owning his boundaries*.

When he started the Community Lab, he did it out of resentment for his town. He had put so much into it, drawing crowds for his fights, helping keep kids straitlaced even when he was still a kid himself, and what had they done? Gone and landed themselves in dire personal and economic health.

Pouring all that rage into his programming, he started high-intensity training to spite them all. The plan backfired. They kept coming back for more workouts, more dietary advice, more, more, more. Someone once asked him how he brushed his teeth—his *teeth*! "Twice a day," he said and described flossing like it was a revelation to the guy.

Boredom came like clockwork. Somehow, he'd started a fitness business, and he had people working for him. It was time for them to sink or swim and for him to walk away. They were still going strong, but growth had stopped. Next, he moved on to home building and was praised for wanting to 'create'. What a load of crap. He wanted to do manual labor and make his own hours.

Then there were women. There had always been women. Womanizing wasn't an option even if he had his pick of the litter. His mama raised him right, and his dad made sure of it. If a woman piqued his interest, he would take her out, but things never got all that serious. His mother, Ivy, claimed that he went for fixer-uppers, like the women he dated were somehow flawed, but he knew everyone had problems. Smart women were sexy, and he didn't mind taking care of them a little, but he liked a woman to have her own life happening. It made them more interesting, for a while, and gave him some freedom too.

Relationships followed a formula, and they all ended with the same conversation. The thinly veiled ultimatum—'Either we get serious or we move on'. He had become a master at letting women think they were the ones making the choice. To his knowledge, no one ever left the relationship unsatisfied. They had good times, great sex, and yet ... boredom. That's what made working with Goldie a treat. Neither of them had ever shown any romantic interest in the other, yet everyone assumed they would end up together, even his mother. This kept some flies away.

He wasn't bored watching Ellie on the field that day. It was clear she hadn't been lying about being a dancer. The only weakness he could find was some tension in her knee, and he only found it because he was watching those legs like they could save his life. Rather than seeing her as an awkward member of the

Lollipop Guild, he saw that she was rhythmic and poised. Boxing drills became a sensual dance rather than a brutal sport. Even with the disgusting sores on her feet, she kept up with the top-level athletes in the crowd and put everyone's form to shame. Maybe it was the Go-Juice, but even during the fastest-paced drills, she floated.

When he saw her body drenched in sweat, it took all his willpower to walk away. What he wanted to do to her, he couldn't, not in front of a crowd. He didn't know how he would get through being alone in his truck with her. The proximity would be electrifying.

Deciding it was time to do something about his newfound appreciation for Ellie, he turned away from the crowd to search her out.

She was gone.

ELLIE WOKE A DROOL-SOAKED MESS. She couldn't tell if it was day or night. Even if she could, she wouldn't have been able to name what day of the week it was. She had been blissfully comatose. Even still, her body wanted to cling to the abyss a little longer. It took her too long to realize that she had been awoken by movement at the foot of her sleeping bag. A shadow hovered over her, and she didn't take any more time to think. She grabbed the only thing within reach that had any weight and threw it at the shadow as she leaped from her cocoon, sprinting down the hall toward the stairs.

"It's me!" A familiar angry drawl burst forth from her would-be attacker. She made it down half of the steps before she processed who the voice belonged to.

"Don't do that!" she hollered as she came back up.

Guy was rubbing his head and carrying a hardcover edition of *David Copperfield* Ellie intended to read on her 'sabbatical'.

"I thought you were some crazed maniac! You're lucky I didn't hurt you worse. I could've had a gun under my pillow, you know?"

"Naw, you're Canadian," he said, failing to defuse the situation.

"What were you doing snooping around my room? You do know breaking and entering is a crime, right? I may be Canadian, but I believe it was an American who coined the phrase, 'Get off my land'!" She was riled up, shaking with adrenaline.

"Now, darlin', where's your hospitality? I came to check to make sure you were still with us. I come bearing doughnuts."

"You gave me a heart attack!" she accused while sniffing for the promised desserts.

"Hey now," he said, his tone softening. "I didn't mean to scare you. Your doorbell works just fine now. When you didn't answer, I thought it best to check on you since you haven't been seen since the lab yesterday. Time to change those bandages too."

As her heart rate slowed, it all came back. She waited for the embarrassment to flood her. She didn't do disgrace well. Instead of embarrassment, something else clicked in place: the realization that Mr. Perfect was trying to fix her. *Oh, heck no.* She was not going to let him Prince Charming her. He took care of the people in this town like it was his job, but she didn't want it. She didn't want to be another smitten damsel in distress and decided right then and there that she was not going to let him off that easy. Even if it was hard to focus with the softened angles of concern on such a rugged, beautiful man. Those molten silver eyes were criminal.

"They're fine, thanks." Even as she raised her chin to him, she felt the scope of the lie. With the adrenaline fading, she found that her feet stung and ached quite a lot, but she was determined not to let it show.

"OK, I get it. You're a tough guy," said Guy.

"Would you mind waiting here while I ..." Ellie realized she was only wearing a tank top and panties.

Guy did a once-over, having missed her situation in all the

drama. His gaze roamed up her body, catching her eye and holding her there, breathless. He broke their connection first. His tongue stroked his lower lip as he nodded like he was tipping his cowboy hat and moved past her toward the kitchen, raising the hairs on her body as he passed.

Ellie shook her head, hoping to clear her impure thoughts before returning to her bedroom. She grabbed a few things from the pile of clean clothes and tidied her hair before returning to him. She stopped halfway to watch his activity.

"Sit," he told her, his first aid kit open wide on her floor.

It took work to check her ego. The fact was, she did have to take care of her sores. He had a first aid kit, and she did not. An answering grunt and an eye roll were all she could think to save an ounce of dignity, which she then lost as she limped toward him.

Sitting on the floor together, she shifted her foot to Guy's lap. She looked away and found herself wishing she'd picked up the country-style table set at Moira's. It was a bit beaten up, but maybe it could be saved. It was easier to get lost in a daydream than to look Guy in the eye. The man was on a mission. The intimacy made her warm and tingly, and she didn't like it one bit. She was engaged, and he was up for sainthood. That was the end of it.

The slow undressing of her foot was to make sure that nothing pulled, but it sent shock waves of goosebumps through her. Turning her attention to her foot was an essential distraction. Some bandages hadn't held on after the workout the day before. *Workout* wasn't a concise enough term. No, it had been borderline torture, but because the entire community embraced it, it still seemed beautiful. It also seemed a little cult-like. She wasn't sure if she should continue drinking the water.

Guy's sun-soaked hair fell forward as he bent to assess the damage in silence.

Ellie was soothed by the warmth pouring from him. The notes of his cologne were fresh yet woodsy when she'd expected pure alpha-male musk. It was so intoxicating that she'd forgotten to brace herself as the old bandages were peeled away, and he treated the blisters with antibiotic ointment. Ellie hissed at the stinging sensation.

"Sorry," he said. "Do you want me to stop?"

Ellie wanted to call him out on his double entendre but was afraid she'd be giving too much away. There was such tenderness in his touch that his kindness was affecting her too much.

"I'm fine," she managed, allowing him to continue his ministrations. Soon her feet felt light with lidocaine numbness. "Thank you. You've played doctor before," she said.

He gave her that sideways grin, pleased as a peacock.

Elmira's cheeks reddened.

"I've had my share of injuries. Your feet are looking better than yesterday. I'll leave you the kit, and they should be passable soon."

"Thanks."

"And again, so sorry about the ..."

"Stop." Elmira held up her hand as she stood and brought the first aid kit to the kitchen where she stored it on the windowsill. There she gathered her strength while appreciating the knots of bushes and trees reaching for one another through the chill morning air. "I appreciate the thought, but I'm OK. You don't need to do this."

Guy folded his arms across his chest and stretched out his legs, crossing them at the ankle. Elmira couldn't ignore how lithe he appeared. Despite his size, she knew he could pounce on her as quick as a lion on an antelope.

"OK." She rolled her eyes and tried channeling someone with actual sass. "I get that you can't help yourself, but I can take care of myself."

"Can't help myself?" he asked, raising his eyebrows, looking entertained.

"Yes. You have a savior complex, and that's great. It works for you, but you already have a whole town under your wing. While I am thankful for your help, I wouldn't want to add more to your caseload."

"Thank you?"

"You're welcome. Now, down to business. When might your supplies be coming in?"

"Having trouble roughing it?" he asked as he stood and shifted the balance between them with his size.

"Not at all." She waved him off. "But it would be nice to have a shower sometime soon."

"Things will be trickling in this week. Hardwood and cabinets should be coming in today, another reason I came by. Once we have everything, I'll call in my guys," he said, scratching his cheek.

Elmira felt like a cad. Here he was being so *nice*, and she was acting all business. They had crossed into new territory. Not quite friends, definitely not lovers, but something was there, something more.

"Great. Would you like some water?" she asked in a weak attempt at kindness. As Guy was about to answer, her doorbell startled them both. She shuffled to the stairs and paused to visualize her descent.

"I'll get it, Miss Ellie. Wouldn't want you to hurt yourself." Guy scoffed.

She accepted the deserved barb.

The next two hours were a flurry of activity. First, her appliances arrived ahead of her hardwood. Then a package arrived for Guy, so he wasn't able to sneak off as Ellie was sure he'd intended. And on it went: the tile, the tub, and all the finery that went with it. Package after package, first for her, then for Guy. Soon she felt buried in boxes.

"My word." She sighed when the bell went quiet. "Where do we start?"

"We?" Guy asked, looking over a packing slip.

Again, Ellie was awash with guilt. "I'm sorry. I don't do well with ..."

"Kindness?"

"I was going to say coddling, but yes, I suppose that's true."

"Who knew Canada was so cold?"

"I apologize."

"You folks usually do, don't you?"

"OK! Fine! I meant every word. Your MO is taking care of people, but I've had to take care of my own well-being for a long time, and when people do step in, I tend to see it as a threat. I know, that's my baggage." Ellie hadn't planned on oversharing, but Guy Manning had made her feel like a bad human being.

While she didn't want to be his pet project, she also didn't want him to think she was an unfeeling control freak either. She heard the whispers of that at work. Men who worked for her claimed she was Titan Holdings' reigning ice queen. Granted that just meant that she had more power than they were comfortable with.

Guy studied her from his perch before sauntering toward her. She swallowed hard. He was majestic, so she didn't much care that he was going in for the kill.

"Do you or don't you want my help, Miss Ellie?" he drawled, looking down at her.

She fumbled on her words, not knowing what to say, her skin growing hot under his scrutiny. "I do ... with the house ... you're not responsible for, I mean ..."

And then he kissed her, pulling her up to him, one hand finding skin under the hem of her shirt and the other catching in her hair. He pulled her against his firm body, and for a second, she didn't respond. For a second, every single reason not to flooded her mind before all capacity to think halted.

She wrapped her arms around his neck, and he picked her up. She braced herself with her legs around him. He bit her lip as he brought his hand up her shirt. She dug her nails into his neck, and he responded by parting her lips with his tongue. They explored each other until they had to part for breath. He brought his hands beneath her, squeezing her bottom as she nipped along his jawline. She felt him quiver and was amazed. Adonis wanted her!

Then her excitement took a nosedive. She was engaged!

She leaned away from him, glad for his support while her knees knocked. His eyes were wild but clearing. He put her down, having registered her reticence. They stood, staring, energy still entangled, his hands in fists against the wall on either side of her.

"I have a fridge," she said dumbly.

He broke eye contact and turned to let her pass. "You do."

"I should get groceries."

"You should."

"You can lock up?"

"I have to call my guys in. I'll schedule your tile in as soon they can get in. I have to be out of town for a meeting today."

"OK, then." She grabbed her purse and slipped into her boots, backing toward the stairs as though she thought he might pounce on her. "Thanks again ... Bye."

She scurried down the steps and out the door, not thinking about her feet while her blood still scorched. Her car was at the garage for repairs making a quick getaway impossible. The only way to maintain a sliver of dignity was to walk without limping and not look back, no matter the temptation.

The initial shock began to wear off, leaving Ellie more confused than ever. Their mutual attraction aside, Ellie didn't just go around arguing with and kissing people. Town messiahs especially. All he knew about her was that she was going through something in the messiest way possible.

Over the past few days, she had gleaned a bit more about Littleton's golden boy. His heart, though guarded with loads of barbed wire, was kind even when he might prefer to be seen otherwise. He belonged to this town in a way she never could. Any attraction she had for the man was moot.

"And," she reminded herself, "you're engaged!"

The truth and guilt stung, but it was also a relief to know that nothing could happen between them, nothing lasting. Any attraction Guy had for her would be from her novelty at best. Ellie had a great many issues to work out, not the least of all her poor fiancé, but she had more pride than to throw herself at any man. Now that she knew who Guy *really* was—hunky Texan builder, former boxing star, forever Littleton god—it was easier. She could be this flighty Miss Ellie. Who would know any different? What a comfort that would be from her responsibilities. The kiss was a natural culmination of a crazy few days. Throw in her need for familiarity and Guy's magical manliness, and all was explained.

And it would *never* happen again.

She made it downtown and slowed her pace to admire a painting in one of the shop windows. It was of a charming toddler leaning against a great beast of a dog. It tugged at Ellie's heartstrings. Would she ever have children? She couldn't see Daniel being an involved father, and she didn't want that life for any child. If she brought children into the world, she would need them to know they were unconditionally loved by both their parents. Children would be an accessory to Daniel, like his tie, like she was.

The store window reflected Ellie back to herself: black slacks, color-blocked turtleneck, hair pulled back in a severe ponytail. She looked too prim. She pulled her hair from the ponytail and mussed it to no avail. Today, she would go in and change things up. Maybe she could get an appointment at the salon in town.

What was soul-searching if not time for a makeover sequence?

CHAPTER SIX

*C*rystal's Salon was girl-glam at its best: soft pink walls and random chandeliers hanging from the ceiling. Ornate, white-framed mirrors hung in front of each station of rosy salon chairs. Faced with a gaggle of women, Ellie realized her blunder in thinking she'd get a walk-in chair. The salon was small and filled with clients getting their nails done, some had their heads in those space-age dryers that look like they could suck a person into another dimension, and a few waited in white reception chairs. All stopped to stare at Ellie who, with all the attention, was now obliged to make an appointment at the reception podium.

"Well, if it isn't the Go-Juice-Girl!" said a shrill voice. "What can we do for you, darlin'?"

"Thought I might make an appointment for a cut?" Elmira said, pushing the conversation forward even though she wanted to hide. The petty sneers the women shared said more than words. Judging by how quiet it had gotten when she walked in, she was the butt of a joke.

"Miss Ellie, you *must* book with Crystal. She does divine work." Looking toward the familiar voice, she found Goldie, having her nails done in an exciting pink that Elmira wouldn't dream of even trying. For Goldie, though, pulling it off wouldn't be a problem.

"You are too kind, Goldie," came the shrill voice again. "I can fit you in at four, if you want to come back."

Her words were sweet as pie in that way women sound when they are playing at kindness. Ellie looked around the room and realized that most of the women wore their hair the same way, various lengths of the same layered shape, near the same color too. Locking eyes with Goldie, who winked at her, she couldn't help but smile.

"Thank you, but I have plans for later. Are there any other stylists available?" A question that earned her a few eye rolls and bursting grins. Crystal had a loyal following.

"I believe Winter has an opening?"

"Yup. I'm free," said a gravelly, bored voice from the rear of the salon. "Come on back." There she stood, the woman in the hoodie from the park who had waved a proverbial finger at the town's health nuttiness.

Winter stood close to six feet tall, thanks to some wildly tall black platform boots covered with zippers and buckles. Her hair was reminiscent of Emily the Strange, but as Ellie moved closer, she realized that Winter's full lips were painted sexpot red, and her ice blue eyes held wisdom in stark contrast to the dark makeup she'd painted on. Despite the clear statement her style made, the woman knew what she was doing with her image, and Ellie's excitement mounted. If anyone could get her out of her comfort zone, it was her.

"So, would you like the town special?" Winter asked with a sardonic grin.

"No," Ellie said firmly.

"What do you want, Ellie?" It was as though a goth queen were looking into her soul, compelling her to be honest.

"Something different. I'm not ... this anymore," she answered.

Winter's perfectly drawn eyebrows furrowed. "All right. Who are you now?"

Ellie laughed in spite of herself.

Winter smiled, leaning in to whisper, "Who do you want to be, then?"

"I want to be sexy and playful. I want to feel confident." Ellie turned a bit red.

Winter nodded. "Color and cut, then?"

"Do your worst," Ellie dared Winter who cackled, turning a few heads as though the sound were rare.

"I got you, girl," she said before she set to work.

CRYSTAL HAD GONE FOR LUNCH, and so, too, had her posse, leaving Ellie in the hands of the Amazonian warrior. Ellie stared at her in the mirror—Winter had so much pull. Her wild persona was executed with such precision that one could regard her as a painting, but there was more too. Every so often, the tough veneer would fade, and Ellie could see a tenderness when Winter's passion for what she was doing shone through.

"Ask." Winter said, startling Ellie out of her thoughts.

"What?"

"Cut the crap. Ask."

Ellie felt embarrassed for having been caught staring. "How do you do it?"

"How do I do what?" Winter stopped working long enough to narrow her eyes at Ellie, as though waiting for the ball to drop.

"How do you stay so resolute? So confident?" Ellie's cheeks flamed red again as she went on to explain herself. "I can tell you love your work, and it must take a lot of energy to put yourself out there in a town like this with such a strong personal image. You radiate this otherworldly connection to what you're doing. I wish I had half of whatever that is. I'm great at my job, and I enjoy it, but I can fade into a group. How do you stay true to yourself, and passionate about what you do, when there is backlash against you and your style?"

Winter raised an eyebrow and took her time to consider her answer. "I don't believe in going halfway. I love my job. Sure, I'm surrounded by lemmings half the time, but I love that I can offer people an alternative to the norm. It's balancing your needs with your purpose. You can live in fear of being judged, or you can put yourself out there, and why not? I'm a bad bitch."

She continued removing the foil from Ellie's hair. "Some people keep me on their periphery because they're intimidated. Or they think I'm weird because of the way I look, and they completely miss out on what I have to offer. But why would I go out of my way to sell myself to people who don't want to know what I'm about? I get the clients who need me. I shouldn't be surprised that you came over to the dark side. You don't fit here either."

Ellie frowned.

"Hey"—she jabbed the pointy end of the color brush in her direction as she tidied her station—"that's a compliment. Now, go to the sink and let's get to phase two. And don't peek until it's done."

Winter washed Ellie's hair in silence, giving a little extra time to massage her scalp. Her touch was gentler than Ellie had expected, and she found herself melting from the technique.

"You have a lot of tension in your neck," Winter stated with muted worry, and she continued working a little longer with the shampoo and the conditioner until Ellie wasn't sure her neck would hold her head anymore. The relief was astounding. As Winter worked her miracle hands through Ellie's hair, she heard the bell on the door ting.

"Forget something?" Winter asked.

"No, I wanted to see how the session was going. I've never seen anyone give you free rein before," said Goldie Morrison's twinkling voice.

Winter laughed. "Pull up a chair."

"I brought some bubbly," she said, followed by a loud pop. "Hope you girls don't mind red Solo Cups."

Ellie opened her eyes, stealing a glance at Winter. She hadn't been under the impression that the two women were friends, but it was a small town and who knew what connections they had? Ellie began to worry that maybe the earlier conversation had all been a ploy to get Ellie alone and vulnerable.

"I won't say no to the drink," Winter replied. "But I will ask why. Back to the chair, Ellie, and don't look yet," Winter scolded like she knew Ellie's intent. Ellie obeyed, accepting a cup from Goldie along the way.

"Because, between your stunt at the Community Lab and Ellie's everyday dive into the absurd, I've decided we all must accept the fact that we are meant to be besties. Cheers!"

Reflexively, Ellie did cheers in return, but she was taken aback. "I thought you hated me."

"Was I pleased when you stood me up and cut me out of a paycheck by buying directly from Guy? No. No, I was not. But I've since learned you are in a tailspin, and friends forgive."

"I kind of thought you would be angry Guy was spending time with me," admitted Ellie.

"Now, why on earth would that bother me?" Goldie asked with a conspiratorial grin.

"Because you two are Barbie and Ken," answered Winter with a steely tone as she began cutting Ellie's overgrown mane.

"Yes, on paper, it would work. Unfortunately, he's like a brother to me."

"Yeah, right! That boy is all kinds of sexy. I grew up with him spreading rumors that I'm a witch, and I would still consider hitting that. Before hexing him, of course," Winter said.

Ellie blushed, prudish as it made her feel.

"Yes, yes, attractive, intelligent, witty, all that. It's a shame. We could have built an empire, if only I were interested in men."

"No shit?" asked Winter, looking genuinely surprised as she sipped her champagne. She put the scissors down and worked styling products through Ellie's hair, followed by the flat iron. The sweet smell of vanilla and fruit filled the air as the iron steamed. Ellie felt awkward with these warrior women sizing each other up.

"No shit," Goldie confirmed. "I'm out, but in a small town like this, it's easier to let people think whatever brings me a regular income."

Ellie picked up her jaw, surprised that Goldie had taken Ellie into her confidence.

"You are masterful, Winter. I think I will be coming to you from now on," Goldie said.

Winter pulled and twisted at strands, making final adjustments before spinning Ellie toward the mirror.

Ellie couldn't believe it. She'd been given a Bettie Page-esque cut, and instead of being terrified, she loved it. The bangs were far less severe than Bettie's, and Winter had left her hair wavy, softening her features. The darker chocolate brown made her look seductive.

"Don't break my heart now, Miss Ellie," Winter said after a brief shocked silence on Ellie's part. "What do you think?"

"Winter ... I have no words ... You made me ..."

"*Sexy* is the word you're looking for," offered Goldie.

"I was going for smutty, but sexy will do," Winter said, relaxing into a chair like a kitten stretching.

"Friday night plans, ladies? I feel like Miss Ellie may need some help adjusting to the style, and nothing gives more confidence than a girls' night out."

"I'm in," Winter said, surprising Ellie with her immediacy. "I'm in a yes kind of mood." She shrugged.

Ellie looked back at herself in the mirror. "Thank you, Winter. Thank you so much." She teared up. Winter had delivered exactly what she'd asked for: something completely different. She hadn't known she could look playful. It was just hair, but it was the start of something. Her mother would hate the waves and would suggest taming it straight. Daniel ... who knew? He'd never comment, but if he didn't like it, she'd be able to tell from his micro-sneer.

Ellie fought the need for their approval, and the wave of distress it brought. This wasn't for them. It might be superficial, but Ellie knew that a piece of her was falling into place.

~

WITH LITTLE EFFORT, Goldie convinced Ellie that the logical next step was retail therapy. They'd driven to the nearest mall, an hour away, in Goldie's adorable red car. The highway driving had been terrifying, as was Goldie's Olympic approach to consumerism. But even she tired enough to stop for a late lunch.

"So, what's it like up in Canada?" Goldie asked as if it were the great unknown.

"Cold ... I couldn't think of wearing any of this back home right now." People were walking around the mall in puffer vests and sweaters to pay homage to the season, but Ellie was sweating.

"Save the pleather for Friday night, or people will talk," Goldie teased her with a wink and a laugh at Ellie's expression. "Come on, now. Enough small talk! Let's get to it. Why are you here?"

Ellie's face fell. She should've seen the question coming, but she'd been so far out of herself that she'd forgotten she'd gone rogue. "Things got complicated, and I guess I needed it to stop," Ellie began, not sure how much of her life she wanted to share with Goldie. It was like a ritual friendship dance she didn't know the steps to. Even in high school, Ellie had been the odd one out because of her devotion to ballet and her studies. She felt stunted, not knowing how to act.

"The man?"

"What do you mean?"

"If a grown woman is on the run, you best believe there's a man to blame."

Was it horrible how little she was thinking of Daniel? She tried to picture him at work, restless and tired, having been up worrying about her. She couldn't picture it. He was always so composed.

Like lightning striking her down, her phone rang, but it wasn't her mother's ringtone. "Oh no!"

"Who is it?"

"Daniel!"

"Who's Daniel?"

"My fiancé!"

"I knew it was a man! Answer it, woman, and give him what for!" Goldie swiped the answer button on Ellie's phone before she could think about it and put it on speaker.

"Hello?" Ellie said, overcoming her trepidation.

"Elmira, I'm glad you answered," Daniel responded pointedly, as though he'd tried calling her all day, which he hadn't done once. "I received our tickets for the hospital gala. Will you be attending? I have to, the firm needs representation, but I'd rather not be seated alone."

"Uh, I don't think I will be back in time—it's Friday evening, isn't it?"

"Yes, that's right. Well then, I will find a placeholder." There was a cold silence that Ellie didn't quite know how to break, but she knew it was her responsibility to try.

"Listen, Daniel, I'm sorry about all this. I would like to explain myself, but I'm not sure how to yet."

"Elmira," Daniel began, "get it out of your system. *Whatever* it is. Sorry, but I've got a meeting to get to. Goodbye."

"Goodbye, Daniel."

"Wow, he's pissed," Goldie said, biting on her fresh nails and leaning in, as though she were watching television.

"You think?" asked Ellie, not ready to divulge that he always sounded like that.

"Well, at least he gave you a hall pass."

"What?"

"A hall pass is when someone in a relationship is given sexual freedom for a set amount of time."

"I know what it is, but how do you figure he gave me one?" Ellie was shocked.

"*Get WHATEVER it is out of your system,*" Goldie said, mimicking Daniel so badly, Ellie laughed despite the implications of what she was claiming.

"I'm sure that's not what he meant."

"Darlin', I have four brothers. I know men, and that one just told you to go get your freak on!"

"No, he wouldn't."

"Jealous type?"

"No ..." Ellie didn't want to say it, but Goldie was going to pry it out of her, anyway. "I'm not good at ... we aren't, um, adventurous?"

It took Goldie a minute to register what Ellie meant. "So you see, he knows that I wouldn't because, well, it's humiliating ..." She chugged down her lemonade as if it were a cocktail.

A sage look came over Goldie's face. "Miss Ellie, I don't believe that nonsense for a second. There are all kinds of kinds out there, but I've never known a man to complain unless they're not getting any at all."

"Well, there's that, too, but mostly, I suck. NO! I didn't mean that, I meant ..." She put her head down on the table in full retreat.

Goldie laughed and laughed and laughed. Ellie could feel people looking in their direction.

"I'm sorry, honey. The last time I saw someone go that red talking about sex was in sixth grade." Goldie wiped a tear from her eye and regained her composure. "Now, why on earth would you think you are bad at ... *it?*" she finished with mock secrecy.

"It's been awkward, and he doesn't ask for it much."

"Let's get specific. I can't help you if you don't speak freely. I promise this is between us." Goldie's turned the most serious face Ellie had ever seen her, and the way she held Ellie's hand made her feel like Goldie was trustworthy.

"We do it when our schedules permit, but … it feels like an obligation. He doesn't initiate it often, so I assume he would just rather opt out."

"Do you come?" Goldie asked at full volume.

"You do know we are in public, right?"

Goldie wore impatience on her brow, a look Ellie was familiar with.

"Of course, I have. We just don't have the blinding passion that everyone gets carried away talking about."

The horror at play on Goldie's porcelain features was almost comedic, but Ellie was mortified. "Wait, was this Daniel fellow your first?"

"No!" she shot back defensively, but it wasn't so far from the truth. There had been a few others in her past, and those experiences had been similar, though the relationships had been much shorter. "I've been with other guys."

"A couple of men can't make you see stars, and you think *you're* to blame? Tell me, do they cum every time?"

"Well, yes, but …"

"No buts about it, girl. Well … there could be." Ellie thanked the heavens when Goldie's phone interrupted her tirade. Goldie's voice went up a few octaves as she sweet-talked a client. It became clear that their day was going to be cut short. "I'm sorry, Ellie," she said after her call.

"It's all right. Business is business."

"Yes, but this is most inopportune. My clients want to view a mansion twenty minutes in the wrong direction from here." She clicked her nails against the table in thought. "I'll call them back to rearrange things. I'll get you home, then come back out."

"Don't do that. How about you go see them, and when you come back this way, you can pick me up?"

"You don't mind?" Goldie looked mighty hopeful.

"I don't mind. I wanted to get a few more things and stop at a bookstore. That will keep me busy."

Goldie left Ellie to her own devices after apologizing again. A couple of hours later, Ellie was beginning to worry. Soon after, Goldie called, whispering that her clients had decided they needed to see a few more places before possibly making an offer that day.

"I'm so sorry, Ellie. I didn't know it was going to turn into an evening affair. If you call a cab, I'll pay you back."

Ellie didn't need Goldie's money, so she assured her all was well and called the cab. It never came. She called another, and it, too, got lost in the ether. Before long, she was frantic enough to call Guy.

"Guy Manning," said the strong Texan drawl.

"Guy, it's Elmira."

"Who?"

"Elmira."

"I don't know an Elmira. Met an Elinor once." He was toying with her, and she was simultaneously annoyed and glad that things weren't any weirder between them after the kiss that morning.

"Shut up, hillbilly," she joked.

"Hey now!" He snorted in mock insult.

"I've got a problem, and I thought I'd ask you, but never mind. It's stupid. I'll figure it out."

"Are you all right? Where are you calling from?" His genuine concern almost warmed her. Then she remembered that wearing a cape was right up his alley. He might as well be looking for a phone booth to change in.

"I'm stuck at a big mall an hour west of Littleton. And my calls for a cab keep falling into the abyss. Forget I called ... I'm sure one of them will show up soon."

"Don't be dumb, Miss Ellie. I can be there soon." Ellie was

about to argue with him when he added, "It's lucky you got stuck today. I just finished a meeting down the highway from you. Be there soon." He hung up.

Alone in a truck with Guy Manning, she thought. *What could go wrong?*

CHAPTER SEVEN

Guy wore a great big grin on the ride to the mall. Of course, Ellie had gotten stranded. He imagined her car breaking down again, but no, that wouldn't be elaborate enough. He chuckled thinking about the possibilities. Maybe she sold her car to stay solvent. Uneasiness washed over him, and not because he was her landlord until the paperwork sailed through. His thoughts began to spiral; she could be in some real trouble. What if her car had been stolen? Had Mark even gotten it back to her yet? It wasn't in the lot that morning. What if she drew the wrong crowd? What if she didn't have any money on her at all, and she was a sitting duck, waiting for someone to pull up and offer her a ride? The damn fool would take up with anyone who gave her the *right vibe*.

No, he thought, taking control of his worry. *She called me.*

Now that brought back his smile. She had been different since the Community Lab. He wanted to chalk it up to minor humiliation but knew he was missing something. They'd bonded, and he'd finally learned something real about her. Then the lab happened, and she tried to push him away, which only made him want to get closer.

He had to remind himself that they didn't know each other that well, and the lab had only been the other day. He wasn't going to be a pup at her heel. Did he still think she might be a psycho, gold-digging fan like Amanda turned out to be? No. And that kiss! That kiss would have been a hell of a lot more if she hadn't run.

Pulling up to the mall's main entrance, Guy saw a flourish of movement and tried to pick Miss Ellie out of the crowd. Too young, too old ... There, in the middle of it all, was nothing short of a sex kitten surrounded by bags. She was a tiny thing with criminally long legs in skintight jeans and a worn-out rocker tee with a blessedly deep neckline. How could a neck look so salacious? Guy began to have some flagrantly impure thoughts as he tried to make out the face behind the sunglasses.

"Like what you see?" she hollered at him with a grin as she threw her bags into the bed of his truck. It hit him like a ton of bricks.

"Well now, ain't it Miss Ellie!" he shouted as he got out of the truck to help, sounding far more confident than he felt. *Get it together, Manning.*

Ellie was a beautiful girl, but this woman in front of him was a showstopper. Guy knew that physical beauty meant jack when it came to anything important, but he was thrown off balance. She was stranded looking like that? His protective instants flared. The more he looked, the more of her he saw. The shy smile she kept, even when she thought no one was looking, her brown eyes seeing everything—but those dancer legs should've been the giveaway. And now she was biting her lip looking at him as he came round.

"I didn't know if I had the right lady."

"Too over the top?" she asked, like his opinion mattered. It warmed him to know that to her it did, even just a little.

"Naw, it suits you." And though he'd have never pegged her as a pin-up girl, he was being honest. She looked like freedom with her new hairstyle. Her face was open to the world, letting those eyes pierce right through, unobstructed. She shifted her weight, at a loss of what to say, and moved toward the rest of her bags.

"Thanks," she said as he helped with her load.

"You clear 'em all out?" he teased, picking up one of her bags. "Whoa, now, this one's the bricks, right?" He two-handed the cloth tote into the truck.

"Well, I'm sure you're not used to girls who read, but I've got some time on my hands, and I intend to do a ton of it!"

To be fair, his longest relationships had been with intelligent women, but he hadn't gotten that deep into it in a long while. Most recent dates were with magazine readers, and while he appreciated a woman devoted to the *Cosmo* sex life, there hadn't been much else there.

"What do Canadian women read? *Igloos 101*? *Texas for Dummies*?"

"HA!" she feigned, and then she went quiet on him. He was expecting a little back-and-forth. That bag was heavy, and he was mighty curious what might be in there. She was usually so open about everything that when she withheld, he grew uncomfortable with the silence. He opened her door for her and helped her in, enjoying the view if not the mood.

The silence continued as he pulled into the parking lot traffic, more focused on Ellie than he should be while driving. Her body was relaxed, her new clothes hugging her shape in all the right places. She leaned her head against the window and had a far-off look in her eye. He'd seen her mad, tired, panicked, like a raving lunatic, near tears, but this was the first time she'd ever seemed plain sad.

Her excitement evaporated. Maybe it was because he was supposed to be watching the road that she let her guard crumble, or maybe it had always been there. Had he been looking close enough? He could reach out and touch her, but her mind was miles away. He felt the distance.

"Come here," he said. He undid her belt and pulled her beside him, wrapping his arm around her. She stiffened at first, as alarmed by the move as he was, then snapped the center belt in place, and slowly melted into the comfort his body offered.

They traveled like this for a while before he spoke. "Want to talk about it?"

"About what?" she asked. To hell if he knew. He let the silence work on her. "Nothing makes sense."

"Those jeans make a whole lot of sense to me," he admitted.

"Thanks," she said, unaffected by the compliment.

"Can't wait to see what else you've got there. Did you rob a bank?" He realized that he'd said the wrong thing as she leaned away from him.

"If you're worried about the payments for the apartment going through, don't. We're clear."

"I didn't mean anything by it, Elle." He tasted the name. Didn't know where the hell it came from. It felt right for this version of her, though. She wasn't uptight Elmira or goofy Miss Ellie. She was womanly, without pretense or distraction.

"I get it. I'm lost. I must seem barely functional to you with everything that's happened, but rest assured, I am more than able to take care of myself."

"Elle ...," he started again, faltering over her name before she cut him off.

"Three missed calls."

"What?"

"I had three missed calls."

"I'm not following."

"Since I left Canada. Three missed calls. Two were my mother and one was my assistant to tell me that my mother had told her the 'situation' and that she would take care of everything at the office for me. It's been a week—a week! And I have had three missed calls. What does that say about me? I bet if you went missing, the town would go into lockdown and they'd release the hounds."

"Yeah, no escape for me."

"My mother figured out within a day that I wasn't going to be back for a while."

"Moms know us best." He tried to soften her mood, to no avail.

"That's the thing. I don't have a mom or a mommy. I have a mother who has run my life for as long as I can remember. She should have been shocked that I'd run from it all. Or at least aghast. She figured it out quicker than I did. It's like I don't even need to be there."

Guy knew it was safest to remain quiet.

"She's taken care of my work, and she's stepped in with the wedding planner ..."

Uh, what? "Wedding planner?"

"Yeah. I know. I am that messed up."

"As in, you're getting married?"

"That's the question, right? I had three missed calls."

"Two from your mama."

"Mother."

"One from your assistant."

There was a long, uncomfortable pause.

"His pride's just hurting," he said, thrown off by her admission. "He'll be calling you soon."

"He called today to see if he needed a seat filler for this gala we're scheduled to attend."

"And?"

"And what? That was it."

"Let me get this straight. You are engaged, soon to be married, and you left without telling anyone. Just took off."

"Accurate."

"He didn't call you till now, and he hasn't cut you a new one or begged you to run back home to feed the huskies?"

"I have never gone dogsledding in my life. It's a way-north thing ..."

"Did he beg you to come back and fill the void in his chest?"

"No ..."

"Dump the prick."

"What?" she gasped.

"If he's pissed you've run out on him, he would call off the wedding. If he hasn't tried to get a hold of you until it's about a damned empty chair, then he's not worth your time." The more he thought about it, the angrier he got. He clutched the steering wheel tighter, releasing Ellie and holding the seat back instead.

"That's not fair. I'm the one who put him in a bad situation."

"Sure. But he hasn't called off the wedding, and he hasn't asked you why you left, has he?" Guy didn't wait for her reply. He didn't want to hear her defend this idiot. "What does that tell you?"

"I don't know, but it sure seems to tell you something."

"Elle, if you ran out on me, I would hunt you down whether I was angry or not and make sure you were OK before killing you myself."

"How sweet ..."

"I'm serious. This is a sign of a sociopath or something."

"Well, if that's so, then I should be glad for the distance," she said.

"Yeah, the more, the better."

"Can I ask you something?"

"Anything," he said, honesty cutting through his rigidity.

"When a man tells his fiancée to 'get *whatever* it is out of your system' ... what do you think he means?"

"He told you that?" Guy wanted to turn the truck north to pop the man one.

"Is it that bad?" She sounded so vulnerable, so innocent.

He relaxed his body and let his arm melt back around her. He smiled, looking down at her. "Naw! It's great news for the rest of mankind!" He could feel her annoyance. "It means whatever you want it to mean, but if you're asking if he's giving you permission to be with someone else, yeah, I'd say so." What a fool. Hell, knowing this woman, her fiancé's actions were straight irresponsible. She would be found dead in a ditch or an alley by the end of the month.

If she were his, Guy would never let her run out on him like that. The lady had no street smarts. Thank all that is holy that he'd been there to keep her out of worse trouble!

The silence continued, but he felt better about it.

"Guy?"

"Yeah?"

"Since when do you call me Elle?"

"I dunno. Why? You hate it as much as Ellie?"

"No. I hate it more."

ELLIE FOUND herself leaning into Guy as they drove back to town. It should've felt awkward for him to have his arm wrapped around her like that. Wrong, even. The truth was that it was nice to have someone comfort her. She couldn't remember the last time someone had held her like that.

Daniel was not an affectionate man, and Ellie was having some trouble remembering the last time they'd shared any tenderness. Every time she tried to picture it happening, her head would hurt. She tried to summon guilt for enjoying Guy's warmth. Instead, she felt sick over ending up in such a cold relationship. How had that happened?

Ellie was also trying hard not to let her mind go back to their kiss. So close to this oversized Texan, while so completely vulnerable, it was impossible not to imagine things crossing the line from this innocent cuddling. She rolled her eyes at herself. She didn't like it but that kiss ... she had to address it.

"About what happened this morning ..."

"You kissing me, or you running for the hills like a scared rabbit?"

"Wait, *you* kissed *me*, mister!"

He laughed, and she knew he was playing with her.

"I'm sorry. I should have been up front about my relationship status. I've been trying to sort some things out, and you caught me by surprise."

"The way I figure it, you have nothing to be sorry about. His permission seems retroactive, and from what you've told me, I don't care much for the guy. But to be clear, it was one hell of a kiss."

They both smiled to themselves, pleased by the memory

"So, how'd you get stuck at the mall?" Guy asked after a long, comfortable silence.

"Oh, Goldie had driven me, but she got called away on business."

"Goldie left you there?" His voice was more apprehensive than skeptical, so Ellie figured she should try harder to save her new friend's reputation.

"She was supposed to come get me, but her clients took her on a joyride."

"She should have been looking out for you. I'm going to give her a talking-to."

"It's fine. She'll make it up to me Friday night."

"Friday night?"

"Mm-hmm ... girls' night," Ellie said with a full dopey smile. Who would've thought she'd find herself some girlfriends on this hiatus?

"You and Goldie?"

"And Winter." Skepticism turned to bafflement on his face. "What? She seems nice."

"Sure, for a witch, but the lot of you don't make much sense. Except ..." He stopped short.

"What?"

"Well, I don't mean nothing by this, but none of y'all fit in."

Ellie laughed at how indelicately he put it. "No, I don't suppose Winter or I do ... but Goldie is like your better half. She's not an outsider."

"She's well liked, and damned good at her job. Her looks don't do any harm neither."

"Like I said. Insider."

"Naw, she's doing her damnedest, but she ain't from here, so she's like the top of the outsider pyramid."

"How long has she been living here?"

"Two ... three years?"

"Guess I'll never belong, then."

"Didn't know you were looking to." He had a mix of distaste and surprise in his expression.

"I don't expect to," she admitted. "But it would be nice to fit somewhere. Girls' night will be a great start. Misfits unite!"

Guy chortled at her geekiness. "What you girls gonna get up to? Braiding each other's hair?"

"Nope, they intend to get me sauced in Hampstead."

"You don't say ..."

She found his sudden lack of interest insulting, like nothing she could do would ever be wild enough to blow his hair back.

"That's right. They figure that I should get drunk, dance my brains out, and hook up." Guy's eyes went huge, and had he been drinking, there would've been a mess on the windshield in front of him. Ellie was proud of herself.

"Hook up?" he croaked. "You?"

"Hey, didn't you say that mankind would benefit?"

"Sure, but you ... I mean ... you're so much more responsible than that."

Ellie groaned. "That's the problem, isn't it? I've always been so damned responsible. No, I think it's time to try living fancy-free. What's the worst that could happen?"

"You lose your self-respect. You get an STI. You end up dead in a ditch."

"Oh, please. Like you've never hooked up with random women before." She put it out there not knowing quite what she was hoping to hear. Maybe that he was the relationship type. Maybe that he wasn't into wild women.

"Sure, I have, but come on, Ellie. I've had a career as a boxer, I can take care of myself. Besides, it's not your thing, is it?"

"I guess I'll find out. Say, you got any condoms I can nab off you?" She managed a straight face and a light tone, but she was furious. How could she have thought that a makeover might change anyone's perception of her? She would always be a messy little egghead.

"Talk big, girly," he said, as if reading her mind. "But there is no way you'd go through with it. You are too decent. Between the idiot back up in Parka Land, and your genteel ways, you wouldn't get past a grope on the dance floor."

Hurt that he couldn't even entertain the idea that she could be reckless and sexy, Ellie unbuckled and was out the door before Guy came to complete stop. She tried reaching over the side of the truck, grabbing blindly at bags most ineffectively due to her height.

"I'm getting the feeling that you're angry with me, Miss Ellie." Guy cautiously stared from the other side.

"Oh no, nothing to be angry about. You don't think I'm sexy enough to pick up at a bar on a Friday night. Not even bottom-feeders will try their luck. Nothing insulting about that!" She stormed up to her door with the few bags she could reach and fought to free her keys from her purse. She could feel Guy coming up behind her, but all she wanted was to get inside to curl up and lick her wounds.

"Leave the bags. Thanks for the ride," she threw over her shoulder as the lock tumbled.

"Ellie, I didn't mean anything like that."

But Ellie didn't want an apology. She wanted him to see her

differently. She wanted to *be* different. And she wanted to kill Goldie for abandoning her.

"It's fine. What do I owe you for the ride?" She pulled out her wallet.

"Put that thing away."

"Fine. Be seeing you, then." She stood a little straighter and pretended she was wearing her work cap. All authority. All at arm's length.

"Right." Guy scratched at the scruff on his cheek, a tell that he was angry ... Ellie's cue to close the door.

"Bye!" She closed it and tripped over the Barnes and Noble bag. Staying on the floor as an admission of defeat, she pulled out a hardcover that stuck her in the back. It was a self-help book. She cursed under her breath as Guy's truck took off.

CHAPTER EIGHT

"*W*ith all due respect, I cannot leave looking like this," Ellie protested as Winter finished her makeup. Winter raised a perfect eyebrow at her. "No! I mean it! I look like a libertine." Winter's eyes disappeared with a roll, but she said nothing as she touched up her own powder.

"Libertine? Really? Someone's been watching Regency romances." Goldie snorted a laugh. "You look perfect. Wait, do you even have a TV set up yet? You do move fast."

"I'll have you know that I read my Regency, thank you. And no, I don't have one yet. But the bathroom tile is done drying, so I don't have to do the guilty tiptoe over wet tile for a shower anymore! Thankfully they offset work so I could use the powder room. Though, I think Guy was angling to get me peeing in the bushes at first. OH! And I have a dining table with chairs... and a bed! I'm off the floor! It came in yesterday, or was it the day before?"

"Time becoming a blur?" Winter asked as she cleaned up her station.

"More like a swirl. The guys kick me out for hours at a time, but it's been good. I've gotten to the library, but they won't let me take books out. Since the paperwork hasn't gone through, they can't consider me a citizen of Littleton yet."

"They're book-blocking you?" Goldie asked, snapping her compact closed with anger.

"That's a new low," Winter said.

"When I first moved to town, I got blocked from town meetings, and the Realty Association luncheons, but the library?"

"You know who's on that board, right?" Winter asked knowingly.

"Who?" Ellie was amazed that Goldie had ever been blocked from anything. She seemed as much a part of the fabric of Littleton as Guy and his family, but Ellie *had* only been there a week.

"Ivy Manning," they both reported, but Goldie continued, "Ivy isn't all that bad, though. I don't think she'd stoop that low..."

"No, but her minions might stoop on her behalf." Goldie tried to cut in, but Winter stood her ground. "That woman is a lot of good Goldie, I know you see that side of her, but take it from someone who saw her take on the school board when Liam first got here and was having trouble adapting. She's a ruthless harpy at heart."

"You sound fascinated," Ellie noted. She had gathered that Ivy hadn't liked her much, but for that to get in the way of Ellie's everyday life was disconcerting. Another piece of small-town living she supposed.

"Oh, I am. Dazzled, even, I'm always in awe of a woman in her full power."

"Me too, darling." Goldie winked. "Now make me beautiful but make it quick. We gotta get moving."

"You already are a knockout," whined Ellie, knowing how petulant she sounded as she stared at herself in the mirror.

"Shut it and put this on," Goldie demanded as she scooted Ellie from Winter's salon chair. Ellie obeyed because she sensed that both women were on a mission, and no one would deny them their vision.

"I still haven't forgiven you for stranding me," Ellie lied.

"Of course, you have. Besides, I still haven't forgiven you for making me the stereotypical gay fairy godmother of hookups. Payback's a witch." She smiled at Ellie, shaking the clothes at her.

"We did not hookup!" She grew red and grabbed the shiny outfit. Ellie retreated to the tiny salon powder room, pulling at the fabric of the silver cowl-neck top, trying to hide her breasts. At least they had agreed to pants—well, faux-leather leggings, anyway. She could see either of the sirens out there wearing this outfit and pulling it off marvelously. There was no avoiding it; she was an impostor.

"Come on out, Ellie girl, or we will have to come in after you!" Winter catcalled.

"VA-VA-VOOM!" Goldie yelled, looking like a gilded Amazonian princess, her blond hair bumped up high the only crown she needed.

"It's too much," Ellie's voice cracked. "It's not me." Winter put her hands on each of Ellie's shoulders and locked eyes like a mythical beast hypnotizing its prey.

"Honey, this is one nanobyte of who you are. Own it and move on." She then brushed past her to get her purse.

Desperation kicked in. "But how will we get home? I mean, maybe drinking out isn't a good idea. We could stay in and get some pizza." Winter and Goldie exchanged smirks. There was no way she was going to win this argument.

"Next week, darling. Tonight, we party. Don't worry, there's a DD program on tonight through the church. I've arranged for a few cars in case we get separated."

"Separated?"

"You're not the only one with needs, Ellie!" Goldie laughed.

"Skank!" Winter shot out, a wolfish grin on her face. It earned her the finger in response.

As Ellie had feared, she, a soft, wooly lamb, was now running with foxes.

"Don't worry," Winter said as she locked up the salon. "I got you."

~

ELLIE WASN'T sure what she'd been expecting. Between the full makeup and the scanty outfit, she could only guess where they were going. She knew they were leaving town because, according to Goldie, it was taboo to do anything but drink beer and watch football at the local bar.

Winter laughed. "Who would I be flaunting it for?"

That had Ellie lost for words. She didn't know who Winter *would* flaunt it for.

They didn't go as far as the mall before they pulled into what looked like a roadhouse. Ellie could've sworn she'd seen this place in a movie. She heard the heavy bass and saw people swarming toward the entrance. The real surprise was that it wasn't country music coming through the walls, and Ellie relaxed, if only slightly.

Though she still felt both over- and underdressed, as she took in the crowd, she realized that at least she wasn't alone. These Texan women took their Friday nights every bit as seriously as Goldie and Winter. She was glad to see it wasn't just a hot spot for twenty-somethings either. She didn't need to feel old on top of everything else.

They joined the swarm, and Ellie felt like an anthropologist watching the women size up one another. Ellie bumped into a woman whose neckline plunged almost to her navel, exposing flawless ebony skin.

"I love your necklace!" Ellie called to her over the crowd, embarrassed to have been caught staring, and the woman smiled.

"Thank you!" Then quick as lightning, the woman made it

through the crowd to the doors where she kissed the bouncer's cheek. Clubbing was a sport, and she kicked all their butts.

The crowd was bottlenecking, and Winter shifted her weight impatiently while Goldie appeared to be counting heads. "What's wrong?" Ellie asked, confused by the shift in mood.

"They might fill up early, and like hell do I want to wait. Should I go work my magic?" Goldie asked no one in particular.

"I'm not kissing the bouncer." Winter chortled.

"Oh, come on, Daryl's a sweetie!"

Their heads twirled at the familiar drawl.

"Guy!" Goldie stepped forward and cheek-kissed Guy, making Ellie uncomfortable with their closeness. Even if they weren't interested in each other, they still looked like people in a music video.

"Let's go, girls. Daryl owes me a favor." Ellie tried to slouch to the rear of their group, but of course, Guy wouldn't allow it. He placed his hand on her back, sending electricity up her spine, and led her forward. Daryl was part of the Guy Manning Fan Club, and with little more than a *hey* and a shoulder slap, they were through the doors.

Ellie went from uncomfortable to seeing red. This was meant to have been a night of recklessness. How was she supposed to let go with him watching? She beelined to the washroom. All Ellie had wanted was some mindless fun, and now she felt like her night was over before it had even begun. Like she had an insanely hot older brother to block her from living a little.

No, even at her most insecure, she knew they had too much chemistry to be that platonic.

Goldie came in looking for her. "There you are!"

"Did you invite him?" Ellie surprised herself by snarling. Goldie stopped in her tracks and raised both hands in defense. "You should know that I don't want or need help getting laid!" She whispered that last bit.

"Whoa, Ellie," Goldie began. "I promise you I didn't say boo.

This is the only place nearby worth coming to." Ellie groaned and leaned against the wall. "Besides, he's met up with his buddies. Not like he's tagging along."

"Really?"

"Scout's honor. I despise setups. You decide your own fate."

"Sorry... I was out of line there... I guess I'm just feeling the pressure."

"Listen, Miss Ellie," Goldie said as she came closer and took Ellie's hands in her own. "I know I come on a little strong, but I am trying to be your friend. So hear me when I say this: I don't give two hoots who you let into your panties, so long as you're happy. Now, let's get our drink on."

The club was rustic, top-to-bottom wood. It was clean but had the same stickiness all bars seemed to have. Regardless of the basic features, the crowd was excited, already swaying to the music. Guy was nowhere to be seen. Winter was easy to find standing at a table, dismissing some poor soul who'd found the courage to talk to her. When she saw the two of them coming, she began pouring crimson drinks from a pitcher.

"Sangria!" she said, having to raise her voice over the music.

"Cheers, ladies!" Goldie howled.

"Let the games begin!" Winter chimed in, lifting her glass. Ellie followed suit, looking around the vast saloon-style room. She saw no sign of Guy and relaxed as she drank. When she returned her attention to her friends, they were slack-jawed with surprise.

"What? Do I have something on my face?" Instinctively, Ellie covered herself with her hand.

Winter broke first, laughing. "Would you like another?"

Ellie looked down at her empty glass and smiled. Between the pep talk in the ladies' room and Winter's surprising warmth, Ellie finally felt in the spirit.

"Yes, please!"

The three women were fast friends. Small talk was put away

with ease, they all wanted to get to know one another with more depth.

"You need to start your own salon," Goldie stated after Winter went on a tirade about her boss's treatment of staff and having customers taken out from under her.

"And take what clients with me? These women are fiercely loyal and have shared too many secrets to jump ship, unless they want Crystal to air their laundry."

"You've got to try," Goldie continued, reaching across the table to hold her friend's hand. "You've got to harness your inner lady boss."

"I don't know. What do you think, Ellie?"

"Starting a new shop in direct competition with Crystal's is too financially risky in such a small town. You need to be more subversive than that. Start with a niche side hustle and build clientele that way." The women stared blankly, so Ellie continued. "For instance, weddings, or with your particular style, you could market yourself online for all kinds of magazines or social media. It depends on where you want your career to go. But you need to build a following, and I would suggest that you start monopolizing the spa angle. You could corner that market by the time they break ground if you play it right.

"If your end goal is to have a salon in Littleton, then work on private affairs that you know Crystal can't touch. I'm guessing she doesn't reach the teen market, so she's missing out on prom season, not to mention photo-day opportunities. Endearing yourself to the younger crowd will serve you well in the long run. But if you want more specialized work, then go freelance. Do you like to travel? You can do this with the security of working for Crystal until you're comfortable with your income, and she won't even have to accuse you of stealing clients because you'll be bringing in your own."

A long silence followed in which both women stared at Ellie as if it were their first time speaking to her. Then Winter's lips turned up from their natural pout into a toothy grin.

"Damn, girl! Where did that come from?" Goldie asked, impressed.

"I'm almost the COO of a major company back home," Ellie responded as she finished the last of the sangria. "How do you ladies feel about tequila?"

After shots, they were on the dance floor. It didn't take long for them to gain a following, which they efficiently shook off. Ellie couldn't remember the last time she'd had so much fun. She laughed at the antics of the men trying to gain the favor of her friends.

"Where all my independent women at? Let me hear you!" The DJ came in over the heavy beat and was met by women hollering back at him. "Where all my bad bitches?" More sassy screams in reply. "Where are all my boss babes? This one's for you!"

The dance floor overflowed with women shaking it and singing the lyrics about getting paid and not needing men to buy their drinks. Most women did not have the luxury of being a boss, making the money Ellie did, especially not while on a sabbatical. Some hit glass ceilings, some didn't work hard enough, and some had dependent personalities. Then there were family women—not even a turn of phrase. Why did *family man* roll off the tongue, but *family woman* didn't? Hustling as a woman was damn hard.

Ellie was a work in progress, but she knew that she was much farther ahead than most of the women in the room. If they could own the song, like hell would she be a wallflower. She worked hard; she would own it too. Feeling more confident than she had in ages, she joined in full force—she let the music take over her body. Nostalgia flooded her system, the freedom she had dancing over a decade before, only without the rules or competitions.

Soon she was playing into the drama, dancing away from men, sometimes with the help of Goldie or Winter. They would take turns pulling one another from zealous men who thought gyration was all they needed to get in. As the night wore on, Goldie carpe diem'd with a tall woman in sequins, and Winter was talking to the DJ like they were old friends. Ellie danced for a few more songs until she decided to grab another drink.

Making her way to the bar, she found that her face ached from smiling so much. Despite the crowd, the bartender came to her first, and she ordered another shot of tequila and a bottle of water. "Is it tacky to do the salt and lime if you're doing the shot alone?" she asked as he poured her drink.

"Darlin', I'll do one with you!" drawled the statuesque person suddenly standing beside her. Their makeup and fuchsia boa surprised another smile out of her. Stealing her shot, they licked the salt off their hand suggestively, tipped the glass back with a flair not to be ignored, and made a feast of the lime as the bartender poured her another shot.

"How are you so fabulous?" Ellie asked. "Please! Teach me!"

"Some things can't be taught. Besides, you're doing well for yourself! I'd have never got a drink without you." They laughed together, looking at the lineup of men along the bar ogling them. Ellie had a new playmate on the dance floor, until they found their own tall, dark, and handsome.

She didn't know if it was the drink or her mood, but she was becoming more accepting of the attention, but things started going too far. While dancing behind her, a clumsy-footed brute kept trying to put his hands down past her comfort zone. Even if Ellie's intention was to have sex that night, it wouldn't be on the dance floor. She pushed the guy away emphatically, but he either didn't get the hint or didn't care.

"No means no," boomed Guy's voice over the music, and a few heads turned. The man, who stood noticeably shorter, put his hands up as he backed away unaffected and probably moving on to his next victim. "You OK?"

"My hero!" Ellie laughed, threw her arms around Guy's neck, and kissed him on the cheek. She continued laughing when she noticed the gravity on his face turn to shock at her advance. She couldn't remember ever needing a white knight more, and there was Guy. The perv had scared her, but she felt so much relief at seeing Guy that it was like nothing had happened. He made her feel that safe.

"Here, have a drink." He handed her a bottle of water. She took a sip to placate him. "Your friends leave you alone?" he asked, looking around for them.

"They're having fun! Looks like you could use some of that too!" she joked, poking him in the chest. His seriousness broke enough to let a grin curl his lips, and Ellie almost melted. He was too attractive, like James Dean with a hard body. Timeless. She looked him over, top to delicious bottom. "Dance with me!" she demanded.

Guy brushed stray hair behind her ear, and she caught the scent of cedar, musk, and something unique to him. What was it? She leaned in closer, breathing him into her.

"I don't think I could keep up with you, darlin'," he growled into her ear, sending warmth deep into her belly.

"Try," she dared him as her heart raced to the beat of the music.

CHAPTER NINE

Guy had been watching from a distance all evening. Had he planned a night out with the guys as a pretense for keeping an eye on Ellie? Pretty much. He kept telling himself that he had to see where her antics would land her and laughed at the visions that came to mind. He'd known his fair share of wild women, dated a few, and was a lot less serious with a few more, and he didn't believe Ellie was cut out for that kind of life. She was too soft, too vulnerable, and not street-smart enough to know when she was getting in over her head. She might look the part with those long legs leading up to that perfectly packaged tight ass, but it wasn't *her*. Like hell was he going to let some asshole take advantage of her buffoonery. He knew she'd regret it in the morning.

He'd invited a few of the fellas out so he wouldn't seem like a complete creeper. Before approaching the women in line, he'd taken his time to appreciate the work Winter and Goldie had put in. Leather pants made Ellie look daring, and that shiny top showed off so much of her creamy, soft skin, it had taken all his self-restraint to not run his hand up her bare back. Winter had done something with Ellie's makeup that made her brown eyes glow. His heart sputtered—she could have disarmed him with those eyes—but she was much less pleased to see him. She disappeared so fast, it didn't take a rocket scientist to get the hint that she did not want him there. And he was offended.

He took the fact that their kiss was a mistake in stride. It was, of course, a mistake; the woman was engaged. But now she was acting like he was an annoying tagalong, big-brother type. He wasn't the enemy. Did she think he didn't get the message? He got it. Hands off. He didn't have to like it.

He wasn't much company for his buddies since he kept his eyes locked on Ellie's every move, scanning the crowd around her for pervs trying to make a play. She was going to be sick by the end of the night, the way she was drinking.

"Who's that with Goldie?" Mark asked, taking a swig from his bottle.

"Freaky Friday?" guessed Grayson, who Guy knew for a fact had been head over heels for Winter since third grade.

"Naw, the sexpot brunette." Mark tilted his head like a hound dog to better appreciate what he saw, and Guy didn't like it one bit.

"It's the Canadian Go-Juice disaster. I believe you're fixing her car right now," Guy drawled, ordering himself his own drink from the waitress. It was going to be a long evening.

"She doesn't look like a disaster tonight," Grayson said. "That why you invited us out? You babysitting your next pet project?"

"Don't know what you mean." Guy shrugged, taking a long draw from his beer, nodding his thanks to the waitress who had slipped him her number.

"Right." Grayson smirked.

"If you're not gonna make a move, mind if I do?" asked Mark, neck still tilted. "She is one fine piece of ..."

"Hey! Mind your manners. Miss Ellie is a nice lady," Guy scolded.

"How nice?" Mark straightened up and grinned mischievously

at his buddies. Guy knew he was messing with him and played along to get his anger under control. Mark wasn't choosy, and he soon had his eyes on some other poor girl. He followed her to the dance floor, making a fool of himself on purpose. He was good at that, girls ate up his lost-mutt routine.

"So, what's the deal?" Grayson asked, chasing a lead.

"What do you mean?"

"Guy, I've known you since diapers. Don't be sly with me. What's going on with Miss Ellie?"

"I don't know yet," Guy admitted grudgingly. "She's a nice girl with a long list of problems."

"She not interested?" His friend was surprised. "A rare woman, indeed."

"Ha, ha. There's nothing there, brother. She's more complicated than I expected."

Grayson leveled his gaze with his friend's. "You ever try noticing someone simple for a change?"

Guy snorted in spite of himself. "You gonna go swoop Winter off her feet?"

Both men scowled at each other while drinking their beers until Mark motioned to a woman and her friend, and Grayson got up to fulfill his wingman duties. "Don't do anything stupid, Guy."

"You don't do any*one* stupid," he returned.

"No promises there." He finished his beer and headed to the bar to meet up with Mark. Guy laughed. Grayson was a good man. Too observant, though. Made sense that he'd become a cop.

He was glad to be left on his own. Once the girls started dancing, it was hard to keep up with them. It was comical how they had to move around the room to avoid unwanted advances. But soon he'd lost track of Ellie. Winter was talking to the DJ—you couldn't miss her in a crowd. Goldie was all over a tall brunette in a flashy dress. That at least made sense. He'd questioned why she'd cozied up to him in public when they'd always been platonic—she was like a sister to him—but people made assumptions. People like his mom. It eased some stress to know that she wasn't after him, and he hoped she'd feel comfortable enough to confide in him someday. Not that she was keeping secrets tonight.

He had completely lost Ellie. In a panic, he stood and surveyed the dance floor, the bar, and the crowds around the exits. He caught sight of her talking to the bartender who was ignoring other customers for her sake. Did the woman know her power? He doubted it, the way she usually held herself had him thinking that fiancé of hers had her living with low self-esteem. She probably didn't realize that she had a huge blinking arrow sign above her head. If she didn't recognize the attention she pulled, how the hell could she protect herself?

As much as he wanted her out of harm's way, he also wanted her to have a good time. It was irresponsible of the girls to have left her alone. As Guy tried to decide on the best way to approach her, someone else beat him to it. The prettiest linebacker in all of Texas started doing shots with her. Guy moved to the other end of the bar to stay out of sight, while keeping an eye on things.

The two of them were having a grand time laughing and fawning over one another. Guy had grown up with Adrian and didn't care that they had on as much makeup as Ellie did, had never been bothered by their flair. What bothered him was how bright she was shining. He was jealous. Guy wanted to be the one to open her up like that. He wanted her to feel at ease around him. And why didn't she? Did he push the teasing too far? Was it their chemistry keeping her on high alert? He wanted her to know she was safe with him.

Guy watched Ellie dancing with reckless abandon. It wasn't the usual drunk girl gyrations. She was sexy as hell, but she could also dance circles around anyone there. Her movements were crisp and intentional. She had footwork rather than the simple sway of the masses, and she kept time with the music. And she was indefatigable, like she never had to come up for air. She was flying.

Soon her new companion moved along, but she didn't seem to mind, so Guy sat back with another beer and watched.

How she managed to walk in those damned high heels, never mind dance, was beyond him. He rolled his eyes. *Women*. Still, his eyes moved up those legs. Those impossibly long legs, fit and firm, yet supple. He imagined how flexible she, a trained dancer, must be. Her tight clothes left no movement hidden; her chest tested the limits of her fancy top. He imagined burying his face where the fabric barely contained her, with those long legs wrapped around him. He imagined what her voice would sound like moaning his name, and he felt himself growing hard. She hit him like a lightning bolt right to his rod.

Closing his eyes, he tried to remember what a mess she was. He tried to remember that she was engaged to marry some Canadian schmuck. He counted the number of times he'd seen this prima ballerina trip over her own feet. It was no good. He opened his eyes and seethed.

Some douchebag had sidled up to Ellie. He'd watched men make their moves on her all night, but this guy was different. He was scum. Guy only had to watch for half a second before he was up and moving. The waitress was coming toward him with his bottle of water, so he grabbed it from her tray while in motion, wishing it were another beer he could crack the slimeball over the head with.

"No means no." He shoved the guy hard enough to get his attention without knocking into Miss Ellie. The snake slithered off into the dark. Guy wished he'd stepped up to him. He'd have loved nothing better than to pop the guy one. "You OK?" he asked, noting that she was quivering despite the heat radiating from her.

"My hero!" She laughed, managing in those heels to reach around his neck and kiss his cheek. He wasn't sure if she was mocking him, but he didn't care. She was smiling. At him. Forgetting everyone else, he handed her the bottle of water.

"Here, have some," he ordered. She needed it more than he

did. "Your friends ditch you?" he asked before she might realize how long he'd been looking out for her. She defended her friends after long-hauling the water, then pushed him playfully. He grinned in spite of himself. Drunk Ellie was a flirt. Who knew?

"Dance with me!"

Guy leaned in and was instantly intoxicated by the smell of daisies, tequila, and sweet lady sweat. "I don't think I could keep up with you, darlin'," he admitted with admiration.

"Try," the goddess demanded, lust clawing its way through him in an instant.

GUY SURPRISED ELLIE. He'd been a boxer, so she assumed he'd have some footwork, but she'd intended to lead. He wouldn't have it. He wasn't a dancer, but the way he held her to him and took control had her full attention. She could be wearing a crimson gown dancing a tango instead of to a grinder tune. Strong and in control, his touch guided her, her every need being met. His dominance sent hot sparks through her body. She ached for him, yet he practiced perfect chivalry. She was torn apart by need; she'd never felt anything like it.

"Let's go to the bar." She tried to save herself, knew that she was going to make herself vulnerable to him if they didn't part ways.

"I think you've had enough," he responded, leading her effortlessly, the calm to her storm.

Ellie pulled him down to speak in his ear. "I don't want your gallantry, Manning," and she let her hands travel from around his neck, down to his shoulders, clutching, exploring. She melted into the heat of his body, testing the waters. Giving herself to him, laying herself bare.

His whole body stiffened. Getting the message, with a dose of mortification, she turned and hurried to the bar. She would get another few shots and refuse to let Guy ruin her otherwise exciting evening. Maybe cozying up to the next horndog to try something was the only way to go. She held her head high, fighting the desire to run to the ladies' room.

The bartender smiled at her, she held up two fingers, and he nodded, dropping off three with a wink. It was getting close to last call, so he was overrun. She held up the first shot to him, and they shared a smile before he was back to work. He was cute, muscular, maybe a little younger than her, but she wouldn't be cradle robbing.

"Ellie, what the hell? Come on, now. I'm gonna get you home." Guy swooped in like the gentleman he was. She stared him down as she licked her salted hand slowly, took her shot, and sucked the lime.

"Listen, Manning, I get it. You're not interested. And why would you be, right?" She went through the shooter process again.

"Ellie," Guy began, but Ellie didn't want to hear about how drunk she was, or how stupid she was acting. What she needed more than anything else that night was to feel wanted, even if it was meaningless sex with a man who would've taken any number of women home. The truth settled in and made her a little sad.

"There has to be someone here who wants to take me home," she said with as much bravado as she could muster, reaching again for the salt, but Guy intercepted her last shot, taking it himself. "Bravo! Wish me luck!"

"Wait, Ellie." Guy grabbed her shoulder, turning her to face him before she could run for it. "You telling me that you are willing to go home with any asshole in this place?"

"Yes, Guy, that's the gist of it." Ellie was losing her temper. "How dare you judge me! I know I'm a mess! But even my fiancé endorsed this decision, so who the hell are you to tell me what I need is wrong?"

Storming back to the dance floor, her mission was clear. It didn't take long before she was hounded once more, but this time she didn't resist. She let this random tall brown-haired guy who smelled of cigarettes and beer fondle her. While it felt cheap, she knew she'd made the choice to allow it. There would be no questions of intentions or hurt feelings.

The body behind her disappeared, and she almost stumbled. Turning, she saw the unfamiliar man gripped by the collar by a gorgeous former boxer. It really wasn't fair that he was so attractive. It was as much a weapon as his fists.

"Take a hike!" he said as he pushed the guy away.

"Hey! I know you!" her would-be seducer bit back. "Guy Manning! Throw any fights lately?"

"I won't tell you twice," Guy told him with a threatening stance that made Ellie's mouth hang open with appreciation. She had never seen him as a fighter. She knew he was strong, and had seen him make the motions, but ready to fight for her? Attraction overload. The brunette retreated with a few profanities along the way.

"Really?" Ellie yelled, fighting her desire to throw herself at him.

He pulled her in close and growled in her ear, "I'm the only asshole you're leaving this place with tonight." And he began to move against her far less subtly than earlier.

Ellie's mind was in shock, but her body knew what to do. He held her hips to him, she praised her high heels for bridging their height difference. There was no question of his need. His hands roamed up her sides, almost caressing her breasts before he pulled her hair away from her face, tilting her head to look at him. He had no glint of humor in his eyes. Usually, she was waiting for his next witticism, but the way he looked at her now was pure hunger. There was no mistaking it.

He ground into her, and her body responded in kind. They entered a haze of give and take, tormenting each other with every caress. Forgetting where they were, he palmed her breast, she swayed, he smoldered, she ached. His mouth found her neck to nip and kiss sensitive nerves that ran straight to her apex. His tongue parted her lips, and she welcomed his warm invasion as her body overflowed with desire.

"Take me home."

"Yes, ma'am." He took her hand and led her out of the bar.

CHAPTER TEN

*G*uy's intentions started out pure, he was almost certain they had. But when Ellie made it clear to him that she was going to be with someone that night, the thought that it wouldn't be him was impossible to reconcile. It was impossible not to respond to Ellie's body. There was her beauty, but when she danced, her confidence was through the roof, exposing more of herself than just skin. And they fit—they shouldn't have, with his height, and their dueling personalities. Their energy synchronized, their chemistry exploded.

"I'm parked over here," he said as he guided her through the lot, past a group of guys tailgating. The night air blew cold as they left the saloon. Guy didn't have a coat to offer, so he pulled Ellie in under his arm as close as he could get her.

"There's the Chump now!" Guy paused as he recognized the idiot he'd peeled off Ellie. The man was volatile, drunk, and ready to brawl now that he had a few of his buddies to back him. Guy knew he would have no problem dealing with these bozos if he had to, but he was more concerned about getting Ellie home, so he didn't engage. Besides, he was secure enough to not have to question his former career every time some jerk wanted to tell him his business.

"What's the matter, Manning? Afraid the skank won't come home with you if you lose?"

Guy turned and caught his opponent mid-stride with a left hook to the jaw that sent him to the ground like a ton of bricks. "Anyone else have a problem?" he asked, ready to throw down. There were no takers, so he turned and wrapped his arm back around Ellie who had gone slack-jawed. He pulled her along.

"You OK?" he asked, uncertain of how Miss Ellie would feel about violence.

"I knew I looked like a floozy!" she proclaimed with pride, unruffled by the altercation.

"You're beautiful. That jerk doesn't deserve to lay eyes on you," Guy answered.

"So, why'd you deck him?" Ellie asked, drunkenly adopting the local twang.

He stopped walking and turned her to him, meeting her eyes with a firm stare so she'd listen. "You have honor worth defending."

She gave him a hundred-watt smile, pleased by his compliment.

Beguiled, he leaned her against his truck. His need overrode everything, and he kissed her with everything he had. Having a taste of celebrity status had taught him the value of privacy. PDA had been a thing of the past, but Ellie was magnetic, and he wasn't strong enough to hold back. He lost himself in her until she pushed away.

"You're drunk!" she accused.

"Darlin', I am not drunk. To be honest, I'm not sure how *you* are standing right now."

"It's a medical mystery, but we aren't talking about me." She folded her arms across her chest. "How many drinks did you have tonight?"

"Three beers."

"And the tequila."

"I'm fine to drive."

"Said every drunk driver in history."

"Ellie, look at me. I'm the size of a damn moose, and we have been here for hours."

She set her jaw and tapped her foot.

They were at an impasse.

He groaned. "Fine! I'll call for a ride." He did, but there were no drivers left for the night that could be there in the next hour. "I swear, Ellie ..."

"Swear all you want, Manning. I will not get in a car with you behind the wheel." Her rage cut through him, and he realized that this was more than Miss Ellie being skittish. She ran her fingers through her hair in a panic as she leaned against the truck, shivering.

Guy opened the toolbox and pulled out an emergency blanket, shook the debris from it, and draped it over her shoulders before she could push him off. He rubbed her arms through it providing her warmth.

"Tell me about it." He braced himself for her words.

She played dumb, but he raised an eyebrow to tell her he wasn't buying it.

"I told you I was a dancer, right?"

He nodded.

"Well, I was actually a *great* dancer. Winning awards at competitions. I told you my mother pushed me hard, but when it came to dance, it was OK. I loved it. It was my life."

Guy groaned as he put it together. It was as cliché as the football hero blowing his shoulder out in high school. The killer of dreams.

"My knee would be fine today if it hadn't been for some guy who thought he wasn't drunk after a few drinks. I would be living the dream that muted all other ambitions in my life if it hadn't been for *just a few drinks*. I would know my life's purpose, if it weren't for some prick who thought he could hold his booze better than he could." She seethed as a few angry tears escaped. She sniffed and wiped them away with the blanket.

"I'm sorry, Ellie. I didn't know. The way you move ... it's hard to believe anything can hold you back."

"Don't be sorry, and don't drive."

He nodded, still frustrated but also deflated. It would do no good to argue. "All right." He kicked the dirt as his phone lit up and vibrated. Looking at the caller ID, he saw that it was Grayson. "Hey."

"Hey, buddy, you still at the bar? Mark took off with a blond, leaving me here holding my dick."

"Yeah, I'm at the truck now."

Ellie scowled at him.

"But I've had a few too many."

"That's fine, I'm sober as all hell."

"Come on out, then." As the call disconnected, Guy turned back to Ellie. "A buddy of mine got left behind. He's sober. He can drive us."

"How do you know he's sober?"

"Because he told me he was."

"Like you told me you were?"

"Listen, Grayson almost lost his little sister in a car accident when they were kids. If he says he's sober, I believe him." Guy's understanding was wearing thin. It wasn't her attitude, because he could see where she was coming from: it was the dwindling possibility of regaining their momentum. Ellie was thinking too much. His whole body felt the disappointment, but it was for the best. Beyond the fact that they were both tipsy, she was engaged. Even if her fool fiancé gave her permission, Guy didn't want her regretting it in the morning.

Before Ellie had time to respond, Grayson appeared.

"Oh, hey, Miss Ellie! Didn't realize you were along for the

ride." He sent Guy a knowing glance that he would pay for at a later date.

"I'm sorry, but how much have you had to drink?" Ellie asked without preamble.

"I had one beer four hours ago, Miss Ellie, and lots of water. And I'm glad you asked. Most folks don't." Grayson held Ellie's gaze, and her shoulders relaxed. "Surprised at my boy here, though. He ain't usually a drinker."

"Miss Ellie got me drunk on tequila."

"You only had the one!" Ellie defended herself, smacking his midsection.

"He's always been a lightweight," Grayson chided. "Y'all ready?"

Guy helped Ellie into the truck, boosting her and kicking himself for having the beers. He'd always intended to drive her home, and while he didn't like to admit it, he might have overdone it. It'd cost him one wild night.

"So, we'll drop you off first, Miss Ellie?" probed Grayson as he pulled the truck out of the lot onto the highway.

"Naw," she answered, still holding on to her drunken twang. "I'm going home with Guy."

Guy coughed in genuine surprise.

"That so?" asked Grayson with an ear-to-ear grin.

"Yup. But I ... oh, never mind," Ellie began but clammed right up.

"Come now, Miss Ellie. You're among friends."

"Well ..." She paused, trying to find the words. "I'm not used to sleeping around, so I don't know how to ask the vital questions."

"Vital questions?" Grayson was having a great time at their expense.

Guy narrowed his eyes at his friend who made sure to ignore him.

"Yeah, like, has he been tested ... when ... is he sleeping with anyone else ... what's his position on protection ... that sort of thing."

"Well, seeing as we are all adults here, Guy, why don't you clear the air for Miss Ellie?"

Trust Ellie to put him through his paces. Guy wished he'd had a few more drinks. "Well, I don't kiss and tell, but you don't have to worry about your health."

"Why don't you want to tell me how many women you've been with?"

"Yeah, Guy, are you ashamed?" mocked Grayson.

"No, it's a moot point because, after the last one, I made sure to get tested. I'm in the clear."

Ellie took a turn narrowing her eyes at Guy.

"How long ago?"

"About a year."

"Bullshit."

"Miss Ellie! I didn't know you had it in you!" Grayson laughed.

"I don't believe it. With all the estrogen in Tiny Town being thrown his way? Not a chance."

"Yeah, I won't deny that I had a wild run, but I wouldn't lie to you about it, Miss Ellie."

"Grayson, is it?" Ellie looked to his friend for verification.

"Yes, ma'am. I've known him all his life. So far as I know, he's truthin'." He would pay for his enjoyment.

"All right, then." Ellie closed what little distance there was between them and rested her head against Guy's shoulder. She dared to blush.

"What are you blushing about? Ready to share your 'vitals'?" Guy teased.

Her face went redder under the glare of streetlights, and she evaded eye contact. "About the same," she muttered.

"What does that mean?" Guy asked. He hadn't wanted to

embarrass Ellie, but when talking about STIs, *about the same* doesn't fly.

She groaned, covering her face. "I'm on the Pill, protection is a must, and I get tested every year I get a Pap."

"Which was when?" Grayson asked.

"About six months ago."

"How many men since?" Grayson asked like he was filling out a form for the IRS, pressing his luck at her expense. If he didn't cool it, Guy would straighten him out.

"None," Ellie answered definitively, keeping eye contact with Guy. He raised his eyebrows, and she nodded.

Guy couldn't fathom it. How could someone be with Ellie every day and not be *with* her every day? He knew it was a crude thought, but he could not imagine going without for a week if he was with her. He kissed Ellie's temple, trying to soothe her.

"Gross," Grayson yelled in mock disgust. "Save it, Guy. I'll have you home soon enough."

ELLIE SHOULD'VE FELT MORTIFIED at all she had admitted. Maybe the conversation had to happen with Guy, but Grayson? Grayson was one of those people who made others feel at ease. He didn't have to coax—words just fell out of her mouth. She blamed the tequila for allowing her to go there with the conversation and thanked the tequila for cushioning her ego. She knew she would forever cringe at the memory of this ride, but the full weight of embarrassment had yet to rest on her.

"So, your lady friends ditch you?" Grayson asked, obviously not at home in silence.

"Shoot!" began Ellie, feeling around in her bra for her phone. "I should make sure ..." She faded out as she held her phone away from her, trying to see the text messages.

Goldie: I'm out, ladies! Good night!

Goldie had made her plans for the night plain from the beginning.

Winter: Are you OK!?

Winter: CALL ME!!!

The phone vibrated wildly, and Ellie nearly threw it up in the air. Regaining partial wits, she answered. "Hello?" she said, unsure of what to expect from Winter.

"Are you OK?" Winter's voice brimmed with concern. "I saw you leaving with Guy and his dumbass friend. Are you OK? How drunk are you? Do you need me to come get you?"

Ellie's heart warmed. "You care that much about me?"

"Of course I do! Now put Guy on."

Ellie handed Guy her phone. When he raised his eyebrows, Ellie shrugged, unsure of what Winter was going to say. As soon as Guy's ear touched the receiver, Winter's voice could be heard laying into him, slowly, firmly, and with insurmountable flair. "Now put Asshat on!" came through loud and clear.

Guy handed back her phone.

"Winter, listen, I'm fine. I—" Ellie began.

"No, put the other asshat on."

"She wants to talk to you," Ellie said, giggling in spite of herself. To have the otherworldly Winter in her corner made her giddy with power.

Grayson went pale as he took the phone, swallowed, then spoke. "I'm driving, so I shouldn't be—"

"PUT IT ON SPEAKER!"

He did as he was told.

"Let me make this clear to both of you. If Ellie is so much as bleary-eyed in the morning, I will hunt you down. Your bodies will never be found. Do you understand me?"

"Yes, ma'am," both men chorused.

"Threatening a police officer is a crime, you know," said Grayson.

"Ellie, take me off speaker." Ellie did while wearing a full smile.

"Are you sure this is what you want? I have no problem picking you up. I know we talked big about you hooking up, but it was for the fun of it."

"I'm good here, Winter. Everyone here is being kind to me."

"OK. Call me if you need anything."

"Want to get together tomorrow?" Ellie could feel the men looking over her head at each other in disbelief.

"Sure. What do you want to do?"

"You into yoga?"

"If wine is involved."

"Or maybe painting?"

Winter laughed. "We'll figure it out. Call me if you need anything."

"Will do, friend."

"Have fun, bestie," Winter said with an eye roll Ellie could feel. Ellie relaxed into Guy as the call disconnected.

"So," Grayson said, "you're gal pals with the resident Satanist?"

"Hey! Don't talk about her like that! I'm at least sixty percent sure she's not into that." Ellie said and stuck out her tongue, not caring how juvenile it made her seem. She leaned forward and played with the radio until she found a funky pop station to put him in his place.

After her bravado cooled, she considered things a little more rationally. She was in a truck with two men she hardly knew. Winter had been right to check on her, and she didn't even ask if she was OK too! What sort of friend was she turning out to be? But what was she doing? This was far from known territory for Ellie. Was she even safe? She felt like she had a grip on who Guy was, and she got good vibes from Grayson, but realistically, she'd been here for a week. What could she know about a person in a week? Sure, he was the town god, but he was also a boxer, and what kind of human being can fight for sport and not have a darker side?

And yet, the way his hand held hers on the inside of his thigh, thumb rubbing warmth into the back of it, heat running all the way to her center ... It was utterly hypnotizing, even if it wasn't intended to be sexual. They were connected. While she was unsure of herself, there was no doubt that she was safe with Guy. The question was: How safe?

Guy was bringing her home. She'd thought they were going to have wild sex with no strings attached, but was that really what was going to happen? He had pulled her away from the other man at the bar. Maybe he was playing like he was taking her home to bed, and when they got there, he'd lock her up until her liquid courage wore off.

With his arm around her, her body melted into his, she could feel his heartbeat, and it was so right. For some inconceivable reason, they fit together perfectly.

She raised her chin to take in that impossibly beautiful face. Strong jaw, blue eyes, sun-kissed hair ...

He caught her gaze and his warm smile had a direct line to her libido. "How you doing, Canada?"

Ellie moved her lips to where she could see his pulse in his neck and kissed him gently. She lingered there before looking ahead at the road as if nothing had happened, even though her own pulse had gone wild at her advance.

Guy had stiffened in response, then kissed her hair and held her closer. Ellie would have paid good money to know what he was thinking.

GUY LIVED in a one-bedroom apartment above the hundred-year-old hardware store along the main street. His stoop was a step and a weather-worn door. It was discreet. Out back, he had a fire escape, noisy, rusty, metal. It was ideal for getaways when fans decided to disrespect his space.

From the front door, they had to climb a narrow staircase. There was nothing fancy about it, but it was well kept. At the top of those stairs was his second door to unlock. He didn't need bodyguards everywhere he went, but he took home security seriously, thus the deadbolts.

Once inside, he could breathe easier. His home was basic but masculine. Cool, dark shades on the walls calmed him. He didn't have a lot of square footage, but he was out of the house most of the time. This was his place of rest, so every piece of furniture served a purpose and suited his comforts. Having Ellie in his sanctuary was surreal.

The ride home had been haywire, and Guy wasn't altogether sure where he and Ellie stood. There was her straightforward questioning about his sexual health, which was classic Ellie. Then hearing she and her fiancé had not been intimate in a while had made him a confused mix of angry and pitying at the same time. The call from Winter was reassuring—Guy liked her more for it. Ellie needed strong people with good values in her life. Then there was the kiss.

It hadn't come out of the blue, per se, but damn, was it sweet. It felt like a dream, but his manhood had let him know it was real. With her leaning into him, smelling like a damn meadow, it was hard to keep his hands to himself. Besides, Grayson would've thrown them out on their asses. Rightly so, they weren't dumb kids anymore. That's what Ellie did to him, made him feel young again, and a little out of control.

Guy turned on the light as he closed the door behind Ellie and locked up for the night. She sauntered in, not asking permission. She appraised the art on the walls where landscapes brought the outside in for him. The small library on the back wall pulled her farther into his space. He felt pride when she ran a finger along a few of the spines with quiet approval. As tiny as she was, they could manage to live here together. They didn't need much space between them. He could picture her curled up on the sofa with tea and a book.

But what the hell was he thinking? She hadn't come here to read. He groaned. It was time.

"Listen, Ellie ..."

She turned to face him, looking vulnerable and beautiful.

"You don't have to do anything here tonight. Take the bed, and I'll bring you some water."

"You listen, Manning," Ellie said, wagging a finger at him. "I did not come all this way to be babied by you. If you don't want me, I can always call Winter and try my luck elsewhere." She was talking big, but he could tell she was hurt. She reached into her shirt to pull out her phone, and his mind stayed there. How would she react to his touch? Would she buck? His jeans were feeling more crowded.

"Look at me, Ellie." He closed the distance between them as Ellie took in the sight of him, eyes resting on his bulge before her cheeks reddened. "How could I not want you?"

Her eyebrows furrowed, like she was waiting for the punch line.

He took her by the shoulders. "You need a mirror, Ellie. You are beautiful."

"Yeah, Goldie and Winter did a great job."

"You were gorgeous before all the extras. They ain't the ones who made those legs come all the way up to here," he said as he stroked her hip.

She shivered under his touch.

He needed to know if she was this sensitive everywhere. "But I respect you too damn much to not give you an out if you want to take it."

Her doe eyes bore into him, forever assessing.

He took her face in his hands, waiting as she leaned her warmth into his palms. When she tilted her head slightly, consent and offering all in one, his self-control gave way. He kissed her supple lips hard, parting them with his tongue, exploring her warmth.

Her surprise faded and her tongue joined the exploration. It had been a long time since he'd been kissed so thoroughly. His body was electric with desire. He ran a hand down to where a pert breast fit into his palm, and gave it an appreciative squeeze before continuing down the curve of her waist, out around the flare of her hips to that cute little ass. She moaned as he went, and that did him in.

He knelt in front of her, helping her out of her shoes, before his hands played at the waist of her pants, teasing her warm skin as he began peeling them off of her. She untied her shirt, and he was mystified. He stood, picking her up by her bottom, and she obediently wrapped her legs around his waist. He groaned with pleasure as she pulled at his lip with her teeth.

"Bed or counter?" he asked as he buried his face in her chest.

"Bed!" she exclaimed, yipping with pleasure at his touch.

Without hesitation, he carried her across the threshold into his darkened bedroom. The curtains were slightly parted, casting shadows around the room. The king-size bed was made, the space tidy, much to his relief. Ellie didn't notice since she was busy kissing his neck, sending surges of need through his body. He set her down, taking his time to appreciate the sight of her. Wearing nothing but a tiny lace thong, she fidgeted under his attentive eyes.

She approached him again, wordlessly undoing his belt, and helping him out of his jeans, trailing her nails possessively down his thighs. He pulled his shirt over his head, tossing it aside. She took in the sight of his manhood saluting her. She licked her lips and wrapped her hand around him with a firm grip, beginning a slow, torturous pumping.

Their breathing was ragged as she brought her tongue to his crown, teasing as she tasted him. He lightly gripped her hair in his fists as she took him into her mouth, warmth enveloping him. She couldn't take him all the way—he was too big for that—but she worked her tongue like magic. With her lips wrapped around him, those doe eyes looking up at him, it was all he could do not to not explode right there.

"That's so good, darlin'."

She hummed in response, almost sending him over.

"It's your turn. Let me taste you."

She was reluctant to give up her feast, but she let him lead her to the bed. She reclined, and he dragged her by the hips to the edge, trailing her thong down her legs to prolong the moment. He knelt, hooking her legs on his shoulders, dragging his stubble along her inner thighs, nipping and kissing as he made his way to her apex.

Sensitive and wanton, she was wet and ready for him as he took his time on her. A brush of his lips over her clit sent her writhing. A rub of his fingers had her cursing his name.

He kissed her there like their lives depended on it until he couldn't take it anymore. He liked to exhaust all areas before going for gold, but it had been awhile for both of them, and Ellie was already panting with desire. Despite her objections to his change of pace, he remembered to pay homage to other parts of her body—her hips, her belly—he took a nipple into his mouth, and Ellie forgot her complaints until he rolled over to reach into his bedside table for a condom.

"Come here." He knew how he wanted her. He was kneeling on the bed, pulling her to sit over him. She took his member in hand, teasing her slick opening, driving him to the edge of his control. He plunged his considerable length into her, and she threw her head back, moaning. He held her hips in place, letting her tight body get used to the hot stretch.

"I need ..." She panted.

"What do you need?" He knew, but he needed to hear it.

"Let me ride you."

He let go of her hips, bringing his hands to her breasts and pinching her nipples as she took control of their pace.

Guy watched goose bumps rise on her skin as he trailed his hands down her sides to her hips, burying himself deeper into her. As they made eye contact, he brought his thumb to her mouth. She sucked it before biting the pad of his finger. He brought it down between them and rubbed her clit as he thrust into her deeply. She gasped as he filled her. She was tight and wanting, and he came apart as her body clenched his.

He lay down beside her, both out of breath. She was a sight to behold in her afterglow, wearing a smile from ear to ear that became sheepish as she watched him gaze at her.

"I'm sorry," he said.

"For what?" she asked, bewildered. "That was awesome."

"I'm going to need a minute before I hit my stride." And he leaned in to give her a round two.

CHAPTER ELEVEN

*T*heir night together had far exceeded Ellie's expectations. As she woke enjoying the warmth of Guy's naked body against hers, Ellie flushed with the memories. Not only had he done things to her body that she'd only ever read about, but her body responded in kind! Who knew that multiple orgasms were a real thing? Ellie had been elated by her first, never mind second or third.

Despite Guy's prowess, her thoughts turned to Daniel. When they went to bed together, it all felt premeditated, like a checklist: This is how it will start, these are the positions in order, then it will finish, and then they will pore over some last piece of work before turning in for the night. It was something Ellie envisioned after years of marriage, but if she was honest, there had never been much excitement in bed, or otherwise.

Daniel was passionate about his work. Daniel was loyal. There simply weren't enough hours in the week for either of them to have a torrid affair. Until now. Guilt soured Ellie's stomach as she carefully left the bed and found the washroom. Despite her flippancy about finding someone to hook up with the night before,

Ellie had run through her conversation with Daniel a million times, coming to the same conclusion as Goldie had. He had given her permission, but she knew that didn't make it right. What if he had been testing her, and she failed?

When she fell in her foyer after Guy dropped her off from shopping, she'd given up on the self-help drivel she'd picked up off the floor. She had lain there, staring at the ceiling, reliving the phone conversation with Daniel until she felt like she was going insane.

"Elmira, are you all right?" Daniel had asked, sounding more distracted and annoyed than worried.

"Daniel, I have a question for you." She paused, waiting for something, not knowing what.

"OK."

"What exactly did you mean when you told me to 'get it out of my system'?"

A long pause, followed by an irritated intake of breath. "I meant just that. Whatever it is that you need to do to pull yourself together, do it."

"So, if I needed to go on a seven-day bender with a biker gang?"

"Now you are being dramatic."

"Yes, I am. Sorry." She closed her eyes, embarrassed by the reprimand. "Did you mean that you want me to sleep with another man?"

"If that is what you need to do, do it," he said curtly.

"You can't mean that, Daniel. I know everything I've done this past week must have hurt you, but ..."

"Elmira, honestly, this was the best week to do it. I've been so swamped at work. But when you do come back, I don't want you to make this a habit. So yes, if you need to sleep with another man, or ten men, go for it. Get it out of your system before the wedding so that we don't have to revisit this."

Ellie couldn't comprehend the words coming out of her would-be husband's mouth, or the tone they came with. It was like he was talking to a child: *That's right, you finish your tantrum, there, there.*

"Daniel, you won't have to revisit this again. The wedding is off. I'm sorry to have to do this over the phone, but if you are willing to let me sleep with other people ..."

"Don't be such a prude, Elmira. Sex is nothing."

"It's not nothing to me," she said. "I'm sorry, Daniel. I will take care of the logistics of canceling the wedding. I wish you well." She'd held on the line, hoping for something, anything, to break through Daniel's veneer.

"Don't be so dramatic. We will talk when you come back."

"Goodbye, Daniel," she said with emphasis before dropping the call and dragging herself up the staircase.

Mechanically, she called the wedding planner and told her to cancel everything. It was done. All that was left was to tell her mother. She was exhausted and decided to send an email. It was cowardly, but it was all she could manage. Then she removed the battery from her phone and returned to the foyer to pick up her purchases.

Now, after her night with Guy, her body was as satisfied as a cat lounging in a sunbeam. The guilt never rolled in. She knew then that she had made the right choice. If Daniel had been the one for her, she wouldn't have been able to sleep with another man. Even Guy.

As she washed her hands, she mustered the guts to check in with the mirror—the woman in front of her had tousled hair, though her makeup had held on for the ride. She went to work trying to tone it down, but she was stuck with the morning-after look. Damn Winter's magic.

Quiet as a mouse, she stood in the doorway watching Guy sleep. Even at rest, he was impossibly handsome. His tattoos and muscles made him look like a tough guy, and he certainly had worked her over like one, but in the soft morning light, he looked too at peace to be a warrior. No man had ever invested that much time in her body. Ellie was amazed by how giving, how selfless and patient a lover he was. He was more experienced, but the care he had given her was more than she could've asked for.

Thinking that way was a bad idea. Last night she had thrown herself at him without any pause for her pride, and that could not happen again. Tiptoeing through his home, she picked up her clothes left in his living room, accepting the loss of underwear. Letting him see how much their night together had meant to her would be too awkward, leave her too vulnerable. Who knew sex could be life affirming? She put on her shoes and made sure the contents of her bra were secure before reaching for the doorknob.

"Good morning, angel," Guy's voice came from across the room. "Tell me you're sneaking away to get coffee. I forgot to pick some up."

Ellie cringed. Having had no experience with one-night stands, she didn't know the protocol or how to act. The struggle with etiquette, along with these new feelings surfacing, were too much for her. She turned to face him, and he overwhelmed her. He even had an inguinal crease below his abs, creating a mouth-watering arrow to what she now knew to be an enormously good time. She couldn't tempt fate.

"I, uh, had a great time last night," she said before giving up. "BYE!" She waved and turned.

In an instant, Guy's hand was in front of her, his half-naked body inches away. His warmth reached out to her, his skin daring her to caress it. "Nope, sorry, little lady, it ain't happenin' like that."

Ellie had no idea how to respond. She was stuck in a nonverbal state of fight-or-flight, but her only exit was blocked. So she avoided eye contact, waiting for him to fill the silence.

"All right, I'll start," he said. "Last night was amazing. I think we should try it sober. Do you need an aspirin?"

Ellie scoffed in defense, but her heart skipped a beat. It was amazing for him too?

"Well now, Miss Ellie, my feelings are hurt. You didn't enjoy yourself at all?"

Her cheeks flushed. *Treacherous body*, her mind cursed.

"I thought so." He smirked and moved in for a kiss. This one was much slower. Much gentler. She realized that he was wooing her as soon as his lips parted hers with a silent request, but as the passion mounted, she broke away. It was time to put her foot down.

"Guy, last night was ..." She failed to find a word for what their night had been, so she changed tracks. "But it cannot happen again."

"Why not?" he asked, leaning his back against the door, crossing his muscular arms.

Her mouth went dry, but she refocused. "Because last night was a fling. I needed to blow off some steam with no strings attached, and if it were to happen again ..."

"You would fall madly in love with me?"

If you only knew. "Or you with me, or maybe because we have a working relationship, or there's the fact that this town would eat me alive. I don't know how long I'm going to be here, but time is limited according to the IRS and CRA, so why risk a perfectly good friendship?" she finished, feeling exhausted.

"You done yet?" he asked.

She nodded and continued, "Besides! I told you this was a no-strings hookup. A one-time deal."

He waited to be sure she had gotten it out of her system before handing her a hoodie hung by the door.

Ellie's heart sank. She knew she was getting what she asked for, but it wasn't what her body wanted. Her body didn't care that she was falling for a man who was impossible to hold on to.

"I'll be seeing you, then," she said as she straightened, ready to pass through the door he was opening for her.

"Naw, you're just thinking too much. Can't leave you alone to do that. Then I'll never see that adorable birthmark of yours again. Coffee's on me." He pulled on a shirt and coat from his entryway closet.

"I can't drink coffee," she said through gritted teeth.

"Well, you can have herbal tea or something. Point is, we gotta sit ourselves down and talk this out like adults."

"That's what we're doing here."

"Naw." He scratched his cheek impatiently. "You'll get there, though. Come on now, fresh scones should be out of the oven." Scones did sound good, and he was so infuriating that Ellie was pretty sure she'd be able to regroup by the time they got to the coffee shop.

She realized her error as soon as they hit the pavement outside Guy's apartment. The night's distractions had bamboozled her: Guy lived in the middle of town. Squat buildings weren't townhomes, or whatever she had thought when she'd climbed out of the truck. They were businesses, and the town was already bustling. She was getting more overt glares than usual. It was the outfit, of course. Guy's oversized hoodie covered her body but highlighted their intimacy. The townsfolk smiled and greeted Guy as he passed, but she only got sour leftovers, at least from the women.

"So, this is what they mean by walk of shame," she muttered to Guy, who was at ease, glib even. "You knew this was going to happen?"

"Well, two and two makes …"

"An outsider messing with their messiah," she said as an elderly woman shook her head at Ellie. She considered running with her tail between her legs—until they were stopped by the one person who could make her feel even worse.

"Hello, sweetheart," said Ivy, her arms wrapped around her baby boy as though he were a toddler rather than a six-foot-tall, trained fighter.

Ellie marveled at their familial tenderness, even as dread set in. Her own mother hadn't ever hugged her that way, only offering Ellie quick embraces as a child. With adulthood came acceptance that while she'd never have a mother like that, she could be that to her own children someday. At thirty-two, with a failed engagement under her belt, motherhood was looking like a remote possibility. It wasn't Ivy's acceptance she wanted so much as a chance at having a family, a chance to give the same kind of love that Ivy gave.

Guy and Ivy exchanged greetings as if all else in the world had ceased to exist. Ivy didn't look once at Ellie until Guy brought her to his mother's attention. "You remember Miss Ellie, Ma?"

Ivy's unlimited love for her son could not warm her features as her gaze shifted to Ellie. As a good southern woman, she did her best to remain polite if not cordial. "Of course, Miss Ellie is not one to be forgotten." She looked Ellie up and down with the barest movement before shifting her attention back to her son. "You haven't forgotten the benefit tonight, have you, sweetie? I know it's not your cup of tea, but the town could use your support."

"I'll be there, but I'm not sure what you hope for me to do. You know you can't get blood from a stone."

"I know, but we can hope. Besides, you always draw a crowd."

"Benefit?" Ellie asked, feeling too ostracized for even her liking. It was one thing to be viewed as trash, it was another to be cold-shouldered by the mother of the man she had spent intimate hours with.

"It's an annual banquet hosted by Mom's charity. We are hoping to attract new money to Littleton to help revitalize the town," Guy replied, lacking passion about having to attend.

"What's the draw?" Ellie asked.

"I run a charity for disadvantaged youth. It raises funds and builds and maintains safe houses for runaways and victims of abuse all over the country," Ivy summarized.

It was clear to Ellie that she should Google Ivy Manning the next chance she got. The woman was proving to be more perfect all the time, but businesswomen, Ellie could handle.

"This year we're also hoping to attract interested parties to the development of the Littleton spa."

"I wish I had known. I would have purchased a ticket," she said, an innocuous apology.

"Tickets sell out fast. But thank you for the thought." The woman's distaste for her was clear, but women like Ivy, like her own mother, could never come out and say exactly what they thought about another person. It was a discreet power play. They were prim and polite on the surface, but venom still seeped from every pore, only to be felt by their intended victims.

"Well, ain't it your lucky day, Miss Ellie?" Guy announced a little too loudly. "I still have my plus-one." His eyes shone with humor.

Both women were struck dumb.

"Well now, there's a lot to do before tonight. I look forward to seeing you." She kissed her son's cheeks and nodded Ellie's way before taking off down the street, as though nothing uncomfortable had happened.

"That was fun!" Guy chortled.

"For you, maybe," grumbled Ellie as she continued walking, still earning the quiet wrath of the townsfolk.

Ellie wished for the strength and composure women like Ivy and her mother had. Especially during these passive-aggressive standoffs. Ellie could fake it, but they always won in the end. She was always left questioning what could have been said or done, and what she'd done wrong in the first place. But why? Wasn't she powerful in her own way? She had been a force to be reckoned with in the ballet world and could soon be the COO of a major company if she wanted—the offer was there.

Bedding the town's god wasn't a shameful thing. They were both full-grown adults, even if she struggled to feel like one at times. Why should she feel ashamed by people who didn't want to get to know her, anyway? Why couldn't she walk away from Ivy with the confidence that all would end well? A grown woman's sexuality was not something to be ashamed of ... now that she knew there wasn't anything wrong with her performance.

She stood tall and walked on like she owned the town.

CHAPTER TWELVE

*C*hecking off another item on her to-do list for the day, Ivy admired the display in the flower shop. Valentine's Day was creeping into the storefronts. She pressed her lips together, trying hard to remember the last time she'd received flowers from Ed. Guy sent them regularly for Mother's Day or her birthday, and Liam would surprise her now and then with wildflowers for the table or her desk. It didn't matter. Ed knew she preferred chocolate or a bottle of wine.

The list she had on her phone was getting shorter. She'd already been to the tailor for the few alterations to her dress for the evening's charity function. Ed's suit was waiting at the cleaners, though why he refused to buy a new tux was beyond her. It wasn't like they didn't go to enough events to warrant one, and it wasn't as if money was tight. No, not tight at all anymore.

She sighed with relief, and the tension carried from her other, harder, life eased. Next, she would have to call her assistant to make sure things were lining up at the venue. There were a few kinks in her speech to work out before going to Crystal's for hair and makeup. Last, she would head to the venue hours ahead to be certain everything was perfect for her guests. But first, she would pick up some scones for Ed. He loved those with his morning cup of tea.

Leaving the café with her bounty, she crossed to her car to load everything. Things were going according to plan until Hellen arrived.

"Ivy! How lovely to see you!" Hellen was ten years her senior and wore her curls a little too tight, in Ivy's opinion. Not that she would ever voice such thoughts.

"Hellen, how are you?"

"A little concerned, I must admit! Now you know how I hate to gossip"—she didn't, it was her joie de vivre—"but I thought you should know who was parading down Main with your son looking like a bucket of sin." Ivy snapped to attention. She would not let Hellen see her squirm. It wasn't a long wait for the silence to be filled. "Miss Ellie, of course! Now, I heard that she was at the club last night ... and she certainly looks like it."

"Thank you for your concern, but Guy is a grown man, and what two consenting adults do behind closed doors is their own business." Ivy smiled despite the bitter taste in her mouth. Hellen tried to hide a scowl and failed.

"Just giving you a heads-up." Hellen puffed her chest like a defensive bird.

"Thank you kindly."

As Hellen moved along, Ivy went toward the drama like a soldier going into battle. She received conspiratorial grins from the young folk and a range of sympathy and pity from the elderly on her walk toward Guy's apartment.

Sure enough, there was her boy, handsome as ever. There was no denying her son was as tough as they came. She'd seen all his boxing matches, no matter how it pained her to watch. Even still, he would always be the tiny baby she and Ed brought home from the hospital all those years ago. So delicate and soft, so sweet and innocent.

She moved her gaze to his right. *Harlot.*

Ivy gave herself a moment to be petty and affected by Miss Ellie's artless and disheveled appearance before they noticed her. Winter had changed her hair, like everyone had gossiped, and it was wild and unkempt. Her pleather leggings left nothing to the imagination, and Guy's sweater on her body spoke volumes. Even with the staining of day-old makeup, Ellie was an attractive woman, as much as it pained Ivy to admit. She didn't trust her with her son for a minute. Guy always did have a weakness for strays. Ivy supposed that was her fault, considering the work she was in. Still, she couldn't find it in herself to look at Ellie with pity. There was something *off* about her.

"Hello, sweetheart," Ivy said, sending adoration her son's way. She reminded him of the evening's function, knowing how boring he found these events. His former career drew more people in, and it was good business to have him show up.

She watched dispassionately as Guy explained the charity gala to Ellie, but then remembered her manners. She was thankful they had sold out of tickets. Ellie would have come and made some sort of spectacle. Her antics were a little much, and frankly, Ivy worried that Ellie would bring the event bad publicity. It didn't matter if it were to happen intentionally or not.

Guy was up to no good when he gave Ellie his plus-one. He was an intelligent man, but whether he was sending his mother a message or having fun at her expense, it took all Ivy's willpower not to shudder. She bid a quick farewell and left before saying anything regrettable.

Once home, she took her time to appreciate her home. She'd never lived in the same place even half as long. The house was as much a part of their family as anyone. There was a feeling hiding in the pit of her stomach, a feeling that asked if the tides were turning. Change was inevitable, but for someone who needed to be in control, it was also terrifying. Ivy hurried up the walk.

Carrying the clothing bags as well as the morning paper and the scones, Ivy managed to unlock the door and avert disaster with the dog like a seasoned pro. She remembered a time when she was less self-possessed and said a quiet prayer of thanks that she had come so far.

She found Ed in the kitchen. He was still in his pajamas, rubbing the sleep from his eyes as he manhandled a tea bag into a mug before the kettle blew a fit.

"Good morning, darling. Did you get Liam to school this morning?" She kissed his cheek before sweeping past to hang their evening wear in the adjoining powder room and closed the door to safeguard against their curious pooch. "I thought you might like some blueberry scones. They're still warm." She dangled the bag in his direction before placing them on the island between them, and he muttered his thanks as he stirred milk into his tea.

"Liam's buddies picked him up early," he said.

"I ran into Guy this morning. He's, of course, still attending tonight."

Ed grabbed for the bag, and his first bite nearly made the treat disappear.

Ivy frowned. She'd hoped he'd take the time to enjoy it. "He will be bringing Miss Ellie as his plus-one."

"That's nice," he said before finishing the pastry.

"Nice?" Ivy scoffed. "They have the whole town talking! You would not believe the scandalous outfit she was wearing this morning while walking with Guy. That woman is sure to cause a scene of some sort tonight." She tried to distance the two thoughts, not wanting to consider her son with that harpy.

"I sure hope so. Could use a little live entertainment." Ed took the newspaper from Ivy as he passed her to sit at the table with another scone.

"Don't you care that Guy is falling in with a bad element?" It wasn't beyond her that she wasn't talking about their teenager, but a man in his thirties.

"What is your problem with that poor girl? Ellie seems all right. A little stuffy, maybe, but she makes up for that in slapstick."

"She's run away from whatever problem she claims to have instead of fixing it. The girl has gold digger written all over her. I'll bet she's cozying up to our son in hopes of paying off some debt. Kelly Ann says she saw Guy drop her off with a ton of shopping bags. You don't think she convinced him to pay for a shopping spree, do you? You should talk to him. Lord knows he won't listen to me about this sort of thing."

Ed raised an eyebrow. "Guy's no chump. He's always been smart with his money. Keyword: *his* money. Besides, I'd bet my left nut that money isn't Miss Ellie's problem." He opened the paper, effectively closing the conversation.

Why he chose to be so crass was beyond Ivy. She stood looking at the wall of print between them before shaking her head and absconding to her office.

SITTING in the small coffee shop should have been stifling, especially since the entire town seemed to make it their pit stop. By now Ellie was used to being stared at by the locals and found that they didn't bother her. As much as she wanted to fit into this little town, chances of that happening were slim, and if she had to pack her bags and go home right then, she would be monumentally happy with the friends she had made. Whatever small-town drama was stirring up around her she could handle later. Besides, she didn't want to give Guy the satisfaction of her mortification.

"You seem to have relaxed some," Guy started, staring over the steam of his coffee, a box of scones between them.

"Yes, well, I've had an epiphany."

Guy raised his eyebrows in mock surprise. Ellie leaned in conspiratorially, smelling only a touch of his vile drink over the intoxicating aroma of the sweets. "Last night was fun, and if people want to judge me for something that is none of their business, they can go ahead and waste that energy."

Guy leaned in almost nose to nose with Ellie. It took all her willpower not to back away. She was feeling daring, but she didn't want a mob on her hands.

"Last night was more than fun, it was amazing, and I won't hear you denying it," he whispered, eyes ablaze. Ellie considered his assessment, took a hearty swallow of her herbal tea, then drummed her fingers on the tabletop.

"You're right, Manning. It was spectacular. So what?" she said, all business, and sipped her tea again, as though she were enjoying the silence instead of bursting from her seams. Why had Guy insisted on coming out with her, unless he'd wanted to watch her sweat the locals? Was it some sick shame game? She was done worrying about them and had trouble seeing him as malicious, so why was he still there, and why was he looking at her that way?

"Why should it be a one-time thing?"

"Slow down, tiger, you're looking a little desperate."

He looked no such thing, and he knew it. He cocked his head, chastising her with an even glare that ran straight to her lady bits.

"I already told you I wasn't looking for anything serious. I needed to blow off some steam ... and thank you. I'm steamless."

"Oh, I think you've got a ways to go, Miss Ellie."

"Is that so?"

"It is. But I know your *situation*. I wouldn't blame you if you wanted to get back on the straight and narrow."

Ellie felt her confidence falter. Had she lost the deal? Had she held out too long, acted too unaffected? A grin from across the table suggested he was playing her.

"I don't want to play games. You're right, Guy. I'm a mess. Why would you want to get tangled up in this? I have nothing to offer you. If we were to continue this, it could never be anything more than mindless, albeit sensational, sex."

"You do know who you're talking to, right? That's every man's fantasy right there."

"Ha, ha, you are hilarious." Ellie was becoming wary of this conversation. It was all too clear that the connection she'd felt with Guy ended between the sheets. Had she even tried to fight it? What else could be expected from a small-town god if not undeniable allure? Feeling the deflation process begin, it was time to gather her tea and scones with her to go. She refused to look back, even if there was no saving her pride.

The bell on the shop's door jingled as she left, and her heels beat the pavement evenly in the direction of her new home. She wanted to run all the way there and take the hottest shower of her life. What had she been thinking? A one-night stand wasn't her thing. Sure, it was the best sex of her life, and there had been more of a connection to Guy than with anyone else, ever. Now she would pay for it, but first, one more walk of shame. Luckily, she was too angry to cry.

She also wasn't about to admit to Guy that she no longer had a *situation,* as he put it. Guy hadn't known that she was a single woman. How could he? And yet it stung. Of course, he knew that a relationship with her would have to be no-strings attached—in his mind, she was engaged! Forget what that said about her. What did that say about him?

"Ellie! Wait!" his voice called from behind her, but she wasn't listening. She wanted to be alone in a hot shower scrubbing off her shame. "Come on now, stop for a second."

"Not a chance."

He easily caught up with her, the blasted heels slowing her down.

"Listen, damn it!" He pulled in front of her, stopping her dead. "I'm sorry. I got a bit mean back there, and it was uncalled for. I don't know what came over me."

She moved past him. He locked step.

"You were right, Guy. What kind of girl gets into this situation?" She would die before admitting the truth. His insinuations and callousness had cut too deep. He couldn't know how much she cared about him; it was too much. She would build the fences as high as ever. Prince Manning wouldn't break her heart. She wouldn't let him.

"The kind of girl who is having a rough time and was given permission."

She scoffed. He wasn't stupid. He had to know how morally convoluted that was.

"Listen, Ellie, I was fronting too hard back there. I'm sorry I hurt you. I know you have this idea of me as a player who's able to cherry-pick the women I want. To a certain point, that's true, but it doesn't mean that I haven't been burned too. You're not the only one with issues here."

Ellie didn't want his apology. It only confused her, softened her. "I don't know how to process that right now! What I do know is that your mom runs the charity, but you're in the same line of work. I'm a technical runaway, and I'm messed up. Sorry to break it to you, Your Highness, but I don't need your help. Except for the plumbing." She turned red and muttered a curse. "I mean, the actual plumbing. The bathroom sink drips at night. I can't get it to stop. It drives me crazy."

Guy pulled her to a stop. Away from the town core, they had room to speak openly. "Now, you have every right to be pissed. I get that, and I'm sorry. I'm glad last night happened. We had a damn fine time, but even if it never happens again, I don't want to leave things like this." He paused thoughtfully. "But I ain't gonna beg for your forgiveness, Ellie. You were posturing back there too."

"Ugh!" she yelled in frustration as she punched him inefficiently in his chest. "What the hell do you want, Guy?"

"Did you hit me?"

"I sure as hell tried!"

"You think hitting a retired boxer is a good idea?"

"You're not going to hurt me. Don't start that macho—"

"That's right, Ellie," he interrupted, dead serious. "I know the score, I know you, and I'm not going to hurt you. So why the hell are you pushing away from a simple thing?"

"Simple!?"

He pulled her into him, his morning scruff abrading her as he took her mouth as much to silence it as to make a point. He pulled away abruptly. "No strings, good ol' fashioned ..."

"Shut up and take me home. I need a shower."

"Not before I help you with your plumbing."

CHAPTER THIRTEEN

Guy should have felt at least a little awkward walking through the town square with Ellie. Her outfit broadcast their night to everyone. Fact was, he couldn't summon any embarrassment. Last night was better than he could've anticipated. He'd expected hesitancy and stiffness on her part when, in fact, she had been quite limber and more than willing to experiment. He smiled to himself at the memory of her taking command, her hair bouncing wild around her face as she rode him. So much confidence! Who knew Ellie had it in her? There were a few more memories he would like to add to the list, but he knew he had to play his cards right, or she would bolt like a scared rabbit.

Even the run-in with his mother hadn't ruffled him as it should have. He didn't appreciate the way Ellie was treated, of course, but he was so relaxed, and she handled it so well that he didn't let it faze him. His mother had always, and would always be, protective of him. It would always drive him a little nuts, but for some reason, he had no desire to shield Ellie the way he might have in the past.

Ivy had always terrified his girlfriends, and Ellie was no different. That was obvious. But the way she recovered afterward was glorious. It was as if the weight on her shoulders was thrown off to expose a supermodel goddess. He had trouble reconciling the vision of her beside him with the antics he'd witnessed in the past week, so he didn't try. He enjoyed the quiet while he could.

Sure enough, she found and reclaimed her crazy, and he should have let her walk away. He didn't need complications. He didn't need crazy women. But he knew he had been a dick, and she had taken all the scones, so he followed her and surprised the hell out of himself.

"Where are you going?" Guy asked, watching as the blanket fell from her body.

"I was serious about needing a shower." She laughed. "I still smell like a saloon. You're welcome to join me." Guy rolled over, checking the time on her phone.

Guy stood before her in the buck, and she stared at him with desire. He strolled up to her, kissing her playfully before walking to the toolbox he'd brought in from another unit. "I'll fix the tap, then I'd better head home to get ready for the benefit tonight. Pick you up at five?"

ELLIE GROANED, having forgotten the mess she'd gotten herself into. Another face-off with Ivy Manning sounded painful, and she wasn't sure it was worth the date with Guy. It was only a friendly date, but given the restructuring of their relationship, she didn't want to risk feeling too cozy. A night off from him, a little distance to get her head back on straight, would be the smart thing to do.

"Naw," she drawled, knowing it was a pathetic attempt at nonchalance. "I'll drive myself. I've got Mark's loaner coming today."

"Afraid you won't be able to keep your hands off me?" He laughed as he fiddled with her plumbing, still naked and glorious. Guy's confidence was admirable, something out of her reach as she threw on her new robe. Anyone would be confident looking like he came down from Mount Olympus and could punch someone out for saying otherwise.

"You got me. Is it black tie or business casual?" There was no way out of it, so she accepted defeat, if only because Ivy would love it if she didn't show up. Small victories were becoming precious.

"Black tie. Need to go shopping again?" he asked, not keen on the idea. He turned the taps on and off, checking his work.

"No, I'd picked up my outfit for the gala back home the day I left, so I've got something worthy."

He caught her eye. Sympathy was there ... a little pity too. "You OK?" he asked, approaching her again, all hard body, soft eyes.

"I'm fine," she purred as he pulled her to him. She felt stirrings. "But I still stink, and I've got plans with Winter, so you should get going."

"Throwing me out, woman?" he joked as he reluctantly reached for his clothes.

"That's right. Must not be too used to that, eh? Girls around here must try to tie you down tight."

"Keep talking like that, Ellie, and you'll never get rid of me." His eyes burned with want.

She threw him his sweater and told him to let himself out as she headed to the washroom at last.

As much fun as it had been with Guy—and he was beyond anything she'd ever known before—the other shoe didn't have to drop for her to know how things would end. Their arrangement was temporary. She was glad he had run after her. Guy had been like an anchor for her since arriving in Littleton, and though it scared her a little, she appreciated his company as much as the sex.

Well ... almost as much as the sex.

ELLIE MANAGED to make herself decent with enough time left to pick up the car and spend the day with the enigmatic Winter. She was nervous as she rolled up to the address she'd been given. The Victorian-style home was beautiful. Ellie had imagined it would be gray on black with a doorman named Lurch and maybe a gargoyle or two.

Pulling up the long, dirt drive, Ellie found a quiet oasis complete with flower gardens and a vegetable garden gated off to the side. The house seemed as much part of the natural order of things as the willow whose branches waved from a spacious back-yard. The light gray of the roof and the white siding and banisters caught the light, while vines grew along the veranda and attached gazebo. Some plants still held onto their leaves; a hint of magic seemed to be at home there.

As admired the veranda wrapping around the home, she noticed movement. First, a black-and-white cat jumped down from the steps finding a sunbeam, then Ellie saw Winter moving things around. She was as dressed down as Ellie had ever seen her in top-to-bottom black—jeans and a long-sleeved shirt— her hair in a topknot and bangs messy. Winter wasn't wearing a lick of makeup, and it made no difference—the girl was stunning. Her skin glowed fresh and dewy, but her eyes were forever coy.

"Hey!" Ellie said, waving meekly as she got out of the car.

"Hey yourself!" Winter came into the sunshine. Both women were a little unbalanced by this next step in their friendship. Thus far, they had only socialized in public, and Winter had been busy fussing over Ellie's hair or makeup. Alcohol had always been present, thanks to Goldie. Ellie was nervous without a crowd.

"Screw it," Winter exclaimed as she gave Ellie a rough-and-tumble hug. "Welcome!"

"Thank you," Ellie said. "Your garden is amazing. I had no idea you were into that kind of thing." Ellie was thankful that Winter laughed instead of fixing her with her patented glare.

"Yeah, well, I grew up with my grandmother, and there wasn't a whole lot to do around town if you weren't into football or cheerleading, so I spent a lot of time learning about gardening. Gran would be angry if I let it go on her."

"I'm sorry for your loss. Has she been gone for long?" Ellie asked, not quite knowing what else to say.

"Feels like forever, but no." Winter chuckled. "Gran is currently on a yearlong adventure cruise. She's supposed to be diving in Australia this week, but knowing her, she's gone inland to find her very own Crocodile Dundee."

Ellie laughed as Winter led her to the spot she'd been clearing beside the house. She unfolded a second painter's easel.

"I know it's presumptuous, but you mentioned painting? It's a little cool today. I'd understand if you want to take things indoors …"

"No, that sounds like fun. I haven't painted since high school. I was never all that good, though," Ellie admitted, crinkling her nose as she remembered the single C- that marred her otherwise perfect academic record.

"Don't worry, this is for fun. I know you've got a lot on your psyche right now," Winter probed delicately, cutting a glance to see if Ellie's guard would go up. It didn't. "Thought this might help. Couldn't hurt, right?"

"I saw this ad for a paint night at a local pub once. I thought it would be a lot of fun."

"Did you go?"

"Oh, no! I wouldn't have known anyone. I usually struggle to get to know other women."

"Me too!" She gave Ellie a smile. "But I'd have gone. I believe we attract the people we need in our lives. It's how you and I met. Other people come and go, and you have to filter out the users and abusers, but the people you need never leave you, no matter how far they travel. If there hadn't been anyone there to connect with, you would still have had a night to enjoy a beer and some art. Nothing lost."

"You don't need to worry about making a fool of yourself," Ellie said.

"Don't I? People get intimidated, sure, but others take my aesthetic as some big joke. Granted, I'm not afraid of confrontation. How people treat you says more about them than you, Ellie. Let's get set up, the paint is in the cabinet behind you." They filled the paint trays, and they placed their easels back-to-back so that their work could be unveiled when they were finished.

For a while, they were both silent. Winter was a flourish of movement. She had sat down with a plan, but Ellie took her time to settle in. Her eyes toured the garden, waiting for inspiration to strike. The breeze shook the ancient trees, and Ellie marveled at how they appeared sentient, reaching toward the sun. She began sketching, and her mind wandered to the memory of Guy stretching, his muscles every bit as taut as the bark of these trees. And she blushed again as other memories flowed.

"I'm sorry about last night," Ellie said, glad to have her canvas to hide behind. "I should've taken better care to look out for you and Goldie."

"Thanks for the thought, but we're good. Goldie checked in with me before she took off with the brunette ... I think her name was Carla? And in the end, I ran into someone from university, and we caught up over tacos."

"What did you study?" They lapsed into easy conversation, as though they had been friends forever. While Ellie had been grinding away at her business degree, Winter was double majoring in art history and sociology, earning some money on the side doing hair and makeup for classmates who couldn't afford to go to an actual salon. They laughed at each other's high school outcast stories and confided their favorite novels that had seen them through the loneliness.

"You going to the charity dinner tonight?" Winter asked as she washed her brushes and put away some of her supplies.

"Yeah," Ellie said with hesitation. They hadn't spoken about

Guy, at all. And strangely, she wasn't bursting at the seams to share. "Guy is taking me as his plus-one."

"Want me to do your makeup?"

"I wouldn't want to impose."

"Please." Winter placed a hand dramatically to her forehead. "From one easel to the next." They tidied, leaving their paintings to dry as they cleaned brushes, and Winter got to work on Ellie's face, not bothering to ask what she wanted. Ellie knew she'd love it, even if it was out of her comfort zone. There was trust between them now, and she knew Winter wouldn't steer her wrong.

"Time for the big reveal!" Winter squealed as they sauntered back out onto the veranda. Ellie's face went red, but she let Winter look at her painting.

"Basic, I know," Ellie said, trying to read Winter's quiet scrutiny.

"Hush now, I like it. That tree is ready to get up and walk away, Tolkien style."

Ellie was pleased at Winter's praise but was wowed as she rounded Winter's easel.

"Oh my ... Winter, it's beautiful." Somewhere between landscape and Impressionist, Winter had drawn inspiration from the garden arbor. All was picturesque around it, but within, the colors set fire to the scene like an intergalactic chaos rainbow. "I knew you'd be good, but this? Have you ever thought about opening a studio?"

It was Winter's turn to blush for once. "There isn't a market for it here in Littleton," she responded.

"No, but you could make it somewhere else." After contemplating, Ellie continued. "As an artist, you can live anywhere, but if your passion is with your work at the salon, what stops you from heading to a bigger city? You've got the chops and the guts, I'm sure of it." When Winter was at a loss for words, Ellie felt a stab of regret for pushing. "I'm sorry. It's none of my business."

"Naw, it's all right, Ellie. I feel stupid saying it out loud is all."

She paused to wipe some paint from the easel. "I've been waiting for the right time. There was this guy when I was younger, thought he was going to be The One. At first, I was waiting on him to wake up, then ... I don't know. It turned out to be a full stop."

"Well," began Ellie, squeezing her friend's arm reassuringly, "think about it. I'd be happy to help in any way I can."

A short time later, Ellie was back at her apartment wearing an ear-to-ear grin, blissed out, heart warmed by her budding friendship, and looking for somewhere to hang her painting.

The simple black dress she'd bought with another charity event in mind hung in the closet. It seemed so long ago, but it had only been a little over a week since she'd picked it up. Already the original shoes and accessories wouldn't suit. She wasn't the same person anymore, or afraid to show a little personality. Ellie paired the posh dress with the exuberant pink heels Goldie had somehow convinced her to buy, a boho purse, and some dangling earrings. If Winter was going to be there tonight, she would make Ellie look tame, anyway. Why hide anymore?

Going into the Littleton lions' den was as bad as it got. Might as well go out as authentic as an aimless wanderer could manage.

Her phone chimed at 4:30 p.m.

Guy: *Sure you don't need a ride?*

Ellie: ...

Guy: *Real mature. If you don't leave soon, you'll be late. It's a good haul. I'll meet you on Main and you can follow me.*

Ellie: *I am fully capable of following my GPS.*

Guy: *Trouble follows you.*

Ellie wanted to deny it, but in retrospect, there had always been *something*. Before Littleton, she had collected big moments—the accident that blew her dancing career, running away from her career and fiancé—and now it felt like she had a little emotional travesty every day. It was exhausting, but it was also freeing to realize that she didn't have to strive for perfection.

How often had the people around her steered her clear of both mishaps and her own selfhood? She wasn't proud of the messes she kept getting into, but at least they were her own. She wasn't afraid of falling down anymore.

Ellie: *All right, come get me.*

When Guy arrived, it was in a sleek black car she hadn't seen him drive before. He wasn't in his usual jeans and plaid either. His face was clean-shaven, and his jawline sent pulses through her body. How could one man be so gloriously beautiful and rugged at the same time? He was dressed in a stylish suit that should have been ridiculous on his muscled frame. The impeccable tailoring made it impossible for Guy to appear anything but flawless.

"All set?" he asked, ogling her.

"Too much?" she questioned in return, unsure of her new style.

"Definitely too much clothing." He offered his arm, and she laughed at his token leer as she got into the car.

Forty-five minutes later, they arrived at a swanky hotel in Dallas. Many stories high, the glass building was modern, sleek, and boasted outdoor terraces and green spaces. It felt odd to see the skyscrapers, as though it had been ages since she'd been in a big city. She was getting used to Littleton, and *that* was something she didn't quite know how to process.

"What is it?" Guy asked after handing off his car keys to the valet.

"Guess I was expecting something more Littleton," Ellie admitted.

"Well, don't you worry, miss. There will be plenty of familiar faces mixed with the hoity-toity crowd."

Ellie grimaced at Guy but felt better when she noted Goldie's car pulling in. "If one of the sharks corners you, pull out that drunken twang of yours, and they're sure to run."

"I'll keep that in mind."

Guy had no idea that these sorts of events were common for her. This one was a bigger deal than Ellie had expected, but it wasn't anything she hadn't dealt with before. He ushered Ellie into the building, and before long, she was holding a champagne flute while Guy introduced her to some so-called sharks.

"Ellie Bondell, is it?" asked Noah Crenshaw, a businessman from New York. "You remind me of someone I can't quite place. Is your family in oil?"

Ellie laughed, surprising Guy with her tone.

"No, Mr. Crenshaw, I'm surprised you made the connection. Our companies briefly shared interests a few years back." When it was obvious that the man was floundering, she offered a life preserver: "I am Elmira Bondell of Triton Holdings."

In an instant, Noah Crenshaw's posture changed. He was no longer talking to the arm candy of a former boxer, as polite as he had been. There was an awkward pause in conversation that Guy, having no idea what was going on, had no idea how to fill.

"Don't worry, Mr. Crenshaw. This may be Texas, but I've come unarmed." Ellie held her hands up in mock surrender. "You enjoy your night now." Ellie breezily led Guy away from the conversation. Shortly after leaving the baffled businessman, they ran into another group of men itching to speak to *the* Guy Manning. Again, gentleman that he was, Guy introduced Ellie.

"Pleasure," one man said dismissively before continuing to chat up Guy. "So, are you planning your return to the ring anytime soon, Guy? Sure would make good business."

Ellie instantly disliked him. Anyone who knew Guy for thirty seconds knew he neither wanted nor needed the limelight or payoff of boxing. He was a person, not an economic device.

"Maybe one day," he said and segued into his business in Littleton, talking up the burgeoning industries.

"It sounds quaint," another woman said, attempting a tone of interest and failing. "Your mother sure knows how to throw a party."

"And for such a good cause too," Ellie enthused, not liking the way these people were maneuvering Guy.

"Yes, of course," the woman said, looking Ellie up and down as if for the first time. "Ivy is a miracle worker."

Ellie was willing to bet the woman didn't even know what charity she was here for. Sure, she knew little herself, but that was because she was afraid if she looked too closely at Ivy Manning's halo, she'd be struck by lightning.

Guy and Ellie moved through the crowd much like this for the better part of an hour before they were left alone.

"This blows. Want to make out in the coatroom?" Guy asked in jest.

"Not your thing, eh?" Ellie asked, sipping her second glass of champagne. "You show well, though, no denying that. The people love you. *Shocker.*"

Guy cursed under his breath.

"What's wrong?"

"Asshole coming over. Sorry ahead of time. Alistair Montgomery!" Guy made like this man was his best friend so Ellie would've assumed he meant money, even if she didn't already know who the man was.

"Guy Manning, how are you doing? Don't let me forget to make you an offer you can't refuse later to get those gloves back on."

Guy's eye twitched as Alistair leered at Ellie too lasciviously for a man with a woman easily twenty years younger on his arm. When he reached her face, he paused as a self-satisfied grin unfolded. "Miss Elmira Bondell, as I live and breathe." He took her hand and kissed it.

Ellie made a mental note to wash with bleach as soon as possible.

"It's been, what, ten years? You are in fine form tonight."

"More like fifteen," countered Ellie, playing nice, if only for the sake of Guy who wasn't one to kiss ass. She knew that this man must be of some importance to him. It didn't surprise her. Montgomery was a billionaire and had his hands in all the cookie jars, and up a few skirts, too, the last she'd heard. A major patron of the arts, she'd met him during a tour she had done in her teens. He gave her the creeps.

"Don't think I forgot about you for an instant after that terrible crash. What a devastating way to get pulled out of your craft. When I close my eyes, I can still see you dancing in *Esmeralda*! A shame! A shame!" He took a glass from a server without so much as looking at him. "But I see you are in good company. A dancer and a boxer. Rather poetic. A tragedy, of course, that neither of you are still players."

"Life is a game, Mr. Montgomery, and we are lucky to still be playing it," Guy intercepted.

"Right you are, right you are."

Ellie turned to the woman on his arm. She was young, salon blond, with the largest brown eyes. She was on edge and fidgeting in her designer emerald cocktail dress. "My apologies, I didn't get your name."

"This lovely creature is my wife, Danika. She, too, was a dancer of sorts, though nowhere near your stature," he said dismissively and turned to Guy, ignoring both women.

"Pleasure," Danika said. "I'm sorry about your accident. I can't imagine."

"Thank you. It happened some time ago now. Life does have a way of moving on. Ballet?" Ellie asked, trying to lock the door on her trauma while warming the timid beauty. She went crimson, and Ellie understood at once what Alistair had meant. What a cruel way to set someone up. "I'm sorry," Ellie apologized.

"It was a long time ago," Danika said sharply, returning her attention to her husband's conversation.

He was speaking of some lavish trip they'd taken before insinuating that his wife needed something to keep her busy, being at home all the time.

"I've found that when women are given the time they need to find their niche, they flourish," Ellie said by way of apology.

"Yes, well, this one glows with beauty sleep," he joked at Danika's expense.

She smiled, but it came nowhere near her eyes.

"Yes, she is quite a beauty," Guy put in, giving the girl a short smolder.

Ellie appreciated Guy paying attention to the mistreated woman. It was good to see his instincts were to soothe rather than ignore. The attention didn't even faze Danika who was pretending it hadn't happened.

"I love your handbag," Ellie said without having to lie. It was a subtle mix of pop art and mosaic pulled off cleverly for a black-tie affair. "Who made it? I'd love to look up the designer."

Danika turned red again. "I made it," she admitted.

"Oh my gawd!" Ellie feigned exuberance as she saw Goldie and Winter at the bar. Goldie wore a white bodycon dress while Winter wore the antithesis: a floor-length, rose-covered dress with a corseted bodice. "I simply must steal you away. Some people I know would love to see your work! You don't mind, do you, Mr. Montgomery?"

While Guy was unnerved by how Ellie was acting, Alistair was hardly aware of her at all. He dismissed them, giving Danika a hard stare before telling her sweetly not to get lost.

"Ellie! You look gorgeous! You have to tell me everything that happened last night!" Goldie demanded as Ellie approached, holding Danika's arm like they were old friends.

"Another time," Ellie waved her off, introducing the young woman. They put her at ease almost immediately, inquiring about her designs. As they spoke, Ellie spotted a few people who Danika and Winter, who shared talent in the beauty industry, should meet. There was a businesswoman she knew by reputation who was always on the lookout for female talent, as well as a fashion blogger that she had by chance met in Toronto a few years before. When she asked him what brought him to Dallas, his single-word answer was: "Cowboys."

Guy rejoined her soon after, standing back and watching Ellie inquisitively.

"Oh! I'm sorry to separate you all, but I know Danika would love to meet Mrs. Manning." Ellie pulled Danika from the group after Parker Talbot, the blogger, exchanged information with her.

"Ivy! I have been looking forward to running into you all night! You look amazing!" Ellie said, caring little for once what the Mannings thought of her behavior. As the front woman for the night, Ivy had to both standout and set the tone. She wore a regal purple chiffon dress, the bodice and sleeves trimmed in a mature lace fitting. "Mr. Manning, a pleasure to see you again. You clean up well. This is Danika Montgomery."

Ivy's eyes narrowed, then grew at the recognition of the name.

"We have met. It's a pleasure to see you again, Danika."

Danika smiled but shrank back.

"Oh, you know each other? Well, of course. Before you do your rounds, I wanted to ask about the organization we're all here for tonight?" Ellie continued like a wild woman, considering their usual stiff conversation.

"Safe Haven," Ivy began. "I'm sure you could find the answer to your question in the literature, darling," Ivy finished softly before making motions to move on. She knew as well as Ellie did that Danika didn't hold her husband's pocketbook, but appearances are everything at these events.

"Of course, but I was curious if your PR firm or advertisers have considered starting a social media buzzword?"

Ivy paused, deciding to indulge her. "In what way do you mean?"

"Well, it's not my area of expertise," Ellie said humbly. "I was thinking about how so many women are afraid to leave abusive relationships. They feel trapped, like their quality of life depends on the people who are bringing them down. Or maybe they are deeply controlled by the men in their lives and can't reach out. It would be nice to give those women some tools they could use to speak out without drawing attention to what they are doing, giving them a second's grace to escape."

"Of course." Ivy struggled not to roll her eyes. "We do try to empower women to make these choices."

"Oh, wouldn't it be great, though, if there was a way of getting a safe word out there, like, a word that is recognizable to people in positions who could help? So that even a server here could lean in to hand over a canapé and whisper, I don't know … *agent orange*. And they would know that this person was in danger and needed immediate help. Because sometimes they only have a tiny window of time, as I'm sure you know."

"Yes, what an interesting idea, Ellie," Ivy said, ready to move on. "I will have to take it up at the next meeting." She had no intention of doing so.

Ellie knew it was an imperfect idea, and that there were many incarnations of the idea flitting across the internet.

"It was lovely seeing you again, Danika. I'm sorry to excuse myself, but I must prepare for my speech." Ivy maneuvered away as graciously as possible.

"She means it, Danika. Good to see you again." Ed Manning smiled at the girl. "Miss Ellie, you look dazzling tonight." He surprised Ellie by leaning in to kiss her cheek. "If you ladies need anything, I will be stage left." He patted Guy on the arm as Danika was pulled away by her *charming* husband.

"What was that all about?" Guy asked.

"Hopefully nothing," Ellie responded, staring after the girl.

CHAPTER FOURTEEN

Ivy was riding a wave of emotion after her speech, her pride swelling. She had hit all her major talking points, had opened up about her past without becoming too emotional, and she had shared some touching success stories and called out the big guns in the room by crediting a few Littleton small businesses who always championed the cause. Her pride made her feel as though she were floating, and the champagne didn't hurt either. She made her way around the room, not settling too long on anyone, always leaving them wanting more.

"Crystal, darling, thank you so much for coming tonight." Ivy took the woman's hands in her own and air-kissed her like they were the best of friends. They were, of course, unless the gossip landed too close to her doorstep. One had to be careful with what they said around Crystal, yet Ivy had only begun to feel hesitancy with her friend, with all the talk about Guy and Miss Ellie.

"Ivy, your speech was beautiful. Thank you for mentioning the salon. I sure do appreciate it. Having my salon and the dream of the spa mentioned so close together got me to thinking ..." Her eyes wandered behind Ivy and her lip curled with distaste.

Ivy didn't need to turn to know what Crystal was witnessing.

"Charming, isn't it?" Ivy said, ignoring the way Crystal was trying to weasel her way into ownership of the resort.

"She's feeding off your poor boy, isn't she? Walking around like she owns the place." Crystal shook her head as though it were the greatest travesty. "I hope Guy knows what he's doing. That girl is after his money, mark my words!"

"I don't know about that," Ed replied as he handed off another glass of champagne to each woman. "She hardly seems ready for the poorhouse."

"Scam artists make it look like they're a part of your world. I saw it on TV. They make you think that you are on level footing, then they take you for all you're worth," Crystal said. "Oh, hush now, here they come. Miss Ellie! What a lovely dress you have on!"

"Why, thank you, Crystal. I like yours too. That shade of blue makes your eyes so bright!" It was clear that Ellie had had a few glasses of champagne herself, her were cheeks rosy. She had a calm about her that Ivy had never seen before.

Ivy thought about scam artists, and about how Ellie had been rubbing elbows with Alistair's wife earlier. She had a vision of her son being paraded around with Ellie as his trophy wife, and she almost choked on her drink. Her son appeared frustrated and put upon. *Good.* This could be the last time they gallivanted together. He was a good man, but he sometimes took his charity cases a little too far. Ivy reached out a hand to him. He took it, of course, the good son.

"Oh, this old thing? You know, I'm glad to be out of the house. I almost didn't make it ... my husband had to stay behind. Our sitter fell through at the last minute. We don't get out together much anymore." Crystal was fishing. Ivy knew that this was the only night of the year Crystal could get her husband to look after the twins on his own. He hated a tux more than Ed did.

"That's a real shame." Ellie sounded genuinely sorry for Crystal. She was either faking or stupid—the con getting conned. Ivy's distaste for Ellie grew.

"It's tough to find a sitter in such a small town. Whenever there's an event, everyone else is there too."

Ivy thought Crystal was laying it on thick, but Ellie was falling for it.

"Well, let me know if I can help. I love kids."

"Oh, I couldn't impose ..."

"It wouldn't be an imposition. Really. Anytime."

"Well, there is a movie I've been dying to see. Do you think you could watch the twins tomorrow night? I know it's short notice, but it's cheap night at the theater ..."

"I would love to." With that, they were exchanging information.

Guy looked as appeased as Ivy felt. She expected her husband to wear the same grin, instead, he was as unimpressed as ever. Clearing his throat, he said his goodbyes to his son, then excused himself to go speak with the Munros. He hated the Munros.

ANOTHER NIGHT, another event, another reason to put on the monkey suit and smile. Ed Manning believed in the cause, of course, but as a rule, he did not believe in tuxes. Wearing one was a metaphysical nightmare every time.

"Dr. Manning, Mrs. Manning," greeted another blue blood. "Business is booming, I hope?" The man's voice came through his nose but was otherwise dry. Ed was sure that these kinds of men perfected the nuance of their tone over the years spent in their towers. He didn't care. He took them at face value if only to ruffle them.

"It is. Never a dull moment." For his wife's sake, Ed tried hard to not pull at his bow tie. He failed. "Thanks for coming out." He guided his wife away.

"That was Finnegan Browning. You could have chatted him up a little, darling. He is worth ..."

"Yeah, yeah, a bajillion dollars. And he will give more to charity to feel more important, I'm sure."

Ivy pursed her lips in that all too familiar way. He braced for the litany. It wasn't only their son who needed chastisement, it seemed. He would say *yes dear* at all the right times, while they both smiled and waved to their guests as if they were having a grand old time, and then he would go find some Scotch. Maybe there was a game playing on a TV in the kitchen. If he tipped well enough, he might not get kicked back out to the party.

"Are you even listening, Ed?"

He wasn't, of course, but he was sure he could recite it verbatim. It was nothing he hadn't heard before. Instead of attempting to, he decided to poke the bear. "There's Guy, honey. Doesn't Miss Ellie look lovely tonight?"

"Oh, that woman ... Shoot, she's coming this way. Quick ..."

Ed laughed as he pulled at his noose of a tie. He hadn't seen his wife run from someone in years.

When Miss Ellie caught up, it was clear to Ed that something was off. He didn't know her well, but she was no fool. Yet she was acting like an excited schoolgirl while discussing safe words with Ivy. He shared a glance with his son, who shrugged, having no idea what was going on.

He noticed that Ellie was being strangely emphatic and looking back and forth between Ivy and himself before darting glances at Danika Montgomery, who everyone knew as Alistair's second or third trophy wife. Soon, Ivy lost interest and walked away. Ed smiled at the women and apologized with a few kind words, something he was sure both women were lacking this evening. He hated how pompous his wife had become and was more annoyed with her than usual. It was the tux. It made everything worse.

GUY HATED THESE EVENTS, always had. Whether it was as the son of Ivy and Edward Manning, or as a boxer promoting himself, he understood why they had to be done, but the plastic smiles and egos burned him out. He'd looked forward to watching Ellie squirm under the pressure. At the very least he counted on her boredom as an excuse to leave early. It turned out that she played the game as well as or better than the giants present.

His mother had them seated with a few financial big shots, but he suspected that she had moved names around once Ellie was added to the mix. He wouldn't have blamed her either, but in the end, it wasn't to her advantage. Miss Elmira Bondell seemed to not only hold her own but was well known to some of the international businesspeople in attendance.

Who is this woman? Pretending to listen to another of his mother's speeches urging people to help America's youth, and thanking Littleton for stepping up, he watched Ellie instead. She was attentive, poised, and ignored the whispers happening around her. He guessed that he didn't have to worry about her payments on the condo coming through. Not that he'd been concerned as of late.

What bothered him was that he'd thought he had her pegged. Was she playing him? No, she wasn't the type ... Then again, he hadn't expected her to be a natural at rubbing elbows with elitist assholes, either, and here they were.

"What?" she hissed at Guy.

He realized he'd been staring. Her reaction was at odds with her composure the rest of the night, and he was ready to throw his hands up in the air. Then he saw his father moving along the wall with a small group he recognized as Safe Haven employees. In the middle was Danika Montgomery. Guy found her husband seated across the room drinking wine and flirting with an attractive young waitress as the speeches continued. *What the hell was that?* he thought as the room exploded with applause and people stood. Ivy Manning had hit another home run.

The rest of the night, he'd stayed as quiet as he could and let Ellie ... Elmira—whoever she was—lead the way. He didn't know how he felt about this new dimension, and not knowing was making him paranoid.

"What?" Ellie asked again once they were in the car, silent, for a few minutes.

"Who the hell are you?" he asked, surprising himself with his own anger.

"You know who I am."

"Do I? Because I didn't know that you were high society, that's for damned sure."

"Really? Because you know I have an assistant, you know I go to galas, you know I can shop without blinking and buy a condo on a whim ... Guy, you didn't want me to be whatever it is you think I am now. You wanted me to be down and out, looking for a prince to ride in on a white horse to make all my problems go away."

"Rich-girl problems," he shot back, knowing he was being unfair.

"That's *rich* coming from you," she returned. The car went silent for a long time before she thawed. "Prior to leaving Canada, I was tapped to become the COO of a major corporation in Canada that has been getting its feet wet in international deals. That's why people knew me in there. After the accident, I went to business school. I got a job, and I worked hard."

"Why didn't you tell me?" he asked, getting to the core of why he was so angry. "You tell me about your fiancé, the accident, your mama ..."

"Mother."

"Why not your career? It's this huge part of your life."

"It's not like we've ever gone the small-talk route. Compared to your own fame and fortune, it wasn't a big deal. I will try to be more forthcoming." She said having taken offence.

He was losing steam but holding on as tight to his anger as he could. "And what the hell was your fascination with Montgomery's wife? You went all fangirl on her. I didn't know you were so hot on fashion. What are you, a talent agent or something? If you're trying to recruit me ..."

"I'm not!" she defended. "How could you think something so crazy? Have I ever shown any interest in your career other than when the hell I can expect my kitchen to be finished?"

"And why did she leave with an entourage and my dad? Don't get me wrong—she seemed nice enough, but come on, now."

"She left with your dad? When?" Ellie turned to face him, a sense of urgency perking her interest.

"She didn't leave *with* my dad. During Ma's speech, they left in a group, and he came back a while later. Don't get all gossipy on me on top of it all."

Ellie leaned back into her seat, tapping a fingernail against her teeth in contemplation.

"What? What are you thinking?"

"I can't know for sure, but I think she safe-worded."

"Safe-worded?" He scoffed, incredulous.

"Agent orange?" she replied.

Guy put it all together—the weird conversation with his mother and Ellie's instant interest in Danika.

"Wait, that idiot idea was a setup? How could you possibly know? You talked to the woman for less than a minute."

"And listened to her husband a little longer. When I was being introduced to him after a show years ago, our artistic director warned me about him. He has a reputation as a womanizer and likes them young," she said with a grimace. "But tonight? Even his compliments to her were backhanded. He spoke down to her, never let her out of his sight, and made sure everyone thought of her as a talentless nobody while he sits up on the hill. Couple that with her meekness, and her knee-jerk reaction to look to him for forgiveness when you flirted with her ..."

"The man's an asshole, don't get me wrong. Trophy wives are kind of his thing."

"I'm sure they are, but it was a gut feeling. I don't know, I could still be wrong. Maybe she left for another reason."

Maybe. Though Guy had his own gut feeling that Ellie was right. But how was this clueless Canuck suddenly so savvy? "What aren't you telling me?"

"Guy ..." She sighed his name, sounding more tired than before. "I don't want to talk about it. I know you're mad at me for not telling you about my job, and I am sorry I didn't warn you, but I didn't realize I would be known in your circle. I thought we agreed we were going to keep things light."

"We're not talkin' about that anymore. How did you know she needed a safe word?"

"I told you, I didn't know for sure."

"What? Is it your fiancé? He roughing you up? That scumbag!" Guy saw red and began plotting retribution.

"No, my relationship with Daniel might be toxic, but he has never been abusive. Leave it alone, OK?"

"Like hell!" Guy yelled, filling the car with raw testosterone. "No one treats you that way. I'm gonna handle this."

"Stop being a caveman. It wasn't him. It wasn't even in this century, so relax! I had a feeling about Danika because Montgomery has always reminded me of my father. Have I told you enough, Manning? Or do you need more? I don't have any memories of the abuse he put my mother through, but she made sure I knew what kind of man he was. My mother is a lot of things, but her one redeeming quality is her quiet devotion to women's charity work, so I have been around victims of abuse a fair bit. You learn the signs."

"I'm sorry," Guy grumbled, anger deflating into something else.

"You should be, but wipe that pity off your face. We live with our parents' scars, but that doesn't mean we have to internalize them. What I want to know is why you are spoiling for a fight? For once, I show a bit of competence, and you get mad about it? What? Did you want me to be a vapid piece of arm candy? Did I spoil your bullshit boxer persona by having a brain?"

"I guess we both have some unresolved baggage," he responded, offering no more on the subject. They rode the rest of the way in silence.

When Guy pulled to a stop at Ellie's house, she hopped out without a backward glance and walked to her door. He wanted to follow her as much as he wanted to peel out of there and never look back.

"Damn it!" he cursed hitting the steering wheel and jumped from the car. "Wait, Ellie, want some company?"

"I'm tired, Guy," she said, her shoulders rolling forward. She looked ready to stamp her foot like a petulant child as Guy caught up to her.

"We don't have to do anything. We could ..."

"Listen here, Manning! It's your talking that has me at wit's end. If you want to stay, you have to promise me you'll keep your mouth—"

He shut her down with a ravaging kiss. She responded immediately, and he took over opening her door as she began unbuttoning his dress shirt.

Once inside, Guy broke the kiss. "Don't worry. I'll keep my mouth busy."

THEY MADE slow progress up the stairs and across her living room, discarding clothing as they went. Ellie cursed her treacherous body. Guy had accused her of trying to poach him with sex. She was beyond hurt and wanted to lick her wounds, but the promise of him licking them for her was too exciting to walk away

173

from. She let her bra fall at her feet, and he pulled her toward the bed.

He looked so eager, like he was going to clap his hands and jump to it. But Ellie's pride stepped in. "Slow down there, Texas." He looked up from the panties he was about to take off with his teeth. "Tell me you're sorry," she demanded in her best girl-boss tone.

"For ..."

"For accusing me of being interested in you for your money and for questioning my integrity."

"Ellie, do we have to do this now?" Guy asked, raking his fingers through his hair.

"All you have to do is say sorry. Until then, my panties stay right where they are."

Guy appraised her, and a cocky grin took up the corner of his mouth. "I'm sorry, Ms. Bondell."

"Ellie will do," she said with a scowl. He was up to something, and she didn't like not knowing what.

"May I take off your panties now?" he asked, his eyes burning into her.

She nodded, and he pulled at her black lace panties with his teeth, nipping her skin ever so slightly.

"What now?" he asked, and she realized what he was playing at.

He was giving her full control. She was terrified. This was his territory, and she didn't want to make a fool of herself. He was daring her to take control—he probably thought she would give it right back to him. After all the games played that night, Ellie didn't want him to win this one so she sat on the bed demurely.

"I want you to kiss my leg from my ankle to ..." She paused for dramatic effect. "Well, we will see how far."

He obliged, dragging his lips and teeth against her ankle, then up her calf, pausing at a particularly sensitive spot on the inside of her knee. His fingers traced the path of her small scar before moving up her thigh, making it halfway before she stopped him.

"That's far enough. Now I would like you to kiss me here." She pointed to a spot on her collarbone.

Guy paused, more tentative than she'd expected. Again, he did as requested, and she arched her back as he nuzzled lower, finding her breasts, cupping one in his broad hand as he nibbled and sucked the other.

"Do you like my breasts, Texas?" she asked, desperate to maintain an authoritative tone.

He smiled up at her and pulled at her nipple with his teeth. "They are mighty fine," he drawled before moving his kisses down to her ribs, his touch sending her nerve endings into a frenzy. He laid her down and continued his kisses to her belly, to her hips, kissing, nipping, stroking, rubbing, lower, lower, lower ...

"What do you say?" she asked.

Guy looked incredulous this time.

"Manners, Manning."

"You're kidding?" His voice was haggard with need.

"No, I'm not."

He considered her. "May I please taste you, Ellie?"

Ellie's mouth went dry. "Only if you're good at it." She felt daring but also uncomfortable. This was a new level of intimacy for them. From her experience, coming this way was a rare happenstance, but she wasn't about to show weakness.

He knew what he was doing.

He began by kissing everywhere but her wanting apex. Her thighs, her hips, the line above her belly. She was acutely aware of the spaces he was missing, and her body bucked with desire. He caught her eye, deviousness and desire darkening his features as he made sure she watched him go down where she needed him most. After that, her head fell back, and ecstasy came hard and fast as she clutched fistfuls of the sheet beneath her.

"I'm sorry," she said sheepishly, covering her face with her hands in embarrassment after the waves subsided.

He raised an eyebrow as he lay beside her. "What for? I'm glad to have been of service," he joked as he took her hands away from her face and kissed her with such compassion. "My turn in charge. Kneel on the bed."

She was shaken, shocked, and had to decide if she was going to oblige. Though she had thought herself spent, she felt a twinge of need building inside her.

Rolling onto all fours, she looked back at him and caught his eyes burning with desire. His fingers traveled her seam, filling her. He pulled her by the hips, backing her to him so that her knees were right on the edge of the bed. The sound of the condom wrapper opening built expectations higher, followed by the silence as he rolled it on his length.

"I am going to push inside you fast and hard. I'm going to fuck you that way, babe, then I want you to finish me in your mouth." He was a man of his word, and she called out his name as he filled her. The sound of their bodies meeting in rough slaps only made her hotter as he kept his pace. She came hard, panting, falling apart, seeing spots.

Although her bones felt like jelly, she knelt in front of him because who could say no to him? Not a mere mortal such as herself. He removed the condom and reached for another but, shyness forgotten, she took him in hand. She licked his crown before taking him into her mouth, doing everything she could think of to bring him to ecstasy. His hips flexed him deeper into her mouth, and she relaxed to accept him. She felt him pulsing as he held her hair tight, keeping her planted until he'd fully released.

Looking down at her, he smiled and ran his hand along the side of her face. Game done, tenderness crept in as he helped her to her feet.

"How'd I do, boss?" he asked.

"You're hired!" She laughed, dazed by their lovemaking. He

helped her to her feet and led her to the bathroom for a soak in her clawfoot tub.

GUY WOKE in the middle of the night feeling Ellie stir in his arms. She spoke nonsense until Guy pulled her in closer. He smiled at the effect he had on her. It softened something in his chest. But the thought hit—what the hell was he doing in this woman's bed?

He liked Ellie and loved spending *quality* time with this virtual stranger. He'd had flings and one-night stands before, but something about Ellie chafed him, and he couldn't put his finger on it. She was intelligent, if naive, kind yet entitled, sexy as hell, though on another planet. Nothing about this woman was simple, least of all her damned fiancé.

Guy kept telling himself that he was OK with being a side piece. After all, what they had wasn't meant to last forever. Yet he still found himself wanting to maul the jerk who would let Ellie run around on him like this. He should think less of her, of course, but he didn't. And the whole thing had started to bug him more than he liked.

It was time to move things along. They'd had their fun, and like she said, this wasn't supposed to get serious. He would do his best to start distancing from her, maybe get her head on a little straighter, and see her off safely back to Canada. Even if it was the last thing he wanted to do.

CHAPTER FIFTEEN

$\mathcal{T}$he ride home was quiet, or it would've been if Ivy hadn't prattled on through the silences. When had Ed become so taciturn? Had he always been that way? Ivy was glad for the hum provided by too many glasses of champagne. It gave her courage.

Early in their relationship, Ed and Ivy couldn't keep their hands off each other. Even after bringing Guy home, they enjoyed more frequent sex than other new parents. Something happened along the way, and their sex life had tapered off. Ivy blamed sheer busyness for the downward turn. When Guy had begun school, Ivy set forth building the charity she had dreamed of through most of her vagabond adolescence. Even alone on the streets, she would try to envision a group that could more effectively offer assistance to kids like her. It kept her from drowning in her own bitterness.

The stability brought by Ed's job as a sought-after orthopedic surgeon enabled her to make a living by giving back. Eventually, she made a career out of helping others start businesses and charities, a career she'd thought she would have to give up once they decided to adopt Liam. He was so young and already had so many behavioral issues that they didn't want to send him to daycare. It was Dr. Manning to the rescue once more.

The man had known how much Ivy's work had come to mean to her and had offered to put his own job on hold to take care of their family. Ivy didn't know too many men who would do such a thing, no matter how much they loved their wives and children. The amount of trust he had in her ability to provide for their family baffled her.

Ivy watched Ed as he parked in front of their home, a home Ivy never dared to dream of owning. The years dripped away. The way Ed turned his key in the lock brought her a vision of the young man she'd married, his dark hair and rugged good looks, and she grew warm deep in her belly for him. She smiled secretly as they walked into their home and greeted Cujo.

"I'm gonna take her for a walk," Ed said simply as he kicked off his shoes, replacing them with Crocs. He pulled his tie and dress shirt over his head in one motion, revealing his flat stomach and broad shoulders before hiding them under a hoodie he kept in the closet. Ivy frowned. She had planned to make a move on Ed, but he was gone so quickly.

Climbing the stairs to their room, she assured herself that once he came back, they could start something. She went about removing her dress and jewelry, tucking everything away in the right place. She put on her robe. Not the plush one with stars that Liam had bought her for Mother's Day, but the charcoal silk one that was bought to match her daintiest negligee. It usually came out on hot summer nights, but it might be enough to draw Ed's eye.

She set to work removing the bulk of her makeup, leaving enough to still be fresh and dewy for her husband when he came home to find her lying in bed waiting. She positioned herself on the bed but felt tacky posing for him like a young fawn. Impatient, she picked up her book and tried to look enthralled.

Becoming bored with her cover story, she watched the street, peeking through the curtains until shadows darkened the walkway. The door closed heavily, and the lock turned as she dived back onto the bed. Cujo lapped up an obscene amount of water. The refrigerator door opened, then closed. The anticipation was electric. It had been too long since they'd last played at seduction, too long since their last sexual encounter, and even longer still since the flames of passion had overcome them.

The television turned on.

Huffing, Ivy knew it was time to be more forward. She glided elegantly down the stairs in their darkened home, stopping in the doorway of their TV room, and posed against the wall in what she hoped was a sufficiently seductive manner.

"Honey, it's late," she cooed to her husband who had yet to deviate from his channel surfing. "You should come to bed."

"In a minute," Ed responded, throwing back a slug of beer, not once looking at her.

Breaking through their old habits was harder than Ivy had anticipated. Her husband was tired, after all. It had been a long evening for him. Maybe a more direct approach would work. "How about I run us a nice warm bath?"

"It's late, Ivy."

"Precisely why I thought we could unwind together." Ivy found herself on the defensive. Here she was putting herself out there in front of him, and he couldn't bother more than a three-word response. "Do you realize how long it's been since we were intimate?" Ivy finished in a whisper, as though her dirty laundry would be aired if she said it at full volume.

"Intimacy doesn't start in the bedroom." Ed clicked off the TV and leaned back in his chair, looking her up and down with much less seductive interest than Ivy had expected.

"We could start here if you like?" She was laying it on thick, but she felt like Ed wasn't hearing her. If she thought it had been too long since they'd been to bed together, then he should be insatiable. Why wasn't he taking her bait?

She sauntered to his chair and perched on its arm, running her fingers through Ed's impossibly thick hair. When they had first made love, she had pulled at it, complimenting him. He'd told her that if she loved him for his hair, she should run. He'd expected a receding hairline that had yet to come.

Ed took his wife's hand and returned it to her lap as he stood without even trying to hide his intention of putting distance between them.

"Ed, what is it? What's wrong?" Ivy began to panic. It was one thing for her husband to roll over in the middle of the night when she'd tried to surprise him in his sleep. It was quite another to be shot down in the face of a sure deal.

"Are you kidding me, Ivy?"

"What do you mean?"

"You tramp around all night like the Queen of England, stomping on anyone underfoot, ignoring the needs of others, and then you think, what, I'm going to be so desperate that I forget all your bullshit?" He turned to leave.

"What are you talking about, Ed? You're not making sense."

"I'm talking about the way you are dismissive of anyone who isn't around to cater to your ego, or to fill your purse. Now, I know that's what these events are for, but you used to care about the people you spoke with rather than prance around the room like you owned it."

"It was my event, Ed. I had ownership over the event, and it was up to me to entertain our guests. I understand your dislike for—"

"I don't think you do. You used to, maybe, but not anymore."

"I'm sorry. I hadn't realized you were having such a bad time."

"Get your head out of the sand, woman! It's not about me. I'm used to being treated like your Man Friday. This is about how you treat others. How did you manage to get so high-and-mighty?" He tilted his head, inspecting his wife like he was trying to recognize her. Ivy felt like she'd been punched in the gut.

"And who exactly did I mistreat?" she asked, feigning indignation.

"You want a list? Well, the top two would be Danika Montgomery and Elmira Bondell."

"Who?"

"Miss Ellie," he answered through his teeth.

"Oh, Miss Ellie, is it?" Ivy laughed in spite of herself. "Since when are you her champion? Don't you see how she's running around with our son? She happens to come into town and buy one of his condos? Come on now, there is something dark about that girl, and I do not apologize for looking out for our son."

"Please, you serve him up to the lions every time you bring him to these events. You know he wants to distance himself from his boxing career, and yet you insist he show up to serve your own visibility. No, I think your problem with Ellie goes a little deeper than that."

"She isn't worth Guy's time, or my own," she spat back.

"No, I've noticed as much. You didn't have time for Danika either."

"Danika Montgomery? What has she to do with anything? I was perfectly cordial to the girl."

"If her scumbag husband had been the one to come speak with you, you would've made time for him. But everyone knows she doesn't hold the purse strings, so what is she to you?"

"What is this all about? I don't know why you are getting so worked up about these ... *girls*." Panic found its way to the pit of Ivy's stomach. She and Ed hadn't spoken this long for ages, never mind argued. What if Ed was more interested in one of those girls than he was in her? Was this what his mood was about? Was he having an affair?

"Do you even remember what Ellie was talking about?" Ed

paused as Ivy scrunched her brow but didn't speak. "No, of course not. She was talking about how nice it would be if we lived in a world where a simple safe word could save a woman's life."

"Oh yes! *Agent orange*, was it? As though abusers wouldn't see such a thing advertised as much as the abused. As though their movement online isn't often monitored and controlled." She rolled her eyes.

"Sure. Large scale. But what you missed while you were playing Miss America was that Danika safe-worded and we had to get her to safety. Miss Ellie knew the woman for five minutes and gave her a way out of a situation she couldn't have even been sure Danika was in. She swallowed her damn pride and pulled you aside knowing damn well you would be dismissive of her, and it made a difference in someone's life. Probably saved the poor girl, judging by how bad she shook on her way to the car. She's at a safe house now, if you care." He took another sip of the beer he'd forgotten he was holding.

"And what? I don't help people every day with the work I'm doing?"

Ed stared at her, mouth slack. "Sure, Ivy. You help hundreds, maybe thousands of people a year. But you don't look people in the eye anymore. You're too busy looking in the mirror. Did you even notice that I was gone for an hour to deal with the logistics of helping Danika? Do you even care if Danika is going to be all right? No, though if she's got a great success story, maybe you'll work her into your next big speech ... Oh! Darn!" He snapped his fingers. "That wouldn't work. Doubt Alistair would put down the big bucks if you outed him publicly for the creep he is."

Ivy was lost for words. "That's not fair," she fumed.

"What's not fair is that you can't see past your own nose and give Ellie even the smallest measure of respect for helping Danika. How many times have we nodded her way without giving her a second glance?"

"Gold diggers must stick together."

"Real cute, Ivy. You're forgetting that the same was said about you when we met. Run along and have your bath. I'm going to wait up for a call from head office to make sure Danika's exit plan is in place. You get your beauty sleep."

Without a backward glance, Ed picked up his cell phone and left the house, leaving Cujo looking up at the door questioning why he didn't take her with him, and leaving Ivy wondering when her husband had started hating her.

FOR THE REST of the night, Ivy tossed around in her bed thinking of all the terrible things Ed accused her of, thinking about how he'd looked at her. She'd gone to him for intimacy and instead received a lashing. Perhaps she'd become a bit birdbrained over the years, but she couldn't pretend that the toxicity of their relationship didn't exist.

It was time to act. Knowing what needed to be done, Ivy managed to get some sleep.

The next morning, she found Ed outside drinking a cup of coffee, talking in hushed tones on his phone.

She felt paralyzed. *What if he's having an affair?* She tortured herself for the hundredth time since the night before. She stepped outside and sat across from him, nursing her own coffee, as well as her frail ego.

"That was Monica from head office. Danika slept at the safe house last night and is being moved this morning. She's confident that the move will be easy, but given Montgomery's financial reach, it's going to be a case to watch."

"I'm glad she's OK," Ivy said, knowing from personal experience that running could be scarier than living in a familiar pattern of abuse. "We will do all we can for her."

Ed nodded, and the air grew heavy with tension.

"Listen," Ivy began carefully, "I've been up all night thinking things through, and I believe we must discuss it."

"Discuss what?"

"Isn't it obvious? I think we should discuss our"—her voice trembled—"well, our divorce."

Silence seemed to linger forever, but Ivy held her tongue. Tired of filling the silences—it was all mindless banter at this point—she just wanted this horrible conversation to be over with. The next chapter, the one without Edward, caused her heartache but it would happen one way or another. It was time to rip off the bandage.

"Is that what you want?" Ed asked, choking on contempt.

"Want? No. Of course not. I want a happy marriage, but what I want and what is possible doesn't always line up. Life is too short to be unhappy, wouldn't you agree? I don't want this misery for you, and I don't want it for me. Neither of us deserves this agony." Ivy paused, waiting for her husband of forty years to say something. To fight for her instead of with her. To problem-solve as they used to when things would derail. She was waiting for him to put forth a compromise.

But he stayed silent, biting his cheek. There had been a time in their lives when they could share a conversation in a glance, a joke with a smile, foreplay with a lick of their lips. That time was gone.

"Well, I suppose we should get a quote on the house. Maybe make a list of your demands, and of course, we will try to do this as amicably as possible. No need to make a scene about it," she rambled.

"God forbid anyone sees you actually give a shit," he yelled, throwing his coffee mug across the yard.

Ivy cringed, for the first time frightened by Ed's anger. She knew the statistics. About half of murdered women in America are killed by a romantic partner. She never thought such a thing would cross her mind about Edward Manning. He was a healer not prone to rages.

"What? Now you're afraid of me? Finally, something authentic! Something rooted in the here and now. Way to go! I call that progress." With that, he stalked out of the yard, slamming the fence shut as he went.

CHAPTER SIXTEEN

*G*uy rose early, slipping his arm out from under Ellie's neck with care. Hunting around her kitchen, he made himself a cup of herbal tea, hoping to fool his body into thinking it was getting a caffeine hit. His gaze flashed around the apartment and was instantly annoyed at the piles of supplies sitting around, waiting to be worked on. As the builder, he should be building.

He began laying out the reclaimed hardwood, planning to make the cuts as soon as Ellie was awake. The noise would chase her from the apartment, giving him the space he needed. Working with his hands brought him peace, but he needed to be alone to think.

He pretended he didn't hear Ellie coming down the hall. Didn't feel her watching him. Or consider whether she'd put on any clothes. His eyes cut to her sharply.

"Don't let me bother you," she said like a morning bird chirping. She poured herself some dry cereal and had the good sense to sit on the couch across the room.

He said nothing as he moved appliances out of his way. He would place the more defective-looking wood pieces where they wouldn't be seen.

"Need help?" she asked with a full mouth.

Guy groaned, acknowledging that he was being ruder than necessary. "Naw, enjoy your ..." Looking at her, he realized what she was eating. "Lucky Charms? Really?"

"What? They have unicorns now." She munched happily in a tank top, pink panties, and weird rainbow knee socks.

He shook his head and continued working.

"It's going to get loud in here with the saw," he said as he measured the space, then the wood.

Ellie's response was a mutter.

He turned on the saw and made his cuts. Then he turned on the air compressor for the nail gun. If that didn't get rid of her, Guy didn't know what would. Without looking up, he lost himself in the intricacies of the work. But he could always feel when Ellie was watching him. Her stare gave him goose bumps. He realized that he was being juvenile trying to get Ellie out of her own home when he was free to leave. Having spent days and nights together, he felt compelled to stay, magnetically held within her orbit. As much as he knew it was time to end things, he didn't want to end them badly. With that knowledge, he recalibrated.

"So, how long you got till you have to be north of the border?" he asked casually.

"Not sure," she responded, looking up from her book. "Depends which way my plans go."

"You think you'll be here long?"

"I'm not sure." She leaned forward, resting her elbows on her knees, her stare averted as she got lost in thought. Her jovial demeanor disappeared behind a storm cloud, and Guy felt more than a little guilty for causing it. He pushed the feeling down and reminded himself that Ellie needed to start thinking through things.

"What about your job? They must need you back."

"Yes. If I take the new position, I'll need to be back before I run short on vacation. I have been able to keep up on the most pressing things from my computer, but it is a part of the equation for sure."

Guy was surprised to hear that she'd been working. He didn't imagine she had time between shitstorms and partying. She carried her dishes to the sink. The scent of her, vanilla and balsam, pulled at him. He wanted to wrap her up tight against him, but he wasn't going to do that anymore.

"And your fiancé?" He'd tried to say it straight, but it rumbled in his chest uncomfortably, and he tensed up. Time to get back to work. He replaced the appliances, then measured and cut another piece of wood before Ellie replied.

"Yes, that's a mess I suppose needs cleaning up at some point."

"Didn't mean to lay the guilt on you," he said, meaning it but grudging it all the same.

"The guilt is where it belongs," she answered shortly.

"Takes two to tango, sweetheart." He gave her a lopsided grin of apology.

"Sure, we had problems, but it's not like he did anything wrong," she said, searching the ceiling for answers.

"Well, where the hell is he then, Ellie? Tell me that. Where the hell is he?" he asked, looking around the apartment, unable to restrain his anger.

"It's not his fault I lost my mind! I left *him*, remember?" There was a crisp pause as the air emptied from the room.

"Oh, I know you're all kinds of crazy," Guy said, pointing his mallet at her before nailing the tongue and grooves together efficiently with his mounting anger. "If he were so smart, you wouldn't have gotten close to that damn border." Guy raised his mallet and brought it down hard. *BANG!* "He would've hunted you down and dragged you back home to your damn igloo and made"—*BANG! BANG!*—"love to you till it melted and you came to your senses!"

"We don't live in igloos."

BANG!

"If he was so perfect, you wouldn't have thought about running." *BANG!*

"Seriously, I've never even been in an igloo."

"Hell, he may have a PhD, but this has got to be the dumbest"
—*BANG!*—"laziest"—*BANG!*—"good-for-nothing man you could come across!" With that, Guy focused his glare on her, daring her to contradict him.

"There was that time when I was eight at Winterlude ..."

"Damn it, woman!" He dropped his mallet and lunged toward her, grabbing her by the shoulders. "This guy is no good for you, not the other way around. You deserve a man who shows up. Someone you don't have to hide your crazy from." Quick as a lynx, she jumped at him. He caught her before her lips were on his, strong, demanding, daring him to prove himself worthy.

He carried her with little effort to the table and set her on it, never breaking from the kiss, feeding warmth into her body, fanning the embers and setting her on fire. She reached her arms around him, drawing his body closer to hers, and the table wavered underneath her. He cursed the lack of craftsmanship and laid her down on it, removing her underwear with one hand while undoing his pants positioning himself against her opening.

Bringing herself on to her elbows, she was ready to comment, ready to take some measure of control from him. He pulled her toward his body, throwing her off balance, pushing inside her.

It was a surprising turn of events, but she was too full of him to consider anything but the punishing rhythm he'd set. She arched her body any way she could to meet him thrust for thrust when the table gave way. She stiffened her muscles, and he caught her. She sat up, wrapping her arms and legs around him again.

His eyes were full of carnal flames, and her smile dissolved. She couldn't look away. Trusting him to hold her, she pulled her shirt over her head as he found the closest wall. It felt welcome and cool against her back as they began again, building, higher and higher.

His heat both overwhelmed and fulfilled her, his eyes never left hers, never showed signs that he was anywhere but there, with her. She came first, falling, falling, as though it had no end, and he followed as she called his name in the throes. Only then did their mouths meet again. A sweet punctuation.

～

"WON'T you be late for church?" Ellie asked Guy. They had cleaned themselves up, dressed for the day, and Guy was determined to finish what he'd started with the flooring.

"Already am, but I can go to a later service."

"I'm sorry."

"For what?"

"I wouldn't want your mother to think I am corrupting you," Ellie admitted, blushing like a teenager.

"Whatever do you mean?" Guy grinned as he tucked his pencil behind his ear.

"Come on, it's obvious she doesn't like me."

"Is it now?" Guy laughed at the daggers Ellie shot at him. "I'm a big boy. I can handle my mother. The pastor is going to be mighty upset if he doesn't see you there this week, though."

"Guess I can cross off the Catholics from joining my squad."

"I'm a Baptist, not Catholic. But don't worry about either. In this town if they think they can save you, they'll always bring you a casserole."

Ellie laughed, and Guy was in awe of her.

"What now? Do I have something on my face?"

"Naw." Guy got back to work before he could tell her how beautiful she was.

"Well, I have some things to do before going to Crystal's this evening."

"Oh, Ellie, you have to cancel that," Guy said with utter seriousness.

"Sorry?"

"The twins. No one babysits them for a reason. They are holy terrors. They'd eat Mary Poppins alive."

"I promised Crystal I'd look after them."

"I know you did, but she will understand that someone spilled the beans about her having twin Antichrists and will adjust accordingly."

Ellie chewed on her cheek.

"You're going to go, anyway?"

"How bad could they be?"

"They once set the church on fire."

"They are, what? Eight years old? I'm sure that was an accident."

"They cut off poor Margret Laney's hair."

"Hair grows back." Ellie's face was paler, but she was choosing to be stubborn.

"It's your funeral, but if things get too wild, give me a call and I'll help you out."

"You'd babysit with me?" Ellie asked, eyes sparkling with mischief.

"Hell no! I mean I will actually help you get out of whatever trouble they've got you in. You get into it, they cause it. All hell is sure to break loose."

Ellie sized him up, realization dawning on her. "Then why didn't you step in last night to stop me from promising?"

Guy went uncharacteristically bashful. "Well now, Ellie, I thought you were a man-eating poacher with a trick up your sleeve."

"Now you don't?"

"I'm not sure what the heck you are, but if you're a talent agent, there's no way in hell I'm signing with you."

"I'll have you know, I'm an excellent businesswoman."

"Know anything about boxing?"

"Let's see ... it's a savage sport." She began ticking off on her fingers. "You wear gloves. 'Float like a butterfly, sting like a bee.'

'ADRIAN!'" she screamed. "I've seen movies," she finished with a shrug.

Guy shook his head as Ellie skipped to her room, where she'd set up her home office. "Don't quit your day job, Miss Ellie." He didn't see her face blanch at the suggestion.

CRYSTAL'S HOME was a quaint brick bungalow with large windows and freshly painted decorative shutters. Though in a less affluent part of town, Ellie felt the same pang of envy she had upon first setting eyes on the Manning residence. There was no tire swing, but the yard was littered with the paraphernalia of boyhood: scorched army men, a magnifying glass, water guns, and bits from burst balloons. Ellie smiled to herself.

Being asked to babysit the twins had taught Ellie a great deal. It had taught her exactly who she could trust when it came down to it. It appeared that everyone with basic human decency had thought to warn her about the reputation of the terrible twosome. Those who were invested in her well-being had begged her to cancel—Guy, Winter, and Goldie. The ones who smiled knowingly were the ones who would enjoy her downfall.

Ellie had played it cool, naive even, like babysitting was a play at gaining an inch with the townspeople. What they failed to note was that in her heart of hearts, she never expected to belong. She never had before, so why now? No, this was something more. This was retribution for all the whispers behind her back.

What Ellie had left out was that she had been a counselor at a camp for disadvantaged youth for three years in high school. The support staff had been made up of former jail guards, parole officers, retired police officers, and Mrs. Kristofferson. With all the pomp and egos, Mrs. Kristofferson, an eighty-year-old widow, had been the most competent of them all. She carried a switch and never had to use it.

There had been one boy Ellie's first year there, Leroy. He was only a little older than Crystal's boys, about ten years old. Already he had a juvenile record, he picked fights at the camp, and even tried bullying the staff. He scared the heck out of Ellie. He stood so tall and was so strong. Being big for his age lent to the feeling that he could take on anyone. It was the look in his eyes that freaked her out; he was so angry and closed off. Ellie had given him a wide berth, not wanting to become his next victim.

One day, he started a fight with another boy and pulled a weapon. Before anyone but Ellie could see it, Mrs. Kristofferson swooped in, pinched his ear, and whispered something into it. The screwdriver was relinquished to the brittle-boned woman who then carried Leroy off by the ear without another word. There were no more incidents with him after that, and Ellie had seen him sitting with Mrs. Kristofferson most nights.

The only person who scared Ellie more than the boy had been the old woman, but Ellie couldn't shake her curiosity. After she saw the boy leave Mrs. Kristofferson's side one night, Ellie approached her.

"What is it, tiny dancer?" she asked, barely shifting her gaze from her knitting. Ellie warmed at the endearment.

"What did you say to him?" Ellie asked.

Mrs. Kristofferson put her knitting down and sized her up. "I told him I had some gummy bears and *Goosebumps* books in my cabin. I told him he was wasting his time, that he'd be sent home if he got caught fighting anymore." Ellie stared at her, slack-jawed. "You can't change the world, Elmira. Don't bother trying. All you can do is show a little kindness."

"But he was going to stab that boy! That can't be all you said!"

The old woman studied her from beneath her thick glasses. "Maybe he was, maybe he wasn't. He's a child. I gave him the opportunity to act like one."

Had it not been for that conversation, Ellie would not have returned the following two summers. She'd followed Mrs. Kristofferson's lead and learned as much as she could from the woman. In her third year, she was voted favorite counselor and felt she'd made a difference.

She continued to write to Mrs. Kristofferson until she passed away years later. Leroy had been at her funeral too. He still stood tallest in the room, but there was a softness to his features, an inner confidence that hadn't been there before. They'd hugged, both with tears ready to fall.

The sound of children yelling and stomping broke through the wall to the street. She rang the bell. Inside fell silent until the clicking of heels came toward the door. "Miss Ellie! Welcome! Don't mind the mess, I sure don't!" Crystal laughed, her voice filled with posturing. Ellie bit her tongue and played along.

"Is Mr. Crystal home? I would love to meet him." Ellie peeked around the room as though he might pop through one of the doorways at any minute. Crystal had a personality as big as her hair, and one couldn't guess what her other half was like.

"The theater is right across from his work, so he's meeting me there. Then he has bowling afterward. I'll have to make introductions another time."

"I hope you don't mind, I brought a few board games. I wasn't sure what you had here." She was grating her own nerves but knew she was hitting her mark when Crystal let a small smirk pass.

"Well, ain't that sweet of you? Jake! Tanner! Get your butts down here and meet Miss Ellie!" The two boys came down the steps side by side, wearing smiles just a touch too wide to be up to any good, their red hair and freckles blazing. They stood like choirboys, but it didn't take a genius to see that they were up to no good.

Ellie smiled back at them because she wasn't either.

"Look, Miss Ellie brought you boys some board games, isn't that nice?"

"Thank you, Miss Ellie," they chorused. The two of them looked downright creepy, but rule number one: show no fear. Ellie wished Crystal a lovely time, closed the door after waving goodbye, and turned the dead bolt.

"Listen here and listen close, because I'm not going to repeat myself. If you boys want to act like hellions tonight and try to break me, go for it. I don't care. Nobody thinks it's going to go any different. BUT. If you want the opportunity to cause some real trouble, you are going to keep the house clean and be in bed, washed, by the time your mother gets home."

The boys, surprised by the ultimatum, took to silent twin-speak before the one Ellie thought was Jake asked, "What's in it for us?"

"Candy." They rolled their eyes. "Lots of it. And firecrackers too." Seeing they wanted the loot but weren't convinced it was enough to keep them in line, she added, "And the chance to freak out your mother and bamboozle the town."

They let this sink in before Tanner answered, "What we gotta do?"

"Like I said, act like basically good human beings for me tonight, fill me in on some details about yourselves that your mother would never suspect you'd tell me, of all people. Then you can use my gifts in whatever fashion you want, as long as it doesn't lead back to me. Though, I do have some ideas." She finished pointing a finger at each of them in turn. "Deal?" she asked, opening her hand.

"Deal!" they both said as they hocked spit into their hands. Ellie didn't let them faze her and spat on her own hand. They shook and got down to it.

She took pictures as she had them help make a simple dinner and dessert. They offered details about themselves: how to tell them apart, favorite toys and movies, themes of birthdays past.

"That's cool, guys, but what else you got for me?"

"What do you wanna know?" Tanner asked, wiping the flour they were using to make a pie onto his brow. He looked so darling, Ellie took another picture.

"Well, given your rap sheet, I'm guessing there's trouble at school?" Ellie asked, being careful not to linger on eye contact.

"What about it?" Jake asked, more annoyed with the situation than his brother.

"You tell me," Ellie said. "What's something, you know, specific, that you've maybe been holding back?"

Tanner looked like he wanted to share something, but he deferred to Jake wordlessly. "This about the fight with Mr. Peterson?" Jake scoffed.

"I dunno," Ellie said. "Is it?"

"Why should we tell you? What makes you special?" Jake asked.

"Sometimes it's easier to tell things to someone you don't know. But you should know that if it's important, like if someone could be hurt, I will have to tell somebody. You don't care what I think, so you don't have to worry about me judging you. The town thinks I'm a fruitcake, so they'll call me out if I try twisting anything you say." They twin-spoke, and Ellie could feel the intensity of the conversation without any sound between them. "So, are you going to tell me about the teacher, Mr. Peterson?"

"That asshole had it coming." Jake was without a doubt the alpha twin.

"Real jerk?" Ellie asked, handing Jake the pie filling to pour.

"Try real creep! He's always touching Maggie."

Ellie's heart sank deep, and it must've shown on her face.

"Not there! Well, not yet, or she'd have told us. She's afraid of lying after we chopped off her hair for tattling on us for something we didn't do. I done told Peterson to back off or I would teach *him* a lesson."

Ellie quietly considered what he had said. Of course, she would have to pass that along. She hadn't thought she would come across anything quite so brutal. She handed him one strip of pie crust at a time to top it off.

"It's cool of you to stand up for Maggie like that. Real brave."

Jake turned red, which was a sight with all those freckles.

She snapped another picture.

"Not like anyone would believe us if we told on him." Tanner sighed.

"Well, I do."

"No offense, but it ain't like anyone will believe you either," Jake said, much less agitated.

"Maybe not, but now it's my job to make them listen. And I can be *really* annoying."

"I dunno, you seem kinda cool too ..."

Ellie was in, and in that moment it was the only acceptance worth a damn.

Hours later, Crystal returned, entering the home tentatively as Ellie read a book on the couch. The boys had been in bed for an hour, and the house was spotless. Ellie pretended she hadn't heard the door open and surveyed Crystal's response from her periphery. It was as though the woman was looking for something, deep confusion written all over her face.

"Oh hey, Crystal! How was your night?"

"Where are the boys?" Crystal asked, skipping the cursory charm she usually led with.

"In bed," Ellie answered. "That Tanner is a real softie. He got me to read *The Story of Ferdinand* about eight times!"

Crystal was shocked into silence, so Ellie continued, "And Jake is as quick as a whip. When we were playing Scrabble, he totally called me out on a spelling mistake. Blew me away!" More silence. "But there's something I need to talk to you about. There's some pie in the kitchen. How about we cut you a slice and talk about Mr. Peterson?"

Ellie led Crystal through her own home and told her everything the kids had said about their teacher as she cut and served Crystal a piece of the pie her sons had baked.

She took the information in stride, but asked, "Are you sure my boys weren't pulling your leg?"

"I didn't get that sense at all," Ellie said confidently, but not wanting to push her too far, she added, "You know them best, but something like this should always be investigated, don't you think?"

She nodded, taking a bite. "This is amazing!" Crystal said, diverting the conversation to something lighter. "You must get me your recipe."

"I'll forward it to you, but the boys are the ones who made it. I've got photo evidence!" Ellie pulled out her phone and showed off a little.

It was clear that Crystal wasn't sure how to process what had happened that night, so Ellie saw herself out. She looked back at the house and saw one of the boys in the window of the front-most bedroom. She suspected it was Jake by the grumpy way he used his fist to rub his eye, and she waved at him before getting into her car, then rolled down the window to make a funny face.

His wave was tentative. Then he turned his head as if someone surprised him and disappeared from sight. Crystal must've been checking on them.

Ellie smiled as she pulled away, feeling like everything was going to be all right.

CHAPTER SEVENTEEN

$\mathcal{I}$t had been an uneventful night for Guy, and he was glad to launch into action on Monday. He had gotten some work done at the office and had a meeting with Edith, the young, forward-thinking teen maven helping out with the Community Lab Group. How she managed school, track, and the Black Student Union was beyond him. Then on top of that, she was bringing him ideas about how to broaden the work that the CLG was doing. He hoped she would be available to do an internship. The girl was going places, and he wanted to help her out if he could.

The rest of the morning, he coordinated his crews to finish up the other units. He was growing bored with the project and needed it done before it turned into tedium. He had wanted to visit with Ellie to make sure she still had all her fingers after minding the twins, but he was swamped until after lunch. When he was able to stop by, under the pretense of checking on his crew, he found two police cruisers outside his building.

At first, he laughed—what had they gotten Miss Ellie into? Then he took a tally of the workmen, some of whom had served time, and while he trusted them all, more than Crystal's boys, in fact, he felt a worry bubble up that one of them might have stepped out of line. He hoped he wouldn't have to fire anyone.

He checked on his contractors first. His foreman was all smiles —Martin Rodriguez loved confrontation as much as he loved gossip. Men let women think that gossip only runs from their lips, but Guy figured Martin could give almost anyone a run for their money.

"You know what two cruisers are doing on my site?" Guy asked loud enough for everyone to hear.

"Boss, it ain't us. It's that cute little thing on the end."

Guy's eye twitched.

"Sorry, boss," Martin continued, attempting to quell his humor on the subject. "Saw Sergeant Wilco and Officer Grayson go in with my own eyes nearly an hour ago."

"Is Miss Ellie all right?"

"Far as I could see, she was still in her pajamas. Looked surprised enough."

"All right, thanks, Martin." Guy tried to put it out of mind. *What the heck has Ellie gotten herself into now?* Guy feigned humor to avoid the knot forming in his stomach. It couldn't be serious. This was Ellie—she specialized in slapstick, not criminal intent.

Still, no matter what he was busy with, his eyes would trail in her direction. When the police officers came out of Miss Ellie's apartment, Guy made it across the lot before they could get into their vehicles.

"Everything OK?" he asked, for once unsure whether to speak to them as friends or as lawmakers.

"Not at liberty to discuss," Sergeant Wilco said as he put on his aviators and got into his car.

Grayson was torn between loyalties—the job and his friend. As Wilco pulled out of the lot, his friendship prevailed. "She's kicked the proverbial hornet's nest, is all." With a shrug, he opened his own cruiser's door. "See you at the gym tomorrow?"

"Sure," Guy responded as he waved off his friend before going to talk to Ellie. He rang the bell before walking right in. Someone needed to teach Miss Ellie to lock her door.

Peering down the walk-up, Ellie indeed looked fine, if a little unsettled. She had changed from pajamas into tight jeans and a lacy camisole, and the light behind her formed a halo. Guy scoffed at the thought. Trudging up the steps, he had become weary of what he was walking into.

He was surprised that Ellie's apartment was looking far more homey than when he'd last seen it. Lace curtains filtered the sunlight from the windows, and a few colorful paintings lined the walls. A chopping block with sliced lemon and a tall teacup sat beside the sink. A sweater hung over the back of a lounger he didn't remember lugging up. All these things should've been endearing, but he was unnerved.

"So, let's have it," Guy said.

"What do you mean?"

"You know what I mean."

She crossed her arms defensively.

"What's wrong is there were two police officers in your home. So let's have it."

"Why are you angry with me?"

Guy rubbed his temples. He understood that he was being short with Ellie, and he wasn't sure why, so he decided to change directions. "I'm tired is all. Did the boys get you into some trouble?"

"No, nothing like that," Ellie said. Guy met her silence with silence, knowing she'd be the one to crack. "They had some information that needed to be handed to the right people."

"The police? You know those kids are con artists, right?"

Ellie's spine straightened. "They may be rebellious, but ..."

"Try holy terrors."

"That's not fair!"

"You walk into town and suddenly, you know what's fair here and what's not?"

"I didn't call them. I told Crystal what they told me, and I guess she thought it was important enough to call Sergeant Wilco about. Maybe you should figure out what's going on before treating me like ... like ... I don't even know what's going on here!" She threw up her hands and went back to the kitchen to fill a pitcher with water.

Guy followed on her heels. "Why don't you clear things up for me, then," he sneered.

"The boys got in trouble for fighting with one of their teachers. They told me that they were trying to protect a girl in their class. They think he's been harassing her."

"So, you're putting someone's livelihood on the line for a couple of degenerates who are probably pulling your leg?"

This stopped Ellie in her tracks. "Excuse me? If this turns out to be nothing, I will be glad to have been duped. If it's between me being wrong about the boys and them being right about the teacher, I hope I'm wrong! But I am not going to risk it!"

"And you say I have a savior complex! You can't blow into town and keep shaking everything up!"

"Are you serious right now? Do you not get what's at stake here?"

"Oh, I get it. Little Miss Canada can't fix her own problems, so she goes nosing around other people's business. Why don't you work on yourself instead?"

"OK, Mr. High-and-Mighty, since you think you know what's going on here, why don't you tell me. Go ahead, lay it out for me!"

"Well, you should start by taking some damned responsibility for your actions. You ran from your job and your fiancé the same damn way you ran from your dancing career!"

Taken aback, Ellie scoffed. "What do you know about it? You've seen my scar."

"I've seen you dance circles around people and make it through a Community Lab on bloodied feet. I may not know ballet, but I do know people. There are people who give up and there are people who fight for what they want. Grayson's sister was in an accident when she was ten, severed her damn spinal cord. You know what she does for a living? She runs a dance studio for kids!" He stopped to regain some semblance of composure. She was dazed—it was time for the TKO. "You talk about how you were forced into things by your mother, but you just ain't got no spine."

"Well, I guess you'd know." Her voice was feather soft, but her eyes scorched. "You quit boxing, you quit college before you even got there, you quit your own organization! You're everything to this town—you know it, you use it, and sure, you help everyone out, but only so far as it keeps you on top. How's that working for you, Guy? No one else sees the resentment you have for this town, not while you're constantly building it up the way you do ... but I see it. You keep giving enough of yourself to say you're trying, but you're miserable here. I may have run away from my problems, but you wallow in yours, and you will wallow until you die and they put up a statue of you in the park!"

"You're right about one thing. This is *my* town. You should leave before you set fire to it. Or are you waiting for that to happen so you can run again?"

She didn't answer, her face red with anger, her eyes welling up. Guy shook his head with distaste before leaving.

ELLIE SURVEYED THE ROOM, making sure she hadn't forgotten anything major before turning out the light and descending the stairs with her second duffel. With the opening of the door, the cool morning breeze brushed a farewell against her cheek, and part of her longed to stay. Though it might reach the right temperature for shorts in Littleton, Ottawa was in the middle of an ice storm.

Winter waved as she pulled into the lot, and Ellie smiled, picturing her in a parka. The woman could work any look.

Locking her front door for the first and possibly last time, she rested her hand against it, already feeling the warmth of the morning sun on the clover green she'd managed to convince Guy to use on all the units.

After he'd stormed out the night before, she had waited—for the slam of the door, and the shock of it to hit. She waited for the tears to come and to wilt from the loss. When it didn't happen, it was time to pack up and put things in order. Winter didn't probe when Ellie asked for a ride to the airport the next morning.

"You need me to come over now?" Winter had asked.

"No, I think I'm OK."

"Need me to beat him up or curse his family for a thousand years?"

"No, I think that might be overkill. But thank you." She was still waiting to feel something.

She then called Mark, the mechanic, to ask if he would be able to sell her car for her. After a few grunts and approximations, he conceded it could be sold for parts. Her mother would be thrilled —she'd never liked the death trap. With that settled, she had called Goldie. They hadn't spoken much since they'd gone out, and as she apologized for that, Goldie laughed.

"It's all good. I'm sorry if I pressured you into hooking up. I must've been projecting or something. Do you want to talk about what happened?" she asked, but Ellie heard a purring voice in the background and told her they could save it for another time.

"But Goldie," Ellie started with uncertainty, "if I decide to sell ... would you be able to take care of business for me?"

"Of course, chica." Goldie giggled, and Ellie suspected it had more to do with what was happening on the other end of the line. "You owe me that listing!" She joked, and they planned to email details soon. They said their goodbyes, and Ellie shook her head as they hung up. Good for Goldie. She waited for a wave of jealousy. It didn't come.

So she called the police station and told them her plans and gave them her contact details for her Canadian address.

Winter grabbed one of the duffels from the ground before resting a strong hand on Ellie's shoulder. "Need me to mess him up?" she asked deadpan.

"Naw." Ellie shrugged. "He wasn't entirely off base."

"Pfft! Like that matters to me." Winter scoffed as she pulled out of the lot and started toward Dallas.

"Thank you." Ellie chuckled, then sighed. "I'm upset, but everything he said was true ... I have been running away from everything, and it's time to face up to my responsibilities. I have to leave Littleton to do that."

They passed the antiques shop where Marlin and Moira were enjoying their coffee on a darling patio set outside their store. Ellie turned—she didn't want to forget the way they stared at each other with adoration one second, then got into a cane war the next.

They passed the salon. Winter honked good morning at Crystal who was jiggling the keys into the door, readying to open in the next hour. She looked more at peace than Ellie had ever seen her, but she knew exactly where the twins got their devious streak. A group of runners followed single file along the footpath, passing the line forming outside the café. Ellie turned forward when passing the unassuming stoop of Guy's apartment.

"Think you'll come back?"

"Definitely. Maybe. I wish he was separate from this town. It would make coming back to visit you and Goldie a lot easier."

"Well, that might not be a problem. I'm looking into renting an apartment in New York."

"WHAT?"

"Yeah, well, I've been talking with Danika, and she's working on ending up there. We've been in touch with Parker, the fashion blogger you introduced us to."

Ellie had followed Parker Talbot for years online until she'd run into him during fashion week. She'd been heading to a board meeting, and he was en route to some runway. Both were more preoccupied with their phones than walking. They crashed heads, and ever since had dinner whenever she came to the *real capitol*, as he liked to call it. Like most Torontonians Ellie had met, he only grudgingly acknowledged the prowess of other places. Except New York City, of course.

"Isn't he something?"

"He is! I guess Danika was pretty open about her situation, and he wants to help her out, so he's going to be covering her handbag line once she's ready. We were talking at the gala too. He's interested in the whole goth fashion mentality thing but doesn't know where to start, so we are going to co-blog ... is that a thing?"

Ellie was glad to hear her friend so genuinely excited for her future. She'd admired Winter's tenacity from the beginning, but the risks she was about to take for her career were nothing short of inspiring.

"What made you decide to leave Littleton?"

This gave Winter pause. "Well, this will always be home base. At least, while Gran is still there. But she's the only thing holding me." She paused, and Ellie could sense her thinking something through. "You know Grayson, right? We were best friends when we were kids. I'm talking from the time I moved here for kindergarten until he hit around fourth grade. I'm talking school yard, sleepovers, tree house in the woods, chasing fireflies at night. That was us. We were going to get married and move to Alaska and raise a team of huskies." She laughed at the memory but sobered quickly.

"One day it was like the switch went off—the day I changed my style. Maybe part of me was sticking around to see if he would get over himself. We haven't had a real conversation in years. It's like it never happened. Maybe it was all in my head ... we were so young. I hadn't even realized I was holding on to it until you asked me the other day. Sorry for unloading on you.

But after all this time, he really was still keeping me from branching out. With Gran on her world travels, I think it's time."

"She sounds like a pip."

"You have no idea!" Winter laughed, launching into story after story about her childhood adventures with her grandmother. Stories that went on until they pulled into the DFW Airport drop-off zone.

"Thank you again for the ride."

"My pleasure. You better call me, or I will hunt you down."

"I promise." Hugging Winter should've brought on the water-works. Ellie knew she'd miss her new friend more than anything. She waved goodbye and waited. Standing there, no tears came.

Could I finally be doing the right thing?

GUY WAS STILL in a foul mood at the office days after his fight with Ellie. He plugged numbers into his spreadsheets like he was poking someone's eye out. His telephone manner was clipped, and none of the foremen were going to be stopping in after the blast they'd received that morning for not having finished the goals from the day before.

At noon, Arleen shimmied into his office, hips swaying her flouncy skirt. Arleen may not have been Romani, but she embraced their fashion.

"Is that really workplace attire?" he grumbled.

"Do you really want to eat today?" she countered, not missing a beat. She held the takeout bag over the trash can.

Guy mumbled an apology, and Arleen shuffled over and began pulling items from the bag. Once finished, she sat across from him and a notebook materialized. "Your three o'clock canceled, but Goldie called. She wants to see you."

"Not feeling like a social call today," Guy managed as he

opened a container of broccoli and shrimp stir-fry. He grimaced and ate the broccoli to get it out of the way.

"Said it was business and that she'd show up regardless of your mood. Thought you'd like to know."

Guy groaned. *Business, my ass*, he thought to himself. He was sure Ellie had gone and blabbed about their fight to Goldie, and Winter too. If it wasn't so infantile, he wouldn't have bothered to be bothered by it. He was done with the drama Ellie brought to his life. From here on out, she was nothing but a customer. Soon the building would be completed, and he wouldn't have to try so hard to avoid it.

"Anything else?" he demanded when he noticed Arleen boring a hole through his skull.

"I'm going home sick," she said evenly, coughing mechanically into her hand before standing and walking out.

Guy seethed at the wall between them as he heard her packing up her purse and tidying her station. Once the door had shut, he got up to lock it behind her. Best not to talk to customers face-to-face today.

Before he could turn the dead bolt, Goldie pushed her way in.

"Thought you were coming at three."

"I come when I can," she responded, demurely sizing him up.

Guy went back to his office and sat, knowing there was no shaking Goldie when her mind was set on something. "Let's get this over with. I got things to do."

"All right, Prince Charming," Goldie answered, cocking an eyebrow at him. "I'll be keeping a key to the unit so that I can stage and have pictures done up. Also, I would like for you to give me the work schedule. I can show around it." She crossed her legs, then noticed Arleen's untouched lunch package and reached for it. "Mmm, orange chicken? You shouldn't have." She opened the container and ate like she hadn't in days.

"The remodel on the Prescott place hasn't even begun. You'll have to wait, or else you'll be showing '70s parquet and '90s rot."

Guy had done a few upgrades for the Prescotts who insisted he keep the key.

"Eww," Goldie said with a full mouth and closed the container with distaste. "I'm not talking about the Prescotts."

"Is Hennessy selling after all, then?" Guy asked, getting a sick feeling in the pit of his stomach. He pushed away the last of his meal.

"Nooo." Goldie realized his hackles were up and spoke softly to him, as if he were a growling dog, ready to pounce. "Miss Ellie's place. She owes me the listing, and that place is going to show like a dream. I'm going to use it as a model home to boost sales for the other units. Which reminds me—word is that Carla Hayworth, Lilly's girl, is coming back with a degree in botany, and she might be interested in one of your storefronts. Granted, the location won't be as ideal as Belle's, right in the middle of town, but I'll send her your way when she's ready. And you better be nice to her."

"Miss Ellie is selling, then? What a shocker!" he said, sneering. He hadn't expected Ellie to be so efficient in her escape. "Tell me— you come here to plant your own seeds to get me to go after your friend for a happy ending? Ain't my thing, Goldie, you should know that."

"Ellie isn't sure if she's selling, but she flew home yesterday to sort some things out. I want to be ready if she does sell. She agreed that I could show the place while the other units are unfinished. I would love to play matchmaker all day long, but you can lead a horse to water ... blah, blah, blah. I have my own burgeoning romance to worry about."

"You're not going to lecture me on how I done her wrong?" Guy accused, leaning back in his chair, assuming an air of nonchalance.

"You know what you've done. When Ellie's ready to talk, I will be there for her. This *is* the twenty-first century, Guy. Even if you pushed her out of town, there are planes and Instagram to keep us in touch. Your drama is yours alone, so stop raining on everyone else before you start affecting your business. That wouldn't be good for anyone."

Her cell phone chimed. He could see her cheeks flaming, despite her downturned face, as she read a text. "Email me those schedules, then I can start showing your building and making us both some money. I've got to go." She breezed out of his office.

He'd been hoping for a scrap to release his frustration. So much for that.

She poked her head back in a second later. "Guy, if your testosterone level comes down and *you* need to talk ... you know where I am."

She left him deflated and nodding stupidly. He tried to get back to work and leaned extra close to the computer screen in hopes of blocking out the rest of the world. Only problem was, he was alone, and what needed blocking was in his head. Then it hit him: she was gone. With all of that woman's posturing, knowing she'd be trouble from the start, he should've felt relief that she'd left. But he didn't.

He drove to her place. Mark's loaner car was still parked in the lot, but it looked cleaner. There was no trash on the dash and nothing dangling from the mirror. He turned the knob on her condo's front door to find it was actually locked. That's when he knew she'd flown the coop.

"What a spineless, two-bit, yellow-belly ..." He got into his car and spun his tires as he pulled out. It was time to pave and be done with this build.

By Friday afternoon, work was dwindling for the weekend. He had some contractors working overtime to finish up the building. The finer details would be left to the future buyers, but he could pawn that off on his design team when the time came. He would only go out there if he had to. Though he was itching to hit something, so manual labor was probably the best idea he'd had since before the Canadian in crisis stumbled into his life.

"Stop fuming," called Arleen from her office. "I can smell you from here."

He grumbled expletives.

"I heard that!" she yelled, and he shook his head with apprehension. Women ... he was surrounded by insane women.

Then his phone rang.

"Guy, darling," his mother spoke in a strained tone. Had she been told about his misbehavior around town? Well, that was too bad. She could play mama duck all she wanted, but it was his damn life, and he would live it as ticked-off as he needed to. "Are you available for dinner Sunday? There's something rather important your father and I would like to talk to you about."

Guy was sure he didn't want to know, and sure that he wouldn't be able to escape whatever his mother had in store for him forever, so he agreed. He expected the usual long conversation to follow but was surprised when she ended with, "Thank you, dear. I'll be seeing you then. Love you."

What was that about? She'd sounded sullen. He could handle his own moodiness, but he couldn't share it right then.

Work was the only thing keeping him sane. He wanted to be as busy as possible, so he made more for himself. Soon he heard a knock at the door. Expecting to see Arleen, he plastered on a polite smile only to find Grayson in his plaid and cowboy hat.

"I'm headin' to Dixon's. I hear you might need a stiff one."

Guy rose, shrugging on his jacket as he waited for his computer to power down.

Dixon's was tied with the bank for the oldest business in Littleton, and the decrepit building didn't pretend to be new or trendy. Spray-painted many times over with most of its windows boarded up, it didn't appear at all hospitable. Neither did Dixon himself. The old man looked as approachable as a pirate with his twisted teeth and affection for chewing tobacco. His son, however, took good care of the place as the old man reached retirement, and where the exterior was weather beaten, the interior was a sports fan's wet dream.

Basketball was on all the screens as Guy took his customary spot at the bar and ordered a whiskey neat. Grayson followed suit, and it wasn't until they both had their second in hand that they even acknowledged each other.

"Rough week?" Guy asked, noting his friend's rumpled appearance for the first time.

"You could say that."

"Wanna talk about it?" Guy asked, bringing his voice up a notch in mock femininity. Grayson scoffed and returned his drink to his lips, changed his mind, and turned back to Guy.

"People are messed up. You know that? You think you live in the most boring town in Texas one minute, and the next you're taking down devastatingly honest testimonies, and you feel the devil himself in the room with you."

"You mean ..."

"Mr. Peterson ... yeah. Don't know if he's touched anyone yet, but he came clean on the nastiness on his computer. My eyes are still bleeding."

"Shit."

"Yeah. There is a lot of BS to sift through before we can take it to the DA. Hoping the kiddie porn is as far as it goes. He's been a teacher for decades. If the media gets hold of this story, I might be getting job offers." There was no excitement in his voice. He was dead on his feet.

Guy decided, despite his interest, and the twisting in his gut about Ellie being right, he would cheer up his friend.

"What, and leave all this?" Guy laughed as pinball machines lit up in the corner.

"Yeah ..." Grayson turned back to his drink. "Maybe. I don't know. What I do know is that I'll need industrial-grade Pepto if I ever work in a place where these sorts of cases are normal." He downed the whiskey and ordered another. "Anyway, I heard you've been throwing your weight around. What's eating you, brother?"

Guy's lip turned up before he took a long sip. "Rough week too, I guess."

"Have anything to do with the tiny tornado who tore through town?"

"Might be. What? You honing your detective skills?"

"Might be." Grayson didn't press. He knew the score. If Guy was going to talk, he'd do it in his own time.

"We might have gotten into it. No big deal. Not like we were *together*. It always had an expiration date."

Grayson looked up at the game, intentionally dividing his attention. "Heard Winter's leaving town too …"

"Women!" Guy said, spitting fire. "They can tell a guy all that's wrong with them, but hold up a mirror and suddenly, you're the asshole." This pulled Grayson's attention.

"Wait, Miss Ellie called you out? No way!"

"Thanks."

"Naw! Someone, other than me, has challenged Mr. Perfect?" He made a *pfft* sound, betraying his low tolerance for alcohol. "You should marry her. She's one of a kind."

Guy turned red, then gray, then green. He raised an eyebrow in defense.

"Naw," he drawled again. "Brother, I'm serious. You get your ass kissed every damn day. Nothing you do ever turns up anything but roses and dollar bills. I've known you a long time, I know your bull, I enjoy it, I laugh at it on occasion, but has a woman—not from the press, mind you—ever called you out?"

"I've gotten in plenty of fights with women!" argued Guy, trying to remember one that didn't end with a roll in the hay or a breakup he'd planned in advance. Was that what he'd done with Ellie? He wasn't sure anymore.

"Right." Grayson raised his hands in front of him. "And how's that working for you?" They both returned to the game on the big screen.

"But, Guy?" Grayson added a long time later as he leaned his head heavily into his hand.

"What?"

"Marry her."

Guy pushed him by the face off his stool. Affectionately.

CHAPTER EIGHTEEN

*T*he Sunday service was too much for Guy. By no stretch a choirboy, he did try to make the most of his time in church and didn't want to be one of the men who slipped in an earbud to catch sports radio instead. He tried to be attentive, but he had this nagging feeling that he was forgetting something. That, and he had a raging headache threatening to overtake him. He knew it was suppressed rage wanting to seep out, but he would have to wait to take it to the heavy bag at the gym later.

Sunday school evicted the children early, and Guy was surprised to see Jessica Jenkins, their teacher, wearing a scowl. The twins must've put the poor woman through her paces if the sweetest Christian woman in town wore that face. Guy tried to refocus on the pastor, but the young ones were uncharacteristically antsy. Some squirmed while others received a firm talking-to from their parents. A few couldn't seem to sit in their seats at all.

Guy surveyed the church, looking for the demon spawn. Usually, they were the ones receiving a scolding, but they were sitting back, arms crossed, smug joy coloring their features, as a handful of their peers were told to wait outside.

It slowed the pace of the service, but Pastor Thomas recovered well overall, to which Guy congratulated him at the barbecue afterward.

"I wish I knew what has gotten into the lot," Thomas said before giving Guy a conspiring grin. "I remember raising hell with Randy McIntyre during Sunday school back in the day. Got a whooping once a week for it. Oh ..." he said, lost in a dramatic reverie, "To be young again. Don't look so surprised!"

"Sorry, Pastor, I can't picture you *raising hell*." Guy laughed for the first time in days.

"Oh yes. Some need to know how it feels to be bad before they can pursue the good with pure intentions." Thomas laid a knowing hand on Guy's shoulder and moved on to say hello to a young mother who was holding on to her son's ear, marshaling an apology.

That's when it happened. Shots went off, loud bangs, cracks. Half the service hit the ground while the other half braced to run. Guy saw Grayson in uniform across the churchyard, hand over his gun, surveying the area on high alert. Parents threw themselves over their children; tables were overturned. Then it became clear that rather than buckshot, someone had set off firecrackers.

All eyes turned to Crystal, who was shouting, "TANNER AND JAKE HERNÁNDEZ!"

"Yes, Mom?" came Jake's voice from beside her, hot dog halfway to his mouth. Tanner was bent down tying his shoe, and Guy thought he could make out a grin. Crystal's shock was palpable, then it gave way to cunning.

"Good boys. Why don't you sit down over there with your father now. Wouldn't want you to get food on your Sunday best."

The offenders were soon found and given garbage duty. The barbecue broke up early as most of the children were either running on high octane or crashing into fits. Guy kept his eyes trained on the twins who acted normal, which was disconcerting. The only giveaway was when they turned to one another in twin-speak. The pride on their faces was too much. Guy couldn't resist having a chat with them while Crystal was busy socializing with the other mothers.

"So, how'd you do it?" Guy asked.

"Do what?" Jake asked, daring Guy to accuse them of anything.

"Turn the choirboys into pyros, of course."

"I don't know what you're talking about." Tanner smiled from ear to ear.

"You pour sugar into the water jug?"

"Weak," Jake answered, unimpressed with Guy's guess. "It would take a lot more than that to get a whole class riled up."

"Yeah, and we don't get an allowance. Only a grown-up could afford that." Tanner elbowed Jake in the ribs, and they exchanged more silent communication.

Guy paused before whooping out in laughter so hard, the boys backed away. "So you've found yourself a benefactor?" he said once he regained control. "Good for you. Too bad she left town."

"Was it our fault?" one of the boys asked in earnest.

"No, buddy," he answered, putting his hand on the kid's shoulder. "It was mine."

"Then fix it," the other twin said, spitting on Guy's shoe and tramping away with his brother.

SOME OF HIS steam had escaped, but he still wanted to hit something, so he headed to his car and drove toward the town's multipurpose gym. Guy lost himself in training on the heavy bag for a long time before he came up for air, and he only did so because the music from his phone kept getting interrupted by calls. He accepted the call while still throwing punches.

"WHAT?" he growled as he threw his famous left hook.

There was silence on the line before Ivy's voice came in. "If I didn't know better, I would think you were raised by wolves. Is that any way to talk to your mother?"

"Sorry, Ma. I'm in the middle of training. Everything OK?" he asked, realizing it was their dinner he'd forgotten about. Wanting nothing more than to revel in his bad mood, he had been avoiding her all week. She would call him out on his behavior, and question him about Miss Ellie, and he wasn't ready for that. So, he'd arrived at church as late as possible, avoided her through the service, and knew she rarely attended the luncheon. The plan was to keep his distance until he got the anger out of his system.

Mothers, or his, at least, didn't allow such things to go unchecked. He knew how she would react when it came to Ellie, and he didn't want to hear it. Not the *I told you so* or the sympathetic mothering that would come with the territory.

"Are you coming to dinner tonight? There's something your father and I would like to discuss with you. Your brother won't be home, so it'll be the ideal time."

"Sorry, Ma," Guy repeated. "I forgot. Made other plans." Silence crackled over the line, like she knew he was lying. "You still there?" Guy asked, stopping his workout at last.

"I would appreciate it if you came to dinner tonight, Guy. I don't mean to worry you, but your father and I have a bit of news we would like to talk over."

That's when Guy noticed the waver in Ivy's tone. It made him nervous.

"I'll be there, Ma." After that, Guy lost his groove and hit the showers. He still wanted to hit other things, but he'd been derailed. What could be wrong? Was she or Dad ill? They hadn't spoken of anything and were typically open about their health. While he hadn't noticed anything askew, he cursed himself for being distracted. He knew whatever needed saying was important by the fact that his brother, who was away for a basketball camp, was not being told.

Kid gloves. Guy didn't remember ever having been handled

with kid gloves before. He'd had a proper childhood, but his parents never shielded him from the world. He'd grown up knowing what sort of life his mother had come from—shelters, foster care, life on the streets. A lot of hard lessons had been taught anecdotally. In the early incarnations of his mother's organization, he'd been forced to realize how privileged he was as there were often young women and children living in their family home, for weeks at a time, in some cases.

The last of these home invaders had been his brother. Liam was nine at the time, had lived through hell with his parents, then worse in foster care. Ivy's organization had found Liam living on the streets, malnourished but filled with joie de vivre. Guy was already in his twenties and had begun his boxing career, and though he had his own place in the city, he still considered his parents' place home.

He remembered his mother cautioning him over the phone about this young boy who was staying with them. Given Liam's history, there was a good chance that Guy's appearance alone would threaten the boy. He'd taken pains to hide his tattoos and cover his imposing physique as well as he could to not frighten the lad, but he wasn't going to give up his home either.

When Guy walked into the house, he was welcomed by his mother who he garnished with love and respect as always. His father had still been working at his practice and wasn't home. Guy remembered the apprehension on Liam's face. It was like he could hear the *whir-whir-whir-click* of his mind deciding on fight-or-flight. Before he could choose, Guy told him he'd brought him a gift, some shirts and other swag from a fight he'd recently won. The kid's smile was currency, and Guy was bought.

A month later, they sat him down and asked permission to adopt him into their family. Liam was blood as far as Guy was concerned. To leave him out of this conversation at seventeen years old seemed cruel, but Guy would wait to hear what was going on before sitting his brother down himself if he had to.

Guy rolled up to the house early, having no need to delay the inevitable. He was surprised to see Goldie's car ahead of his. Journeying through the house without being accosted by Cujo could only mean that his father had taken the dog out for a walk. Unless ... had something happened to him? Liam would be heartsick.

Goldie was in the yard with her fuchsia clipboard, and Guy's stomach sank. The house. Much better news than he'd been expecting—it was only the sale of the family home they wanted to tell him about. But *why* would they sell? If they were having financial difficulty, they had to know he would bail them out, no questions asked. He grew impatient and called a hello across the yard as they had yet to realize he was there.

"Guy!" his mother exclaimed in joy before remembering herself or the occasion. "You're early!" She came across the grass, arms outstretched, as if waiting for her little boy to run to her.

"Ma, Goldie ..." Guy gave his mother a hug and nodded toward Goldie, still feeling suspicious of his friend.

"I heard about Miss Ellie leaving, son. I know you were ... well, I'm sorry it didn't work out." His mother attempted to soothe him, but he knew, despite what had actually happened between him and Ellie, his mother was nothing but happy that she'd flown the coop.

"Sure you are, Ma," he responded, feigning good humor.

"Oh, Guy. I won't pretend I understood the allure. But I don't like to see you unhappy."

"I'm fine, Ma," Guy said through a clenched jaw.

"She was so ..."

"Spineless?" Guy jumped in, trying to move this part of the conversation along.

"Adventurous?" Goldie suggested, smiling widely.

"Immature," Guy added, darting a sideways glare.

"Fresh?"

"Calculating."

"Clever?" Goldie showed so many teeth, her smile was menacing.

Ivy was oblivious to the feud playing out in front of her.

"Contrived. I think that's the word I'd settle on. I'm sorry, Goldie, I know you were fond of the girl." Ivy patted Goldie's shoulder apologetically.

"Doesn't matter much what she was, only that she's gone." Guy hoped that would be the end of the subject.

"Yes, onward and upward," Ivy agreed. "I never knew what you saw in the girl."

"Aw," Goldie cooed. "Protective mama duck."

"Oh, I know Guy can take care of himself. I'd much rather if he ends up with someone with integrity, someone who knows up from down, who doesn't posture so much. Someone like you, Goldie. Now there's a connection I'm surprised hasn't yet come about. You two should go out on a date sometime and see what comes of it."

Guy was as near shocked as he could be while Ivy took a long draw out of her wineglass, but Goldie didn't miss a beat.

"Well now, Ivy, you know I love Guy."

"Yes, you two have always got on well, haven't you?" Ivy agreed.

"I'm in a fresh relationship right now. I'm pretty sure me having a date with a man would scare her off." Goldie paused as she put her clipboard back into her gargantuan purse, allowing Ivy to absorb her words. "And despite what you think of Ellie, she has become a good friend. I couldn't do her wrong like that, now could I?"

"Good on you, Goldie," came Ed Manning's voice as Cujo hustled to her water dish, also known as the birdbath. "You best be bringing her around one Sunday."

"Yes, sir." Goldie was overjoyed. "I'll crunch some numbers, Ivy, and get back to you tomorrow afternoon at the latest." With that, the Mannings were alone.

"Well, I guess I stepped into it." Ivy shrugged. "Think she'd take cookies as an apology?" she asked, though the space was now electrified with nervous energy.

"I think she'd take an apology as an apology," Ed said with a short tone that cut Guy's attention from the now-soaked dog at his knee.

"OK, let's get to it, then," Guy said, breaking the tension. "Why are you selling the house?"

"We're not selling the house," Ed said through gritted teeth.

"Not yet, anyway. We need an approximation of worth because ..." Ivy's voice faltered, and she took her son's hands and led him to a chair, sitting him down.

"Here we go." Ed threw his hands up with exasperation.

"Guy, your father and I are getting a divorce."

"No. We aren't."

"I'm sorry it has come to this. We can answer any questions you might have about it," Ivy's soothing, motherly voice finished, completely ignoring Ed as he stood head down, fingers on the bridge of his nose.

"Naw, Ma, it's OK. I get it."

Ivy's eyes shot open with shock.

"It's not like it's a huge surprise. Y'all haven't been getting on the past few years. I'm glad you're not wasting your time anymore. You can both try to be happy now."

Ivy BLANCHED as though she'd seen a ghost. How could her son have seen it all this time when she herself had only realized in the past week? Was Ed's unhappiness so obvious to everyone but her?

"Listen here—" Ed started toward their son, angry as a bull. "You think that's what marriage, what love, is all about? Happiness? Sorry to break it to you, but happiness isn't all that new age crap. Happiness is a *feeling*. Nothing more, nothing less. If you aren't happy, you wait for it to pass, and it always does because there's football, and children, and kittens, and gawddamned truths that make all the drama you both love to steep in mean nothing. Or, if none of that warms your heart, you go to therapy and get medicated need be.

"You two try so damned hard at being perfect that when you realize you're as messed up as the rest of us, it's like a fall from grace. No one is perfect. No relationship, no man, no woman, no one. You wanna be happy? Go get a snow cone. You wanna stay married? You work at it."

"I've done nothing but work at it!" Ivy muttered.

"Have you now? Did you quit the job you'd worked your whole life for to give your partner a chance at their dream? Did you hold them up to the world as a prize, or did you let their name get reduced to *Ed*?"

"I'm going to leave you to it," Guy said, trying to keep the anger he'd been carrying for the past week from spilling over.

"Get back here, son. You could learn a thing or two," Ed called.

"Like what? How to whine and hold other people accountable for choices YOU made?" Guy struck back.

"I don't regret a single choice I made. I wish I'd quit doctoring earlier to raise you too. Maybe you wouldn't be teetering on your damned pedestal. You're missing the point, and tell you the truth, I'm not surprised."

"Well, why don't you tell me all the ways I've let you down? Don't hold back now, old man." Guy and Ed were nose to nose.

"You didn't let me down, son. You couldn't. I love you like I love your mother and your brother—soul deep. You can't cut out a love like that. Naw, you let Miss Ellie down by being a self-important fool, too afraid to step up."

Guy turned away from his father with a sneer. "What do you even know about it? Not like we've had a heart-to-heart on the subject."

"I know you. And I've got a pretty good estimation of Miss Ellie too."

"Oh yes. You are quick, Ed. You manage to know Miss Ellie, even though she swept through town faster than the Road Runner." Ivy rolled her eyes deeply as she moved to the bar cart and poured herself another glass of rosé.

"Are you blind AND deaf, woman? *That* woman may have her demons, but she managed to touch so many lives, and save at least one person before our son made the biggest mistake of his life."

Guy laughed. "And you call *us* dramatic. Miss Ellie was always going to leave. It was only a matter of time."

"Then why are you so angry?"

When Guy couldn't find an answer, Ed continued with tenderness. "Son, you aren't angry at anything that woman did, or even that she left. Naw, you're angry because you are too damned afraid to drop your defenses and love someone other than yourself. People bend over backward to build you two up, and all you are, are sledgehammers. Miss Ellie didn't want you for your money, your station, your family, or the town that loves you. You two clicked, and that's all there is to it. Now you want to burn her for her shortcomings? Go for it, but you'll be hurting yourself because it's her damned quirks that you are in love with." Ed was no longer looking at his son but at Ivy who held her glass halfway to her mouth. Neither of them noticed when Guy left their yard.

"So, you're still in love with me? Is that it?" Ivy turned back to the cart, refusing to look at him again.

"How could I not be, Ivy? Because you're a self-absorbed twit who cares more about how things seem from the outside than how they are? Or because you would rather pretend than have it out?" He came up behind her, and she felt the static between them. "Ivy, you are a pain in my ass. And I am genuinely unhappy with the way things are, but I love you. Once you get that through your head, we can move on to the next step."

"What's the next step?" She sighed as he wrapped his arms around her.

"Lots of booze. Lots of raunchy, angry sex," he growled. She began to speak, but he wasn't done. "Followed by makeup sex. From there? Who knows? Couples' therapy? But I won't give up on you if you don't give up on me."

"What if it's too late for us?"

"It's only too late when one of us is in the ground, and even then, I can't be sure."

Ivy turned to face her husband and trailed her hand against his face, gifting them both with her tenderness. They kissed, slowly exploring each other, tentative, waiting for traps to trigger. When they parted, Ed offered a lopsided grin and chose a bottle from behind his wife. He began walking into the house, and Ivy watched him go, unsure.

He stopped at the door and turned back to her. "Pick your poison and meet me in the bedroom." He went inside without another word.

Ivy chugged her drink and grabbed blindly as she moved past the cart onto the next step.

CHAPTER NINETEEN

*E*llie unlocked the door to her condo with a mild sense of foreboding. She didn't know what to expect—possibly a lot of dead houseplants. Everything appeared to be as she'd left it, if not tidier. Maybe the housekeeper had been by or maybe her mother? At the thought of the latter, Ellie's ears perked, listening for telltale signs of her mother—the pages of *Forbes* turning, the hum of her curlers heating, anything. The condo was silent.

Careful not to get any snow on the tile, Ellie removed her boots on the narrow rug, and hung her coat in the closet. She could do with the chill no longer and set to work boiling the kettle for cocoa. She went to her room to throw on a sweater and stood in her walk-in, dumbfounded. Her clothes were neatly pressed and color-coded, which was laughable considering they were all essentially one tone. She realized this wasn't her anymore and frowned. Had she been sleepwalking through life all this time?

She hastened her retreat, going for her duffel, sorting clothes into clean and dirty piles—shorts, tanks, tees, all still smelling of sun, sweat, and him. That's when she found his hoodie, the only thing she'd ever stolen in her life. She considered the emblem of the town's mascot, a longhorn, touching it gingerly with her fingertips, afraid it might fade at her touch. She put it on and curled up on her bed, alone, waiting for the tears to come.

Soon the kettle screamed. Dry-faced, Ellie got to her feet to cross to the kitchen as the front door unlocked and a dark figure walked in.

They both stood completely still. Shocked to see one another.

"You're back," said Daniel, breaking the silence with his even voice.

Ellie had almost forgotten that her ex was handsome, tall with dark eyes and hair, a chiseled jaw, and he always dressed in fine suits. Ellie felt nothing for him, no lingering attraction at all.

"Yeah," she answered.

"Good, then. You should get the kettle."

Startled by the sound, she hustled to the kitchen and unlatched the whistle, almost burning herself with the steam as she turned off the element. When she turned back, he was putting down his briefcase and setting her mail on the table. "Listen, Daniel, I—"

"Before you continue, and I know you must need to share your little adventure with someone, I need to mention that I'm expected at the Renalds' home at seven. You are welcome to join, but that would give you little time to prepare," he finished, motioning to her attire.

"The Renalds?" was all Ellie could muster.

"Yes, they have invited me, and by proxy, you, to dinner to cele-brate the merger. I realize you must want to *talk*. However, to be honest, the past few weeks have been busy and had you been here, I might have been too distracted."

"Merger."

"Yes, thanks largely to *this* deal, I have been named partner. Tonight is a celebration of both, and of course, no one would be surprised to see my fiancée there with me. As such, might this awkward moment pass? At least for the evening so that you might …"

"Dress the part?"

"So to speak."

"Daniel."

"Elmira?"

"Did you miss me at all?"

"As I said, I have been busy. Though I can't say that I enjoyed your theatrics, the timing was rather perfect. But you are back now, and time marches on."

"Do I really allow you to speak to me this way?"

"Excuse me?"

"Do I let you address me as if this is another one of your mergers? Forgetting, of course, that I called off the wedding, do you care that I have been out of the country? Do you care what I've been doing? Why I've been doing it?"

"I'm sorry, Elmira, I forgot that you like to play the victim. You leave for a month—"

"A few weeks!" Ellie argued.

"—and I'm expected to, what? Sit and pine after you, forgetting about my own responsibilities and ambitions? And now that you have reappear, what is it you want me to do? Fall to my knees and sob like a child? Beg you to never leave my side again? I get it, you want a romantic reunion, but maybe you can think of someone else for the evening, and then we can play out some more theatrics for you later."

"So, you *are* angry with me?" Ellie honestly couldn't tell. She knew he was chastising her and was almost certain he was propositioning her, but she was not sure what the emotion behind any of it was. She felt like she was having an out-of-body experience. There was no connection here whatsoever.

He considered her as if looking over a set of glasses. "Elmira. You've had a long ride by the looks of it. How about you draw a bath, have a cup of tea, relax into yourself again? I will stop by after work tomorrow, and we can get the ball rolling. I know your mother can repair the relationship with the wedding planner, and there has been no real damage." He gave her a chaste kiss on her head, collected his case, and walked out of the apartment just as he had come in—unconcerned.

Ellie quit her cocoa, brought her mug to the cupboard, and found some old cooking sherry to fill it up.

ELLIE HAD MANAGED to put off another meeting with Daniel. Though it might have been cruel to string him along, in her defense, she wasn't sure how to be any clearer. It was like he plugged his ears and started yodeling when he was told point-blank where they stood, and she didn't have the energy to figure out how to cement it in his mind, or if it was even her job to do so.

Her days were spent straightening out issues at work and detailing her counteroffer to move forward in the company. More time off and fewer hours in office were some of her demands, but she also wanted to develop a charity organization to give back to the community. If nothing else, the Mannings lit a fire in her belly to help others.

A meeting had been scheduled with the CEO for the following morning. In the past, all this might have been nerve-racking, but at this point, she was prepared to walk if her needs weren't met. Work wasn't enough for her anymore, and although she loved her job, she would no longer compromise on her priorities, even if she wasn't entirely sure what they were yet.

The rest of her time, she spent researching. Guy had spoken of Grayson's sister, and she couldn't help her curiosity, so the Google stalking began. Her crash had made the papers and looking through the pictures triggered Ellie's emotions about her own accident. Soon she came across a new phrase: *integrative dance*. There was even a strong presence in her own city that she'd never realized was there. Researching brought up words that seemed counterintuitive to her own experience as a dancer, words like *diversity*, *difference*, and *acceptance*.

How that would translate onstage became an obsession until Ellie sat in the middle of the growing audience in one of Ottawa's larger theaters. Living down the road, and often finding herself peering into the building, she'd never found the guts to go in. Theaters gave her an unnerving pang of nostalgia that she'd tried to avoid at all costs.

And the fact was—Guy was right.

Physical therapy after her accident had helped her regain most of her dexterity. A career in dance might not have been out of reach, likely not at a competitive level, but she had *chosen* not to try. She had used her injury as an excuse. Had she sabotaged herself with perfectionism? Or maybe she hadn't wanted to let her mother down. Ellie suspected that it had been much more about the fear of not being as good as she once had been. She felt regret as she questioned, finally, whether it was dance or competitions that she'd loved so much. Admitting that possibility had uncoiled some of her reluctance to be involved in the arts. It was, however, curiosity that had gotten her in the door that night.

The lights dimmed, and she was transported to another world. The show opened her up to laughter and tears, in complete awe of the performers. Her heart soared with them and fell too. When the performance was finished, she hid in her jacket with a plan to escape into the night, head buzzing with re-education—all bodies can dance, all bodies can create art.

Ellie's mind was blown. She felt stupid for wasting so many years avoiding what had once been her dream as a matter of pride. Art was not about being the best—it was about overcoming, about inspiring others, about broadening minds rather than limiting them. She had been a complete fool.

"Here." A young man still wearing stage makeup shoved a pamphlet at her before turning to the next person and doing the same. Ellie read the tagline: *Dance lessons*. She couldn't ... could she? This part of her life was over, wasn't it? Her world wasn't feeling so black-and-white anymore.

ELLIE'S BRAIN was still addled the next day, but as her week was ending, the possibility of a career change sat on the horizon. This day, more than most, she had to hold together her fracturing emotions. She dressed smartly in an outfit she planned to donate to a women's shelter and did her hair and makeup in a style Winter had shown her over a video chat. Heartache was setting in when her phone pinged with a text.

Winter: Knock him dead.

How that woman always knew the right thing to say was ominous. Ellie strung together a thanks and told her how miserable she was so far away from her.

Winter: I'll visit soon. I'm checking out apartments today.

Ellie wiped a stray tear, so happy that Winter and Danika had hit it off. They would take good care of each other in the big city, but she also felt a surge of jealousy. Maybe by day's end, she would be free to run off to New York too.

A quick Uber ride took her to the downtown office where, unloaded of her purse and jacket, she hugged her assistant. Ellie thanked her again for covering for her, and apologized for her mother's intrusions, before meeting with her boss at the end of the hall.

Wyatt Wright had been young when he amassed his fortune, and he still looked like he could be a twenty-something playboy. With his dark features and roguish hazel eyes, he could mesmerize from across any room, but Ellie had only ever seen him use his powers for good. He was a savvy businessman Ellie suspected was just getting started. While other young entrepreneurs might be found in one questionable establishment or another flaunting their money while throwing it away, Wright invested it. His net worth had skyrocketed in a few short years.

"Elmira, welcome back. You look stunning. The South treated you well, I hope?" From any other man, this might have been idle chit chat, but Ellie had been working for him long enough to know that if he asks you something, he is interested. He never wasted words.

"More or less," Ellie admitted. "I'm sorry for my lack of notice."

Wyatt waved off her apology. "We all need a break sometimes."

"You give yourself permission yet?" Ellie laughed, accepting the glass of water his assistant silently offered her.

"If I had my right-hand woman, maybe I would." He chortled, bringing them back to the matter at hand. "I've looked over your requests. Driving a hard bargain."

"Well, that depends," Ellie told him.

"On?"

"On how badly you want to keep me. I mean no disrespect. I know what an enormous gift this job is ..."

"Nonsense. Your work is brilliant. You are the asset here."

"But this can't be all I do anymore. I've had to think about my life these past few weeks, and I feel like I need more balance. I love this company and I love the direction you are leading it in—"

"But if your demands aren't met, you will walk?" Wyatt raised an eyebrow, giving her a stare that would've had any imaginative woman fanning themselves. Ellie found herself immune. There was a time when she'd fantasized about her boss, knowing full well that he was out of her league, but now he couldn't hold a candle to Guy. She frowned and pushed the feeling down.

"I'm sorry to say, but yes, I will."

"OK."

"Pardon me?"

"I'll send the contract to your office before lunch. There will be a few details to iron out, such as what kind of charity work you specifically want to get into. We have people on staff who are qualified, but I have a feeling you might want a hand in selecting your team. A far as I'm concerned, it's damn good business to keep you on. Let's do some good, shall we?"

They stood, and Wyatt walked her out of his office.

"Thank you, sir."

"No, thank *you*. I would have been disappointed if the South had won you over. Also ..." His smile grew lopsided then, and he wore a mirth she'd never seen on him before. "Thank you for hiring Alyssa Stinton." In the whirlwind of running away, Elmira had forgotten all about the woman she'd helped in the door.

"She's working out well, then? I'm glad. I think she needs the opportunity as much as the job."

He nodded in response, tucking his smile away. "This is just the beginning," he said with a firm handshake. Whether he was speaking of the good they would do or about Alyssa, Elmira couldn't say. She was eager to find out.

ELLIE SAT in front of her new TV with an immense sense of pride. It had taken all afternoon, but she managed to mount it to her wall *and* set up both Netflix and her DVD player. After a last-minute shopping trip, she'd found exactly what was needed—all the fixings for a pity party: every romantic comedy she could find, nail polish, a facial kit, a six-pack, and snacks, but decided against sorbet. It was close enough to ice cream for her night of breakup clichés but reminded her too much of downing milk at the Manning's. Other people might think it healthier to be celebrating this huge career win, especially after Wyatt had given her the afternoon off with a bonus check. Ellie, however, knew that she couldn't move forward until all the feelings were sorted through.

The focus of the films would be on the actresses because on top of everything else, she was missing female camaraderie. She'd been in touch with the ladies back in Littleton, but it wasn't the same. The three of them wanted to have a grand pity party but that couldn't happen in Ottawa. They promised to call, and they would plan trips to see one another, but Ellie's heart ached over the distance between her and her friends, the first true ones she'd ever had.

And so, the films were about relatable women like quirky Meg Ryan, intelligent and self-deprecating Sandra Bullock, and free-spirited Drew Barrymore. The weekend would be devoted to these actresses who played characters Ellie saw in herself and her friends, to their heartache, to their love stories. There would be laughter and tears and maybe even some drunk dialing. Then, it would be time to move on. But first, she would allow herself one weekend to grieve hard and messy.

She got into her oversized T-shirt and knee socks, applied the mud mask, and began the first film while painting her nails each a different color to keep her rebellion alive. She was blowing on her fingernails when she heard the dead bolt tumble, and in walked her mother looking like a Kennedy in her pink wool suit and kitten-heel boots. Even the chill of winter had nothing on this woman.

Ellie was glad to have the element of surprise; her mother took her time sizing up her daughter's appearance.

"Don't bother to get up to greet me. I can see you are wallowing. Let me make you some tea, dear."

"No thank you, Mother. I'm fine," Ellie said, sipping her beer, sounding more confident than she'd expected. But her mother continued to the kitchen, turned on the kettle, and put together a pot of tea.

"Chamomile with a spot of honey." She placed the tray in front of her daughter, tidying the table as she went. "Now, darling, I know that it has been an eventful month for you. There is so much on your plate, but now that you are back, I think it's time you recommit."

"Indeed." Ellie scowled, *recommitting* to the bag of nacho

chips, and trying to focus on the movie. Her mother set her jaw and clicked her tongue, a habit formed during Ellie's teen years. Ellie knew it took all her mother's self-restraint to not comment on the snack she was gorging on, so once her crunching was done, she decided to give a little. "I'm sorry, Mother, I was expecting a quiet night. What brings you here?"

"Can't a mother look in on her child?"

"Of course, and you know you are always welcome, but ... is something on your mind?"

"Elmira, I am worried about you. First you disappear, and now that you're back, you seem to have ... what's the word I'm looking for? Regressed? I'm sorry, I cannot focus with whatever that is on your face. Could you please take it off?"

"It's supposed to be rejuvenating."

"It looks like you should be dipping those chips of yours in it." She left the room and returned with a warm wet cloth.

Ellie accepted it and wiped her face clean while responding. "Mother, thank you for worrying. I appreciate it, but I need some room to ..."

"You've been gone a month, Elmira! You've had time to do or to process whatever it is you needed to. Now is the time to get back on track."

"It was two weeks," Ellie said, hardly believing it herself. "And I don't think you understand. Things happened in Texas that I haven't had a chance to talk to you about." Though given her mother's attachment to Daniel and the wedding, she hadn't planned to broach the subject of her love affair.

"Do you think me a fool, Elmira?" Eliza's face softened uncharacteristically, and she sat beside her daughter, taking her hands into her own. "There was a fling, and I understand."

"You do?" Ellie asked, genuinely flummoxed.

"Of course, I do. Whatever happened in Texas, with whoever it happened with, I don't need to know the details. I know you, darling. Affairs aren't your style. You convinced yourself that this man was your soulmate or some other romantic contrivance. When it ended, you were, of course, left in a state. This state," she said, motioning to the paraphernalia of heartbreak. "You have a gentle heart, and you let it get the better of you. Now it's out of your system, but you are processing, dear, trying to justify it to yourself. You don't have to—what's done is done. You tried on a different lifestyle, and it didn't fit. The life you worked so hard for is still here waiting. Although, some aspects might need a bit of legwork to bring back into order."

Ellie was shocked that her mother had gotten so much of what had happened right. The more she thought about it from her mother's perspective, the more nachos she wanted to shove in her face. Her heart *was* gentle, and even after years of digging a moat to protect it from anyone coming into her life, it was still there on the floor, sputtering but pumping.

"You're wrong."

"Pardon me? Speak up."

"I said, you're wrong. The *lifestyle* I tried on suited me fine."

"Well now," Eliza huffed, "then why are you here? I'll tell you why. Our plan isn't moot because you've decided to go Bohemian or what have you." She motioned to Ellie's outfit with her hands as she spoke.

Our plan. There it was. Ellie kicked herself for having let her mother into her head. It was laughable at this point, and she did let a smile pass, but the giddy sensation fell when there was a knock at her door.

"Expecting company?" her mother asked with bells in her voice.

Ellie narrowed her eyes—she knew those bells. Her mother was up to something. The knock came again, and Ellie stood, but Eliza intercepted. "Come, dear, you should put something else on. Let me get the door."

"I'm sorry, but you have the wrong apartment." Eliza's words carried a command.

"This is Miss Ellie's home, is it not?" The voice of a lilting, slurring southern belle.

"No, it is not," responded Ellie's mother, not bothering to hide her distaste for the scene before her.

"Ivy?" Ellie gasped.

"I knew we had the right place. Didn't I say so, Ed?" Ivy pushed her way through. "Miss Ellie, your home is lovely, though not as colorful as I'd expected. I hope you don't mind us stopping in," Ivy said as though they lived down the street from one another ... and were on good terms.

Ellie looked from Ivy to Ed and back again. Ivy's face had the flush of a woman on a bender. Ed, still appearing stoic, had a peaceful smile and a twinkle in his eye.

"Sorry for barging in on you, Miss Ellie. Ivy had something she wanted to say. I told her a phone call would do, but ..." He shrugged dramatically.

"BUT it simply would not do," Ivy finished for him. She took Ellie's hands and led her back to the couch, sitting her down and looking her dead in the eye. "I apologize for being judgmental. I realize now that I misunderstood your intentions with my son, and I am sorry that I didn't allow us to become closer so that we might have discussed whatever it was that brought you to Littleton."

"That's kind of you, Ivy." Ellie appreciated how hard it must've been for Ivy to apologize but was not expecting the hug that flew her way.

From across the room, Eliza made the clucking sound that signaled her patience was going to blow. "Elmira," she began pointedly, "who are these people?"

"Where are my manners?" Ivy jumped up and moved to her husband's side, dizzy from the quick motion. "I am Ivy Manning, and this is my husband, Dr. Edward Manning."

"Charmed." Eliza was anything but. "Elmira, I think it best if we find your friends a cab?"

"And you are?" Ivy asked, straightening, ignoring or oblivious to Eliza's insistence that they leave.

"Eliza Bondell," she responded automatically. "I am Elmira's mother."

"Well, that explains a lot." Ivy laughed. "Oh, nachos! May I have some? We flew out of Dallas before dinner and only had an hour layover in Washington, only had enough time to stop at the bar. It's a good thing we didn't bring any luggage, or I might have sobered up." Ivy helped herself to a handful of chips.

Ed and Ellie shared a smile.

"Little chance of that with the wine on the flight." Ed eyed his wife lovingly.

"Oh, those were tiny little cups." Ivy flapped a hand at him. Remembering her mission, she continued with utmost seriousness: "I promised my husband that I would not let another day pass without righting my wrongs. I promise you, Miss Ellie, that my days as an uptight socialite witch are through. Oh, that's a great movie!" She leaned forward, distracted by a DVD case.

"I'm sorry how things went before you left," Ed said, turning away from his wife for the first time since they'd arrived. "Guy is hurting, too, not that the cad doesn't deserve it."

"He is?" Ellie's heart lurched. No, he couldn't be. Ed was just being polite. Guy had told her to leave. He thought she was worse than scum, not that she had done anything to prove him wrong.

"He's been moping around town all week," Ivy said through a full mouth. It was too much to process. Ellie couldn't comprehend having the Mannings in her home any more than she could picture Guy moping over her. She was sure he would've been glad to be rid of her.

"It was nice of you to visit and make amends." Eliza tried again to bid the unexpected guests farewell. "But as you can see, my daughter is distressed and was planning a quiet evening of ..." She faltered, motioning around the room.

"Wallowing?" Ivy guessed like she was playing charades. Eliza huffed. "Ellie, are all Canadians as unwelcoming as your mother? I had no idea that the north was so inhospitable."

"It's like rolling the dice up here," Ellie admitted.

"There is nothing wrong with my hospitality!" Eliza was immediately tested on her proclamation. Before she had said the words, Guy Manning, small town god, Viking of a man, shouldered his way through Elmira's door. He wore a grim face, which only made his masculinity pulse through the room more.

"Does security have the night off?" Eliza seethed.

CHAPTER TWENTY

The air crackled with electricity. It was surreal to see him there, like a celebrity showing up at her door, which she supposed he was. A big, hulking missile pointed in Ellie's direction. Her body quivered with awareness. He was swoon worthy.

"Guy! You're here! What a surprise!" Ivy smiled happily at her husband, who took a seat beside her, grabbed a handful of snacks, and leaned back to watch the show.

Guy was shocked that his parents were there, but as soon as his eyes landed on Ellie, nothing else mattered.

"Do you have any idea what you've put me through?" he asked, bristling.

Ellie hoped it was a rhetorical question because she couldn't figure out how to speak. He was in her condo. Had she hit her head?

"I drove twenty-four hours through rush hour in multiple damn states, and a godforsaken snowstorm, just to be stopped at the border where they searched my truck and my person. They almost didn't let me through until one of the managers recognized me!"

"You should've flown, dear," Ivy said.

"You"—Guy pointed an intimidating finger at Ellie—"you have to stop running from all of your damned problems."

"Need I remind you that you told me to leave?" Ellie answered, refusing to be bullied.

"Do you realize that it's minus forty out there?"

"That's a little dramatic. It's winter. And it's only minus thirty-five. Welcome to Canada!"

"I couldn't get coffee because the drive-through window froze shut!"

"Should I put on a pot?" Ellie asked ironically.

"No, damn it! I'm trying to tell you something." He paused, swallowing his aggravation. "When you were with me, I was looking for reasons to push you away. My mind couldn't get what my body already knew." He moved closer to Ellie. "You might be the most frustrating female on two damn fine legs, but we belong together."

"Say what?" Ellie asked as her mother cringed, not quite brave enough to step in.

Guy looked formidable. Despite the weather, he was in a simple Henley with the sleeves rolled up, showing the starting point of the tattoos that could be found all over his muscular body.

Ellie remembered licking the contours of both sinew and art. She felt the room growing hot and tried to put up a wall. He couldn't mean what she thought, she couldn't wrap her head around him being there.

"Ellie," he said, cupping her face as though no one was watching, "we are meant for each other. You know that. I know I messed things up, but I need you."

"I am not going to abandon my company, Guy." She was too proud to cave, not while waiting for the other shoe to drop.

"Of course, you're not. I'm going to abandon mine." Guy shrugged his wide shoulders.

"I won't be able to live in Littleton full time. It wouldn't be fair to either of us to do long distance. Plus, there's the issue of you not trusting my gut with the twins."

"You were right, Ellie. You did the right thing. And screw long distance. I will move into this froufrou modern casket with you. Besides, Goldie will have your place sold in no time."

Ellie saw her mother's gobsmacked expression but didn't have time to cater to her at the moment.

"You hate Canada," she pointed out.

"You've got cable. I'll live."

"I don't have cable."

"Now, that's some new age, trendy bull—"

"You would hate it here, Guy. It's cold most of the year, and the people can be too. When I'm working and you're not, you will start to resent me, and I don't want that. Part of my job is galas and social events, and I know how much you despise those. I would never force my life on you. Listen, I get it. When we were together ..." Ellie paused with a quick glance at the crowd around them.

"Don't mind us, dear. Is that beer taken?" Ivy slurped, not waiting for a reply.

"When we were together, fireworks went off," Guy finished for her.

"Sure, but it was temporary. We both knew that. You don't owe me anything, Guy. Why would you put yourself through misery for something that may not last?"

"Not going to last? Listen here, Miss Ellie, I'm not going anywhere until you agree to marry me and have my babies."

"Marry?"

"Babies."

"Baby?"

"Babies ... plural. I'm thinking five, but we can see how the ratios turn out."

"Did you hear that, Edward? Sweetheart! We are going to be grandparents! Isn't that incredible, uh—" Ivy snapped her fingers at Eliza, having forgotten her name. Eliza was slack-jawed. A sound at the door alerted them to Daniel, who stood in the frame holding a dozen red roses.

"Is this a bad time?" Daniel asked, surveying the room full of people he'd never met. His eyes found Guy and burned dispassionately.

"Yes!" everyone exclaimed, except Eliza, who had paled.

"I'd say you are right on time, Daniel dear," she said, emphatically darting her eyes back and forth between the flowers and her daughter.

Ellie stood in the middle of the room, staring up at the ceiling, grinding her teeth.

"Would you like us to leave?" Edward asked with as much kindness as he could muster while marveling at his wife, now elbow-deep in the supersized bag of nachos.

"No!" Ellie seethed. "All Texans and my mother, stay here. Daniel—" Ellie thrust her thumb toward her bedroom. Ellie stalked in and Daniel followed.

Only a word here and there could be heard. The rise and fall of a hushed argument had everyone wanting to hear, but none wanted to be the first to put their ear to the wall.

Minutes later, though it seemed like a lifetime to Guy, the door opened, and Daniel left, throwing the flowers to the floor. Eliza chased after him, chirping at him for information, already trying to salvage anything but her dignity. Ivy stumbled toward the entryway, closed the door, locked it, and put a chair in front of it. Ellie didn't emerge from her room.

"You're up, buddy," Edward said, like it was his turn at bat.

"Any advice?" Guy asked, not once turning from the doorway.

"You'll do fine. Good luck."

From the entry, Guy saw Ellie lying face down on a pile of fluffy pillows. He knocked gently. She grunted something inaudible as he entered, closing the door behind him. He took in starkness of the room. There were none of the quirky furnishings that had grown synonymous with her since they'd started playing house together. Beige walls made boxes labeled *KEEP, GIVE,* and *TOSS* the focal point of the room. Give and Toss were overflowing with clothing, while Keep was empty. Hangers were strewn all over the floor, but a computer desk on the other side of the room had impeccably organized piles. *This was so Ellie*, he thought. *An organized mess.*

"You OK?" he asked, stuffing his hands into the pockets of his jeans. Not quite knowing where to stand, he leaned against the wall while Ellie found her composure. "Lover boy couldn't take the heat?"

"Technically, you would be the lover boy, no?" she shot from her nest of pillows and blankets.

"What did you tell him?" Guy asked. Though he gathered that Daniel was upset for a reason, he didn't want to get his hopes up. He would fight to the death for Ellie, but he couldn't do that if Ellie had told Daniel to leave so she could get rid of her Texan lover.

"What do you think I told him?" She seethed.

Guy had a few jokes on the tip of his tongue, but he bit them back. It was time to get serious. He waited for Ellie to be ready. She rolled over to glare at him, and her nightshirt rode up to the top of her thighs as she brought her legs over the side of the bed to sit. It took all of Guy's willpower to focus on her face. Her *very* angry face.

"I told him that when I broke up with him a few weeks ago, I meant it. How could I be with someone who would rather I sleep around than ask about my emotional well-being? I told him that I was sorry for having done it over the phone, beyond sorry that my mother was stringing him along, but that it's over."

"Weeks ago?"

Ellie bit her lip.

"So when we hooked up, you were single?" Guy asked with a relieved laugh. It had bothered him knowing that Ellie was someone else's all the times they were together. It hadn't changed anything, but it was exactly what he needed to hear.

"What do you take me for?" she shot at him, betraying her mood with an ounce of good humor.

"You are sun-kissed skin, dusty boots, and a right ol' mess of paint everywhere. Organized chaos. You are warmth, quirks, and blind freaking passion."

"Who are you?" Ellie asked, mind blown. "What is it you want from me, Guy?"

"I'm the one who will make you a pot of namby-pamby herbal tea whenever you want it. I'm the one who will make sure the power restarts after you blow the fuses with whatever harebrained idea you come up with. I'm your security system, your chef, and your blanket when you need one. I'm the one who is going to curl your toes and throw your head back. I will take care of our babies when you're off making hostile takeovers. I'm yours, damn it!" He was missing something. He began to panic until he felt his heart break at the sight of her, eyes red with unshed tears and slack muscles. He sat on his knees in front of her.

"Elmira, I love you. I've loved you all along, but I didn't think I was allowed to. Hell, I was scared to, but I promise I will love you fiercely for the rest of our lives together. Please, baby, forgive me for being an idiot." The silence went on between them, bringing him close to madness.

"OK," she responded, voice cracking. "But calling me Elmira is grounds for divorce."

Guy rushed over and lifted her into the air, laughing with triumph.

"Put on a dress," he said after kissing her soundly.

"Why?" she asked, wrapping her legs tighter around him, making sure he knew her intentions.

"Believe me, sweetheart. I want to lock that door and have you every which way till you're passed out sated."

"Then what is it? Are our parents still out there?"

"Well, mine are ..."

"Right. I guess we could go out and celebrate." She hesitantly climbed down and riffled through the Keep box for something to wear.

Guy snorted. "Are you kidding? Ma is going to be passed out by the time we leave this room, and I don't think my dad would leave her here alone. Naw, I was thinking we should go to city hall."

"That's sweet of you," Ellie laughed, a bit uncomfortably. "But I'm pretty sure it's closed on Friday nights. Besides, we should talk about only having known one another a short time, and it being too soon for marriage. Especially since I just canceled one. I've made some huge life changes here. How can you even be sure about what you're getting yourself into?"

"Do you love me?" He was raw vulnerability.

She knew she'd never said it, hadn't dared to think it. She had a lump in her throat the size of Texas.

"If you're not there yet, sweetheart, we can wait."

"I love you. You're a bulldozer, but I love you. How could I not?" She began to weep, finally finding emotional relief.

"I sure hope those are happy tears." Guy wiped them away with his thumbs. "Marry me, Ellie. I'm willing to be a little crazy. I know you're the one for me. We can work through anything that comes up along the way."

Ellie considered the play of emotion on Guy's face. Tired, elated, but he was also feeling thoroughly insecure. It almost broke Ellie's heart. "Did you know that the easternmost point of North America is Cape Spear, Newfoundland?"

"I did not know that." Guy stared at her blankly.

"Logically, their town hall would be the first to open Monday." She watched as his expression turned to glee. "But don't you want a church wedding?"

"I want you to be my wife as soon as possible," Guy said without hesitation. "But you deserve better than Vegas."

"And you're willing to move to the land of ice and snow?" she asked, a blush warming her as his proclamations of love sank in.

"Yes," he answered firmly. "But, for the record? Your mother scares me."

≈

ON MONDAY MORNING, Guy stood at the head of the chapel-like room in St. John's City Hall. Ivy and Ed cuddled together on a bench, inseparable since making up back in Littleton. The cold only gave them an excuse to touch each other constantly. Liam, having flown in the day before, stood bleary-eyed and ecstatic at being his big brother's best man. Winter and Goldie couldn't make it on such short notice. Winter had booked the flight, but a snowstorm grounded it. She and Goldie promised Ellie a late bachelorette party as soon as they could manage it.

Initially, Eliza had flat-out refused to come, citing the fact that they had only known each other a couple of weeks and that to marry so soon was foolhardy. They figured she must've Googled the Mannings and found the match agreeable, after all. She was the first at city hall, making sure that if it was to be done, it would be done right.

Guy watched as Eliza walked Ellie down the aisle holding her head high and biting her tongue, which was more than either of them could've hoped for. Ellie hadn't wanted to go wedding dress shopping on account of it being too cold to leave their hotel room. Forgoing the traditional gown was a sacrifice Guy was willing to make, but one his mother was not. Ivy had managed to get a stunning dress that fit Ellie like a glove, not surprising since Eliza had her daughter's measurements on file.

Ellie was beautiful. She glowed like heaven shone down on her, and Guy felt warmth growing in his chest. She was here—he hadn't messed it up after all. He smiled wider, remembering breakfast at the hotel.

They'd needed room service to refuel after another night of vigorous making up, since they weren't traditional enough to wait to get naked until after the ceremony. As such, Guy had a breakfast buffet delivered to the room. When he offered her milk for the cereal she was eating dry, she told him she was lactose intolerant. Her eyes went wide with mortification as it dawned on him what that meant about her first dinner with his family. He laughed until he was in tears. This woman was a lot of things, but she would never be boring.

Ellie stood before Guy and the officiant, happy tears welling in her eyes, wearing a grin so large her face hurt. She didn't know what her future was going to look like. She hadn't figured it all out yet, but she knew that the man before her would be there, no matter how impulsive or nitwitted she might be. They would take care of each other.

A calm swept through her like a warm breeze. She had finally found home.

ACKNOWLEDGMENTS

It takes a village to raise a child, and this has been a lengthy birthing process.

Thanks to my family, without whom I wouldn't have any concept of happily ever after. My husband for making space for me and to my children who had to wait for snacks more than once. You have been as much a part of the process as breathing. I love you all to the moon and back, forever.

Jennifer Sommersby Young, my editor, thank you for your guidance through the whole process. I've had a lot to learn and you've been so patient and kind while getting me up to speed.

To my Beta Readers: Natalie, Rose, Haley, Kim, and Renée Gendron. Thank you for gifting me with your time and insights. To Jon for guiding me through my website options—not my comfort zone—thank you.

Zoe Dickinson, I can only try to convey the confidence you've given me. You've been feeding my creative soul since second grade and continue to guide and motivate me. Thank you for saying it was decent even when we both knew it was a mess.

Eternal thanks and gratefulness to my friend and emotional support person, Haley Deladurantaye. You get it. You get me. Your support has been everything.

ABOUT THE AUTHOR

Mary Lavoie grew up in Aylmer, Quebec, where she became a voracious reader. Love stories always drew her in, whether it was a rom-com or a wrestling event.

After a stint in Theatre Arts, she earned her B.A. with a specialization in English and a minor in philosophy at the University of Ottawa.

Mary is living happily ever after with her husband, daughters, and fur babies.

For more books and updates:
www.marylavoie.com

facebook.com/Mary.Lavoie.Author
instagram.com/marylavoieauthor